The Lithmern lay, still blindfolded, bound, and gagged, in the center of the circle Illeana had scratched in the hard grey soil. Worrel crouched uneasily beside him, holding an unsheathed knife in one furred hand.

Illeana threw back the hood of her cloak and loosened her hair to fall in silver waves over her shoulders. From under her cloak she drew a thin circlet of silver twined with gold; this she placed about her head, settling it firmly onto her brow. The Shee woman turned to the seated humans. "Do not stir or speak until we finish," she warned them. The two Shee walked to the edge of the circle. Then they began to chant, an eerie keening sound that rose and fell in waves over the barren mountaintop.

The others watched, silent. This was the first they had seen of true magic. Alethia, despite the Shee's warning, crept closer as the chant went on. Maurin sat bemused as the legends of his boyhood walked the earth in flesh before him. Tamsin the minstrel watched hungrily, with an intense longing, as the Shee wove their spell, for magic was his heart's desire . . .

*Ace Fantasy Books by Patricia C. Wrede*

DAUGHTER OF WITCHES
THE HARP OF IMACH THYSELL
THE SEVEN TOWERS
SHADOW MAGIC
TALKING TO DRAGONS

# SHADOW MAGIC

A Lyra novel by
## PATRICIA C. WREDE

ACE FANTASY BOOKS
NEW YORK

SHADOW MAGIC

An Ace Fantasy Book / published by arrangement with
the author and the author's agent, Valerie Smith

PRINTING HISTORY
First printing / September 1982
Second printing / March 1984
Third printing / October 1984
Fourth printing / August 1986

ISBN: 0-441-76014-7

Ace Fantasy Books are published by The Berkley Publishing Group,
200 Madison Avenue, New York, New York 10016.
PRINTED IN THE UNITED STATES OF AMERICA

*DEDICATION*
*For David, my brother, who loaned me the typewriter.*

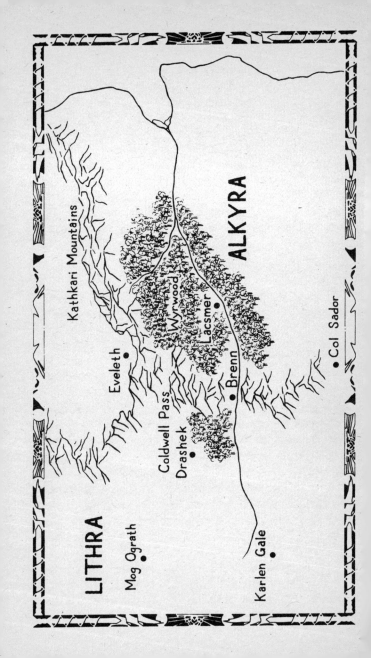

# CHAPTER ONE

The caravan wound slowly through the woods along the riverbank and broke at last into the fields surrounding the city. Except for a few wooden shelters near the gates, the city itself was invisible behind massive walls. Not even the roof of a tower showed above the smooth grey stone.

Though they were now within sight of their goal, the dust-covered guards continued to ride restlessly up and down the long chain of wagons, watching field and forest narrowly for any sign of unusual activity. Travel here, at the western border of Alkyra, was relatively safe, but the Traders generally preferred not to take chances.

When the last of the wagons had entered the city, the guards relaxed at last. Their far-flung riding pattern contracted into small eddies of motion between the lumbering wagons. The iron-rimmed wagon-wheels were noisy, and conversation was minimal. The horses seemed to find the stone pavement, rough as it was, an improvement over the deeply rutted dirt road outside the city, and it was not long before the caravan had reached the wide courtyard of the inn.

The hypnotic rumble of the wagons gave way to a cheerful bustle of securing goods and stabling horses. Everyone took part, from the most exalted

1

of the Master Traders to the lowliest apprentices. As each finished his appointed task, he went in search of friends or pleasure, depending on his inclination, and soon the courtyard began to empty.

Among those remaining was a tall, black-haired man in the utilitarian leather of a caravan guard, his skin tanned by the sun and wind of the trails to a deep bronze under its coating of grime. The uniform suited him well, and he carried himself with an easy confidence that proclaimed him a veteran despite his relative youth. He was checking the ropes securing one of the wagons when another man hailed him. "Maurin!"

The dark-haired man at the wagon rope looked up. "Greetings, Har. I thought you would be away home by now."

Har made a rude noise and looked at his friend with disfavor. The two were of a height, but Har's slight build, accentuated by the leather uniform, made him appear smaller and younger than he was. An unruly shock of sandy brown hair added to the effect, and made the straight black brows and slightly tilted grey-green eyes more startling.

"I've been hunting all over for you," Har said when Maurin made no response. "I invited you to visit when we got to Brenn; did you think I would forget? Haven't you finished with that yet?"

"I'm just checking the knots," Maurin replied. "Last stop we nearly lost three white fox pelts when the wind blew the canvas off, remember?"

Har grinned unrepentantly. "This is Brenn, remember?" he mimicked. "That can't happen in town, and anyway the light stuff has all been unpacked. So won't you come on?"

"A journeyman can't leave the caravan without the permission of one of the Master Traders. You know that," Maurin answered.

"So let's get it! They won't deny it; there's nothing more to do here." As Maurin still hesitated, Har frowned. "I'm beginning to think you don't want to come. I tell you, Maurin, you work too hard. Take the whole week and stay with us and relax for a change. Or isn't the Noble House of Brenn up to your standards?"

"I don't want Master Goldar to think I'm trying to curry favor," Maurin admitted. "And what will your family think? It's all right for nobles and journeymen to brush cloaks on a caravan trip, but even the Master Traders don't visit lords in town unless they're invited."

"Well, I invited you, didn't I?" Har said. "You don't have to worry about my family; Mother won't mind, and if she doesn't, no one else will, either."

"There's still Master Goldar."

"Fear not, my friend," Har said, striking a theatrical pose. "We shall yet win for you the freedom of the city, overcoming all objections of . . ." His speech was abruptly stifled by a heavy wool horse-blanket, thrown accurately over his head by the friend he was addressing. Har emerged a moment later, grinning broadly.

"At least there's one good thing about being heir to a Noble House," Har said as the two set off in search of the Master Trader. "I know more about protocol and persuasion than just about anybody. We won't have any trouble with Master Goldar; you'll see."

Whether because of Har's vaunted diplomatic talents or for some reason of his own, the caravan master not only released the journeyman for the week, but went so far as to give him the freedom of the town for the entire month of the caravan's stay in Brenn. The two guards set off, with Har making much of his own skill in achieving such a desirable result. Maurin pointedly ignored him until he changed the subject. By that time, the two had reached the wide avenue that led straight from the western gate of Brenn to the large stone building in the center of town. They turned away from the gates, and Har darted a sharp look at his friend.

"Now what are you shaking your head about?" he asked.

"That," Maurin said, waving toward the building in front of them. Even from this distance, Styr Tel loomed above the jumble of homes and shops and inns. It bore little resemblance to the ornate palaces and castles of Alkyran nobles in other cities.

"What's wrong with it?" Har demanded. "Hurry up; I don't want them to find out the caravan's in before I get there." Har started toward Styr Tel. Finding no adequate reply, Maurin followed.

The street was full of the cheerfully miscellaneous crowd of a trade city. Peasants, guildsmen, merchants and Traders jostled visitors and townsfolk alike. A man from Rathane in gaudy robes walked past the deadly, black-clad figure of an assassin from beyond the Mountains of Morravik. Three dark-skinned desert people bargained in loud voices with a man who spoke with the accent of Ciaron. And everywhere there were men in soldiers' dress. Some, like Har and Maurin, wore the leather of caravan guards, but many were dressed in the colors of the city. Several times Har and Maurin had to stop and wait while a band of soldiers marched by.

During the third such incident, Maurin looked at Har and said, "I have never understood why Brenn has so many more soldiers than the other trade towns. It isn't *that* much more dangerous to be right on the border."

Har laughed. "As well ask why a fortress has so many caravans passing through!"

Maurin frowned in puzzlement. Har looked at him. "You really don't know?"

"If I did, I wouldn't ask."

"Unless you had some other reason," Har grinned. "But I'll tell you anyway. Brenn is both fortress and trade town, but it is a fortress first. My great-grandfather founded it about two hundred and fifty years ago, right after the Lithmern invasion was stopped at Eirith. The idea was to prevent the Lithmern from ever overrunning Alkyra again; Brenn sits right in the gap between the Kathkari Mountains," he waved to the north, "and the Snake Mountains." Har waved toward the south. "Nobody can get into Alkyra from the west without passing Brenn, so of course it became a trade town too. But it is still the first line of defense for northern and western Alkyra."

Maurin found it easy to believe Styr Tel had once been a fortress. It was surrounded by a high stone wall, set back from the houses of Brenn as if to prevent an attack from the upper stories of the homes and shops. Above the wall, two tall black towers rose to command a view of the entire city; from this angle, they were all of the Styr that could be seen.

Time and custom had made a marketplace of the open area between the low buildings of the town and the walls of Styr Tel. Maurin and Har wove through the merchants and townspeople to the gates, ignoring the persuasive calls of the dealers. The guards recognized Har at once, and let him and Maurin through the gate without challenge. As they entered the courtyard, Maurin got his first close view of Styr Tel.

Black stone, polished smooth, filled his eyes. Styr Tel was made of it. The place was enormous; Maurin's head bent back as he tried to see it all. He could easily imagine a company of troops vanishing inside without disrupting any of the gentler pursuits of the nobles who lived there. The lines of the building were clean and practical, but the dark stone gave it a dignity lacking in the airy palaces Maurin had seen in other cities. This was a strong place, an armored place, a home for a soldier. Maurin found himself admiring the man who had built it.

A long whistle from Har brought Maurin's eyes down, and he blinked. The Styr courtyard was full of activity. Servants were bustling about with buckets, rods, stacks of cloth, brooms and articles of furniture. Everywhere people were cleaning, polishing, and scrubbing; the atmosphere fairly reeked of soap, and the strong scent of Mindaran wood-wax.

"Looks like we've arrived in time for spring cleaning," Maurin observed as they threaded their way through the crowd.

A shout from the doorway ahead spared Har from responding to this obvious comment. A tall girl with pale gold braids hanging down nearly to her knees ran forward to throw her arms around the young noble. "Har, you're back!" she exclaimed.

"Just barely," laughed Har, swinging her off her feet in a wide circle. "We came straight here as soon as the caravan got in." He set her gently back on her feet and turned. "Maurin, this is my sister, Alethia."

"I am charmed," Maurin said, bending low over Alethia's hand. Privately he thought that the introduction was nearly unnecessary; there was no mistaking those tilted green eyes and straight black eyebrows. Alethia was clearly Har's sister.

Alethia returned his courtesy absently, and linked arms with her brother as they started for the house. "I'm so glad you got back in time for my party," she said as they mounted the stairs. "But you could have sent some kind of warning, couldn't you?"

"Party?" Har said blankly.

Alethia laughed. "You don't even remember! I'm twenty tomorrow; it is my birth eve."

"Well, I didn't forget entirely," Har said. "I got something at our last stop in Karlen Gale. I'll give it to you tonight, after I've unpacked."

"Thank you in advance—I think!" Alethia replied. Then, turning to Maurin she added, "You will come to the party too, won't you? It won't be more than dinner and songs, really; the Lords Armin and Gahlon are coming at the end of the week to talk to Father, and it would be hard to have two large feasts so close together."

"Lord Armin and First Lord Gahlon, here? Together?" Har exclaimed. "What do they want to talk to Father for?"

His sister smiled mischievously. "I'm not supposed to know, so you'd better ask him. The Lithmern raids, I think," she added innocently.

"But the raids have practically stopped!" Har said.

"I know," said Alethia, and grinned again.

"You must tell me all about it after he explains to you."

"What makes you think he will?" Har countered.

"Well, aside from being his son and heir, you've just come back from three months with the caravans, haven't you? And your last stop was Karlen Gale, which is the only Free City anywhere near Lithra. So if Father wants to know about the Lithmern, who else would he talk to?"

"Who indeed?" said a deep voice behind them, and Alethia jumped. The three turned to find a tall, dark-haired man of middle years looking at them with a smile. "Father!" said Alethia and Har together.

The man's smile deepened. "Welcome home," he said to his son, and there was no mistaking the deep affection in his tone. For a moment they stood silent, then Har shook himself and turned to introduce Maurin.

"I am honored; I have heard a good deal of you, Lord Bracor," Maurin said when the formalities were finished.

"Nothing too intimidating, I hope," Bracor responded. "Come into my study where we can talk." He turned toward Alethia and studied her for a moment. "I don't suppose you would like to go on and tell your mother that Har has returned?"

"Mother probably already knows," Alethia said, and smiled.

"And you would rather join us," Bracor finished with an answering smile. "I don't quite see why; you probably know all about it already."

"I know just enough to be interested, that's all," Alethia said. "Of course, I can find out from Har later, but it would be easier if you'd just let me stay.

Har leaves things out sometimes."

Har's face reddened, and Bracor shook his head in mock resignation. "Very well, then, since you are so determined." He stood aside and let the others walk past him into the room, then entered and closed the door behind him.

"I suppose that Alethia has already guessed that I wanted to talk to you about the Lithmern," Bracor said when they were all seated inside.

"Well, she did say something about Lithmern raids," Har said, glancing at his sister. "But I don't see the point; they've practically stopped."

"The Conclave of First Lords feels the same way, I'm afraid," the Lord of Brenn replied tiredly. "But raids are not the only thing to fear from Lithmern."

Har looked puzzled; Bracor continued. "Do you know that the Lithmern now control, either by outright conquest or by more subtle means, most of the countries to the north and west of Alkyra? They are far stronger than you may think."

"Then why aren't they raiding more instead of less?" Har said stubbornly. "If they thought they could get away with it, the Lithmern would be attacking every caravan that takes the northern trails!"

"Not every one," his father said. "Only a few that they can loot completely. Your Trader friend knows what I mean." Maurin looked at Bracor in surprise as Har and Alethia turned their heads.

"You must have excellent sources to have uncovered that, my Lord," Maurin said with new respect.

Har made a frustrated gesture. "What are you talking about?"

"Three caravans have disappeared completely in

the past six months," Maurin said.

"Disappeared?" Har asked skeptically. "How can fifteen or more wagons and sixty men just vanish?"

Maurin shrugged. "They are certainly gone. No trace of men, horses, goods, or wagons has been found, not even the Traders' family gear. And all of them were passing near Lithra. At least, that's where we think they were."

"You don't know?" Alethia asked.

"Caravan masters can be very secretive about routes and destinations, especially if they think someone else wants to cut in on their profits," Maurin explained.

"But how could the Lithmern do it?" Har puzzled. "And why would they take everything that way?"

"How, I do not know," Bracor said. "Why, I can guess. They wish to keep us in doubt of their numbers and their intentions. Until now they have been afraid of Alkyra; they remember their defeat at Eirith too clearly to take chances with us. Now I think their fear is passing; they have been preparing carefully for years, growing stronger while we bickered among ourselves."

"Then you think the Lithmern are planning to attack Alkyra!" Alethia said.

"I do," her father replied. "I have tried to tell the Conclave that, but they will not listen, and the Regent has too little real power to compel the lords, much less the Nine Families. We have kept them safe too long. Oh, there are a few who suspect, who build their own forces, but Alkyra has no unity."

"Can't the Regent do anything?" Maurin asked.

"He never does," Alethia said. "I think he's afraid to offend the First Lords, because they might decide to replace him if he tried to make them do anything."

"Alethia is right," Bracor said. "The Regent's power depends on the good will of the Nine Families, and he knows it too well. The last regent, of course, was not a strong ruler, and he allowed his authority to be eroded by the nobles."

"Then what are you going to do?" asked Har.

Bracor straightened. "Lord Armin of Lacsmer and First Lord Gahlon of Meridel will be coming here in three days on a courtesy visit." He smiled wryly. "Protocol has its uses, after all. They are actually coming to discuss an alliance among us to meet the threat of the Lithmern. If we can come to an agreement, Brenn will have some support, even if the Conclave of First Lords does not act."

"I do not know either of them," Har said. "But the Nine Families have always been independent. Do you think they will agree to work together?"

"First Lord Gahlon is young, but he is reasonable. Armin has something of a temper, but things should go well if I can show him how great the danger really is." Bracor looked sharply at Maurin and Har. "That is why I wish to talk to you; your caravan is the only one in the city which has taken the trade route just south of Lithra in the past month. So tell me about your journey."

For the next hour, Har and Maurin talked, describing the cities and towns they had passed through. Bracor had many questions, from how many men-at-arms they had seen in the streets of Sormak to what welcome the Traders had received from the people in Karlen Gale. To Maurin's surprise, Alethia's comments were more intelligent and informed than his small experience with noble ladies had led him to expect.

Finally, Bracor sat back. "That is enough for to-day, I think. I need some time to consider what you have told me before we continue; we can talk more tomorrow." He rose and nodded as the two younger men stood and followed Alethia out.

It was over an hour later that Alethia descended the stairs to the great dining hall. Bracor was there before her, standing at the foot of the stairway talking with Maurin. As she came down, the men looked up. Bracor stepped forward with an exclamation. "Alethia! You look lovely; you could be your mother twenty years ago."

Alethia laughed. "Mother doesn't look any older now than she did then. Where is she?"

"She hasn't come down yet," Bracor replied; "but she should be here any minute." Turning to Maurin, who was staring almost rudely, he started to ask a question, but he was interrupted once more by the entrance of a tall, gracious woman with silver-white hair. She wore a simple gown of grey, trimmed with silver, and she moved like mist on the water. She came directly over to Bracor and placed one slim hand on his arm.

"Isme! I have been looking for you," Bracor said with a smile.

"I was delayed helping dress Tatia," replied the woman. "I am sorry to have kept you waiting."

At that moment a small bundle consisting mainly of arms and legs came flying down the stairs and struck Bracor at about waist level. He staggered, but kept his feet. Bending down, he picked up the missile, which resolved into a small girl in a blue dress. The child was about four years old, with blond braids and Isme's slanted eyes. "Tatia, have you been keeping your mother upstairs?"

"No, she was just dressing me. Don't I look pretty? Where's Har? I want him to see my dress. It's new. He is going to take me fishing tomorrow. He didn't come see me when he got home. Who is that?" She pointed to Maurin, who was standing in awe of the flow of words. Bracor laughed.

"He is a friend of Har's and he will be staying here with us for a few weeks while Har is home. Har should be over there; see if you can find him."

The Lord of Brenn placed his youngest child on the floor. She stood and stared at Maurin for a moment, then tore off at top speed. Isme shook her head. "After all the time I spent dressing her . . . It isn't worth it. But who is our guest?"

"Forgive me; I should have introduced you earlier. May I present Maurin Atuval of the Traders?" Bracor said, turning to her.

"Har has told me much of you already," said Isme in her musical voice as she nodded. The years had indeed been kind to the Lady of Brenn; she could have passed as Alethia's twin sister easily. Maurin bowed courteously, wondering where the Lady Isme's native land was. He had never seen the combination of white-blond hair and tilted green eyes before, though he knew most of the peoples of Lyra after his travels. "I hope Har's report was favorable, Lady," he replied.

"You need have no fear on that score," Isme said. "Har is not likely to speak poorly about one whom he holds in such high regard. You are welcome in Styr Tel." She nodded again. Smiling slightly, she moved off on Bracor's arm before Maurin could think of an appropriate reply.

"It is time to seat ourselves." Maurin turned to find Alethia beside him.

"Allow me to escort you to dinner," the Trader

said formally, wondering if he was being maneuvered into taking her in. Alethia's eyes glinted with amusement; then she inclined her head gracefully. The jewels in her hair flashed as she took Maurin's arm and they went together toward the great hall.

# CHAPTER TWO

Candlelight and color filled the banquet hall of Styr Tel. The black walls were hidden behind tapestries in rich hues depicting history and legend. In front of them, the notables of Brenn stood in small knots of conversation, or filed toward seats at the linen-draped tables. Over half the places were already occupied, and serving-boys with silver decanters moved along the tables, pouring wine.

Maurin felt out of place among the richly dressed men and women. He tried to ignore the feeling, and concentrated on observing people instead. He was successful enough that it was a moment before he realized that Alethia was speaking to him.

"I am sorry," he apologized. "I'm afraid I didn't quite hear the question."

"I asked what you find so fascinating," Alethia said. "Now I am doubly curious."

"I was watching your guests," Maurin said. "You said this would be a small party, just dinner and songs, but it looks like a feast to me."

Alethia laughed. "Just wait until First Lord Gahlon and Lord Armin get here; then you'll see a feast! Everyone in town will want to come."

"I don't see why; the guest of honor tonight is far more attractive."

"Very nice!" Alethia said approvingly. "Are all Traders so courteous?"

"Oh, most of them are much better at it than I am," Maurin assured her solemnly. "I am only a journeyman, after all."

"Only a journeyman? After everything Har told me, I thought you were a Wagon-master, at least!" Alethia's eyes danced wickedly; Maurin shook his head in mock sadness.

"Har tends to exaggerate," he explained.

Alethia laughed again. "I see you know my brother well."

"Well enough; we stood watch together from Ciaron to Karlen Gale."

"Stood watch?" Alethia looked puzzled. "But you're a journeyman."

"Trader caravans can't afford to carry dead weight," Maurin said. "Everyone does something; journeymen earn their keep as guards while they're studying for full status."

"What do Traders study?" Alethia asked curiously.

"Customs and languages of the largest cities, and tables for converting the coin of one realm to another," Maurin said. "Some of the Master Merchants can speak and write in twelve tongues, but a journeyman is only required to learn five. It is not really very interesting."

Har heard this last remark and leaned forward. "Don't let him fool you, Allie," he advised. "Maurin is one of the youngest men ever to master all of the tables and scripts, but he is too modest to mention it. And he wasn't even born a Trader!"

"What?" Alethia looked at Maurin. "Then how can you be a journeyman? I didn't think the Traders let people just join!"

"They don't," Maurin said. He shot a deadly look at Har, who grinned unrepentantly. "But I've been with the caravans since I was fourteen."

"If you aren't a Trader, where are you from?" Alethia asked.

Maurin hesitated. "I was born in one of the seacoast towns; my parents were killed in a fire at the docks when I was an infant."

"Oh. I'm sorry." Alethia looked as if she really meant it. "How did you join the Traders, then?"

"I was raised by a couple who took me in for charity and never let me forget it," Maurin said. He was surprised at how easy it was to say. "I ran away when I was fourteen. One of the south-bound caravans picked me up. I suppose I was useful; anyway, they let me stay."

"Ha!" Har leaned forward again and grinned at his sister. "Let him stay? Maurin's one of the best swordsmen in the guard; I'll bet he was good even then. Of course they let him stay!"

"I suppose that is another thing he is too modest to mention," Alethia said. "Go start your own conversation, and stop listening to mine!"

Har grinned and turned away. Alethia looked at Maurin speculatively for a moment. When she was sure Har was occupied elsewhere, she tilted her head to one side and asked, "Are you very good with weapons, then?"

"Some think so," Maurin replied cautiously.

"Do you know how to throw daggers?"

"Yes, of course; all caravan guards learn that," Maurin said, puzzled.

Alethia glanced down the table. Maurin's eyes followed hers; he saw that Lord Bracor was turned away from them, talking to someone on his other side. Alethia turned back.

"Do you play san-seri?" she asked.

Maurin nodded, still wondering where this was leading.

"Then would you play a match with me?" Alethia asked, leaning forward anxiously. "Har won't any more, so I hardly ever get a chance. Please?"

Whatever Maurin had expected, it certainly wasn't an invitation to play an intricate knife-throwing game with the daughter of one of the Noble Houses of Alkyra. San-seri was played by professional soldiers and the Traders who had brought it to Alkyra from the lands west of Ciaron.

Aware of Alethia's expectant eyes on him, Maurin finally asked, "But where could you set up a san-seri target? The courtyard is much too crowded."

"I knew you would!" Alethia said happily, and Maurin realized with a sinking feeling that he had just committed himself. "The target is no problem; Har and I set one up behind the stables when he was learning swordcraft." She laughed. "When I started beating him, he decided to teach me archery instead, because he was better at that than I was. Father would be terribly upset if he knew; he is always telling me to be more ladylike."

She gave Maurin instructions on when and where to meet her, and the conversation turned to other things. Maurin found himself hoping that something would happen to put off the proposed match, such as the ground opening up and swallowing him before he had to arrive at the stables. A clandestine meeting with a noble's daughter was a good way for a Trader to get into trouble, and he was not quite sure how he had been maneuvered into such a breach of common sense.

The dinner ended, and Bracor rose. After the obligatory toasts to his daughter and his guests, he said, "We are fortunate to have in town a man who has just been accepted by the Guild of Minstrels. He was only passing through, but I have heard well of him, and I persuaded him to play for us tonight."

A ripple of anticipation went through the hall as Bracor signaled to the man and re-seated himself. Full-fledged minstrels came seldom to Brenn.

A young man stepped forward, dressed in the blue and green of a traveling minstrel. He carried a melar, the stringed instrument that most wandering musicians used, and the hall hushed in anticipation.

"Now will I sing for you the song of Gasinal and her love for Kellingarm the Kulseth seafarer," said the minstrel, and he drew his hand across the strings and began. Though all had heard the song before, and knew it well, the hall was silent as he played. For the minstrel was he who was later known as Tamsin Silver-Tongue, and though he was not yet at the height of his power, still he held them. Even Tatia kept still, without fidgeting, until the song was done.

When he finished they would not let him go, but showered him with praise and begged another of him. And so he sang for them the greatest lays of Alkyra, one after another, on into the night while the candles burned low in their sockets. When at last he ended his songs and bowed and slipped away, the guests shook their heads and gathered in quiet knots to speak of older things in low voices until the close of the eve was upon them, when they went their several ways.

* * *

Shortly after noon of the following day, Maurin picked his way across the courtyard of Styr Tel toward the stables. He was still not certain how he had gotten himself into this ridiculous position. Fortunately, Har was out with Tatia on the promised fishing expedition, so he had needed no excuse to slip away from the young noble.

The stables of Styr Tel were built in a corner of the courtyard. On one side they extended up to the outer wall, but on the long side there was a gap of six or seven feet between the stable wall and the fortifications. This was partially roofed over, so that it was not clearly visible from the towers of the house, and it was one of the most popular trysting places of Styr Tel.

Maurin rounded the corner of the stable to find Alethia waiting for him. Her hair was braided again, and she had tied the plaits back to keep them out of her way. The severe style emphasized her high cheekbones and the slant of her wide eyes. She held a rack of daggers in one hand: twelve of them, with green handles.

"I am so glad you came," Alethia said as soon as she saw Maurin. "I was afraid you weren't going to show up."

"I almost didn't," Maurin admitted.

"Are you worried about getting into trouble with Father?" Alethia asked. "Don't be; he will know exactly who to blame if he finds out. But if he does, you must promise to smuggle some pastry up to me after he locks me in my room; I don't mind missing supper, but not Ceron's pies!"

Maurin grinned back at Alethia. "But what if he locks me in, too?"

"Oh, Father would never do that," Alethia said with mock seriousness. "You are a guest!"

"Then you have set my fears at rest," Maurin said, and bowed with a flourish.

"Are you ready to start, then?"

Maurin nodded, and Alethia waved toward a second rack propped up against the wall of the stable. This one held red-handled daggers, and on closer examination they proved to be exceptionally well-made and balanced for throwing. Maurin tossed one in the air, enjoying the feeling of quality.

"They are good daggers, aren't they?" Alethia said with some satisfaction. "Har brought them from Col Sador the last time he rode guard."

"No wonder they are so well-balanced!" Maurin said as he rose, holding the rack. "Where is your target?"

Alethia nodded toward the end of the alley. Someone, probably Har, had fixed a large board in position against the stone of the outer wall. On it the square, circle and diamond shapes were drawn roughly but clearly. Maurin nodded. For a few moments they took turns making practice throws, and Maurin found the red-handled daggers just as good as he had expected. Then the game began.

They flipped a coin for the first throw, and Alethia lost. Maurin stepped to the throwing line and, with the ease of long practice, brought his arm down. The dagger flew in a perfect arc, turning in mid-air to strike point-first at one of the four intersections between the three figures. Alethia nodded in appreciation and stepped forward to take her turn.

The green dagger placed itself perfectly in the next intersection, and Maurin raised an eyebrow in surprise. Alethia was better than he had expected, unless it had been a lucky throw. The game went on, and it soon became clear that Alethia was not going to be easy to defeat. Maurin was hardly a novice player, but Alethia matched his throws with an ease that surprised him, and she was no mean strategist.

They reached the final throw, and Maurin paused to study the board. The pattern of red and green was nearly complete. Carefully, he aimed and placed his last dagger. It flew true and fair, and Maurin smiled. The pattern of red was complete. Green could best it by completing its pattern, for Alethia had chosen a more difficult design, but her final dagger would have to be placed almost on top of Maurin's last throw. If Alethia knocked the red dagger from the board, she would lose.

Alethia stepped up to the throwing line. She frowned slightly, then in a single, fluid motion she raised her arm and threw. The green dagger came to rest a hair's-breadth from the red, quivering slightly, and Alethia smiled.

"What a throw!" Maurin exclaimed in genuine admiration. "Har should have warned me. You have won, I think."

"Har doesn't like to admit that he can be beaten by his younger sister," Alethia said, smiling.

"If you always throw like that, I can't imagine why," Maurin said. "Where do you get your skill?"

"I suppose it runs in the family; Father and Har are both very good. Besides, I have a lot of time to practice," Alethia said. She looked at the board critically. "I must admit, this is as close to a perfect game as I have ever managed."

"I would like to see you in competition," Maurin said thoughtfully. "I don't know ten men who could have made that last dagger."

"You flatter me, sir," Alethia said, sweeping him a dignified curtsey.

"No, it is true," Maurin protested; then he saw Alethia's grin. Together they walked toward the target. "We must have a rematch," Maurin said as they retrieved the daggers.

"Not today, I am afraid," Alethia said with some regret. "Mother and I are going down to the healer's houses for our weekly visit. If I stay here to play another game, I'll be late."

"Then I suppose we must wait," Maurin said. "Tomorrow, perhaps?"

Alethia nodded, smiling. "Tomorrow."

The rematch was not held. Alethia was caught up once more in the whirl of preparations for the visit of the two lords, and she was barely able to snatch enough time to let Maurin know that she could not make it to their appointment. Maurin would have been disappointed if he had not been busy with Bracor and Har, going over and over everything that was known about the Lithmern. As it was, neither of the two found time for regrets.

# CHAPTER THREE

Alethia hurried down the back stairs of Styr Tel, skirts lifted high to avoid catching dust on the green silk. The slippers that showed as a result were in the latest style; spangled, with narrow heels. Normally she was not quite so careful, but it was only an hour before the feast Bracor was giving for the two nobles and she wanted to look her best.

Har had persuaded Bracor to invite Maurin to the welcoming feast, even though the unexpected addition gave the preparations a last-minute touch of confusion. Adding two more to a formal banquet was a far cry from setting two more places at a birthday party, however elaborate. As she reached the foot of the stairs and turned toward the Styr kitchens, Alethia frowned. Maurin was undeniably a personable young man, and she would be glad to see more of him, but she wished he would not monopolize Har so thoroughly. She had hardly seen her brother since the two men arrived. Of course, some of the fault was Bracor's; he kept the two men studying Lithmern for hours. Still . . .

The door to the kitchen swung open, cutting Alethia's reflections short. She found everything in a predictable and unalarming state of chaos. She waved to Ceron, the head cook. He grinned broadly in response, but he made no move to leave the large kettle he was stirring. One of the assistant cooks came hurrying up.

"Anything we can do for you, my lady?"

"Mother sent me down to see if things were going well. She would have come herself, but she has too many details to see to upstairs." Alethia did not mention that her mother seemed more apprehensive than usual about the evening. Isme's hunches were known and respected by the members of the household staff. To allow her nebulous fears to be known would insure a disaster, so Isme had reluctantly allowed Alethia to take her place for the customary visit to the kitchens.

Things seemed to be well under control. Alethia settled several small quarrels, checked the wine, and informed Ceron that he could begin serving upstairs in one hour's time. The whole tour of the kitchens took only a few minutes, and she left quite satisfied.

Just outside the kitchen door Alethia paused for a moment to dust off her skirts. As she did, she heard a muffled thumping coming from the courtyard. She turned uncertainly, and the noise was repeated. Frowning, she reached for the small side door that led to the yard.

Outside it was very dark, though the sun had set only a few minutes previously. Alethia peered into the shadows. "Who is there?" she called, and stepped forward. There was a movement on her left, and she half turned. At that moment a heavy cloak dropped over her head, and she felt herself being grasped and lifted. Through the folds she heard a hoarse chuckle.

Alethia fought and tried to scream, but the folds of the cloak hampered her movements and muffled her voice. Someone wrenched at the throat of her gown; then the cloak was wrapped more tightly.

Despite her struggles, she was picked up and thrown unceremoniously across a saddle. She heard the noise of hoofbeats as her kidnappers started off. Alethia kicked and tried to slide from the horse's back, but the rider who held her was strong. She kicked again and heard his breath hiss as she connected, then she was knocked senseless by a blow on her head.

On the second floor of Styr Tel candles smoked and flared as Bracor paced the floor of his study, sending dark shadows leaping about the walls of the room. Isme and Har sat near the door, watching. Tatia, oblivious to the tension in the air, played happily with a paperweight and Bracor's official seal.

"Where *is* Alethia?" demanded Bracor, for the seventh time at least. "She knows how important this banquet is; we can't keep the guests waiting much longer. And Gahlon made a point of mentioning his desire to see her."

"She knows, and she promised me she would be as pleasant as she could to First Lord Gahlon," Isme said soothingly. "I'm sure she wouldn't start by being late without a reason."

Bracor stopped pacing and turned. "I know, Isme, but that girl finds the most unusual reasons!" Isme smiled, but her husband continued, "Armin and Gahlon have come specifically to talk about an alliance between our cities against the Lithmern. You know how touchy they are, how quick to sense insult. I can't risk anything going wrong now."

"I sent Alethia down to check on things in the kitchen," Isme said calmly. "Though that was at least an hour ago . . ."

"Har," Bracor snapped. "See if you can find her. And make sure *you* get back here on time!"

Har nodded, and rose. Tatia looked up from her play and said with round-eyed seriousness, "Something bad happened to Alethia."

"Hush, brat," said Har, taking a swing at his youngest sister. Tatia ducked under a chair to escape him and stuck out her tongue. Bracor bent to retrieve his erring offspring before she tipped the chair over, and Har proceeded on into the corridor. Turning right, he headed toward the back stairs and practically tripped over Maurin.

"Where away?" the young caravan guard asked.

"Alethia is wandering around somewhere, and Father is having fits, so he sent me to find her," Har said inelegantly. "You look splendid," he added as Maurin fell into step beside him.

"Splendidly uncomfortable, maybe," Maurin said with a grimace. "Give me a nice, practical uniform over these any day. I can hardly move." He indicated his tightly fitting garb of wine-red velvet and silver. The black cape he wore was held at the left shoulder by a round silver clasp which bore a lighted candle in its center. Around the candle a stylized shield, sword, cup and staff intricately entwined with vines formed a circle. He did indeed look a splendid figure, and just as uncomfortable as he claimed. Har laughed.

"I hate to mention it, but that *is* a uniform. The dress uniform of a Captain of the House Guard of Styr Tel, to be precise."

"What!"

"It was all I could find on short notice. Did you want to go to a formal banquet in caravan leather? Quit complaining and let's find Alethia before Father blows the roof off. Mother said she was heading for the kitchen."

Together the two men headed down the stairs and through the passage at the back of the house. Just before they reached the kitchen doorway, Har paused with a frown.

"That door shouldn't be open at this time of night. Wait just a minute, Maurin; I'll be right back." Har stepped through an archway towards a small side door that was half ajar. As he pulled on the handle something jammed, and he bent to examine the frame. He straightened with an exclamation. "Maurin! See here."

The other man hurried over. Har held out his hand. In it was a bent silver clasp similar to the one which held Maurin's cape, but with two leafy branches emblazoned in the center instead of the candle. "This is the badge of Styr Cisek, at Meridel," Har said.

"What would one of Gahlon's guards be doing . . ." began Maurin, then stopped abruptly. Through the open door he had seen a flicker of movement in the shadow of the house. Motioning to Har to continue, Maurin pulled his black cape over the betraying silver of the dress uniform and slipped like a shadow out of the door into the darkness.

With scarcely a pause, Har opened the door slightly wider and, raising his voice, continued, "I don't know, but this undoubtedly belongs to one of them. Perhaps he had an overwhelming desire to sample our dinner, or maybe he came courting a kitchen maid. Still, he must be found; we cannot have such—Maurin, have you got him?" he broke off as the sounds of a scuffle came from the courtyard.

The noise subsided, and Maurin reappeared,

grinning broadly. "Here is our spy," he said, lifting up a small, squirming boy about six years old.

"Lemme go!" the prisoner cried. "I didn't do nothing! It wasn't me. Lemme go!"

"What are you talking about?" demanded Har as Maurin set his captive on the ground once more. Without a word, the child darted away toward the courtyard, only to be scooped up once again by Maurin. "Lemme go!"

Maurin set the boy in front of him, this time keeping a strong grip on one skinny arm. Squatting down to look directly at the child, he said, "Look, we aren't going to hurt you. All we want to know is what happened. What is your name?"

"Ancel," sniffed the boy.

"Well, Ancel, what are you so afraid of?"

The boy trembled, but under Maurin's steady gaze his eyes fell and he mumbled, "The guy with no face that took the lady."

Har and Maurin exchanged frowns. "What happened?" Maurin asked urgently. "Did you see?" The child nodded. "Tell us!" The boy gulped twice and began.

"Cook told me to get out of the way, so I came out here. Then a whole bunch of men sneaked around the corner, and I hid. They waited for a while, and then one of them made a noise. The lady from up in the house came out to see what it was and they put a big cape over her and took her away. She looked awful pretty, all in green. Then one of the men stuck something in the door and they all rode away. I was scared so I stayed hid. Then you came."

"What did these men look like?"

"Mostly dark, like the traders when they come in. And they had their hair chopped off around their ears. I didn't like them. But the big one didn't have no face. He made it dark. They were all scared of him. I was scared too."

The boy began to cry again. Maurin and Har looked at each other. "Lithmern! And they've kidnapped Alethia!" Har exclaimed. Maurin turned back to the boy.

"Ancel, do you remember if they said anything?"

"They didn't talk much and I didn't understand what they said. They didn't talk right," the boy sniffed.

"Well, at least we know who they are," Maurin said to Har. He turned his attention back to the boy. "Now, Ancel, you come with us. I want you to tell this to some other people. Come on."

Maurin led the boy back into the house, while Har lingered behind for a few moments. Har caught up with the pair at the head of the stairs, and they made their way rapidly back to the room where Bracor and Isme waited. As they entered, they saw that Bracor had been joined by his guests. The lords were not in the best of tempers.

"I say there is no reason for this," Armin was saying as they entered. "The girl is making fools of us all, and I for one will not stand for it."

"Your pardon, Lord," Maurin interrupted firmly. "I do not think this is by her choice."

"What do you mean?" Bracor said, stepping forward anxiously. "Where is she?"

"Alethia has been kidnapped," Har stated flatly. Isme turned as white as her hair, and the two visiting lords looked at Har in consternation.

"We found this jammed in the door," Har went on. "I believe it belongs to one of your men, First Lord." He handed Gahlon the silver clasp.

Gahlon held the clasp without looking at it for a full minute as the implications of that statement sank in. "Are you accusing me of this?" he asked quietly.

"No, but we were meant to," Maurin said. He pulled Ancel forward. "Fortunately, this boy saw the whole thing. Alethia was kidnapped by Lithmern, who deliberately planted First Lord Gahlon's insigne to throw suspicion on him and cover their traces. Possibly they also intended to make us waste time arguing among ourselves."

Bracor, somewhat recovered from the initial shock, nodded thoughtfully. "Such an accusation would ruin all chance of an alliance between Brenn and Meridel for years. The Lithmern would seem to be well informed; I had thought your purpose here was unknown." He gazed absently at the other two lords. Abruptly, he came back to the present. "Under the circumstances, speculation can wait. I trust you will excuse me, my lords, but I must go after these men."

"I have already ordered a party of guards to prepare, and our horses should be waiting now, Father," Har put in. "We only came back to tell you."

"Well done. We go, then," Bracor said. Turning to his guests, he continued, "You are welcome to stay here and enjoy the feast that has been prepared for you. I must hold myself excused; do not think me a poor host, I pray." Bracor bowed and started for the door. He was brought to a halt by the sound of Armin clearing his throat.

"I may not speak for First Lord Gahlon," the Lord of Lacsmer said rather gruffly. "But for myself, I would consider it a poor return for your hospitality if we were to remain here at our ease while you ride out to danger. I would join you."

"I also." Gahlon spoke quietly, but there was no doubt of his sincerity.

The grim expression on Bracor's face lightened a little. "I accept," he said, and the three men left the room, followed by Maurin and Har. As Maurin turned toward the stairs he caught a glimpse of Isme's white, strained face as she slipped away toward the tower stairway. His sympathy went out to her for a moment; then he was hurrying on toward the courtyard where the horses waited.

Shadows danced over the stone walls of the castle and stable as men and horses moved purposefully about the courtyard. When Maurin arrived, a troop of guards was already mounted. Three horses stood waiting to the left of the door. Bracor was speaking with the gatekeeper. Maurin saw him shrug and turn to Har, who nodded a little reluctantly. The Lord of Brenn motioned to his two guests, and the three Nobles moved together to the waiting horses and mounted. Har came over to the doorway where Maurin still stood.

"The Styr gatekeeper swears he didn't see anyone come in or go out since the last of the guests arrived late this afternoon," Har informed him. "I don't quite understand it; the captain has found the tracks and they are as plain as a fire on the top of Shadrock Mountain."

"Never mind that. What about us?" Maurin asked, indicating the departing party of guards.

Har's reply was drowned for a moment by the noise as the pursuers started out the gates of Styr Tel into the city. Then he said, "They are saddling two more horses for us now. Father wanted to start at once. We can catch up without too much trouble once we get outside of Brenn, and he thought it important not to antagonize Gahlon and Armin by leaving them behind to wait for horses."

Maurin snorted disgustedly. "Politics at a time like this! I'd never make a noble, that's certain. Well, come on. We'll get started faster if we don't wait for the horses to be brought to us."

The two walked across the courtyard to the stables. They were met just inside the stable door by a groom leading their mounts. With a nod of thanks, Maurin took the reins from the man and led the animals outside.

"They'll head for the West Gate," Har said as they mounted. "It is closest, and the kidnappers wouldn't want to attract attention." Maurin nodded, and with barely a backward look he and Har galloped out into the city.

Maurin and Har did not catch the larger party within the city. Outside the West Gate of Brenn, the trail of the pursuers turned northwest, toward Lithra. As the two turned their horses to follow, Maurin reined in suddenly. "Wait a minute," he said. Har obligingly brought his mount to a halt and turned to look inquiringly at his friend.

Maurin sat bolt upright in the saddle, staring at the sky. "We are going in the wrong direction," he said slowly.

"Why do you say that?" Har asked.

"The Lithmern were trying to throw the blame on Gahlon. If they left the city and headed straight for Lithra, it would give the whole thing away. Suppose they went east, toward Meridel, to lay a false trail instead? They could drop something of Alethia's, just to convince everyone, and then double back toward Lithra. If that's what they're doing, Bracor and the rest will never catch up with them the way they are going."

"Maybe," Har said, running a hand through his hair distractedly. "But do you really think they would take such a chance? It means they will have to slip past Brenn on their way back, with the whole city looking for them."

"Not if they go through the Wyrwood," Maurin said grimly, swinging his horse's head around.

"Impossible."

"There is a pass they can use if they take that route; they wouldn't have to come back this way to get around the mountains."

Har's eyes widened. "A pass? Are you sure?"

"It was used in the days of the old Empire," Maurin said. "The Wyrwood wasn't as overgrown or dangerous then, and they say the caravans used the pass to trade with the Wyrds and the Shee. It has been abandoned for at least two hundred years."

"Wyrds and Shee!" Har said impatiently. "My sister kidnapped, and you talk about children's tales."

"The past exists. Traders don't lie about making money. Not in their own logs, anyway. And I suppose the Wyrwood gets a bad reputation by accident?" Maurin asked politely.

"A couple of travelers get killed by robbers, somebody has a nightmare, and all of a sudden the woods are filled with Wyrds," Har muttered. "I hope this pass of yours is not some minstrel's tale as well."

The two paused briefly to leave a message with the gatekeeper, then urged their horses to a faster pace. When they reached the other side of the city, Har dismounted and studied the ground carefully, but he rose shaking his head.

"Too much traffic," he said. "If the Lithmern

did come this way, their tracks are buried. We must head further east to learn anything." He remounted and they moved away from the city at a slow trot. Har dismounted frequently to study the tracks in the road, but always remounted with the same negative headshake. Both men were growing frustrated, and Maurin was ready to admit he had been mistaken, when he caught sight of something lying in the middle of the road, glinting in the moonlight—a brooch, gem encrusted, bearing the arms of the house of Styr Tel.

# CHAPTER FOUR

When Alethia regained consciousness, it was nearly dawn. Her captors had stopped, and she was propped with her back against a tree at the edge of a clearing in a forest. The horses were tethered in a group to a clump of bushes directly across from her. She craned her neck, but there was no sign of a road; they must have left the highway hours before.

Her hands and feet had been tied tightly in front of her, and her head ached. She was cold and stiff, for the cloak she had been wrapped in had been repossessed by its owner. The brooch she had been wearing was missing; the lace of her dress was torn where it had been ripped away. She felt a pang of regret, but stifled it and turned her attention to her kidnappers.

They wore heavy cloaks against the early morning chill. When they spoke, it was in low, growling voices in a language unfamiliar to Alethia. Most of them were dark men, with straight black hair chopped off raggedly just below their ears. Their eyes were brown or black; several had scars running across their faces, giving them an even more sinister appearance. Their hands were large, and looked almost out of proportion to the rest of their bodies. They moved constantly about the clearing, preparing a temporary campsite. A large fire was already blazing in the center of the clearing.

Alethia thought she counted eleven men, but in the poor light she could not be sure. She noticed that one man, who seemed to be the leader, stood apart from the others, and she studied him carefully. He wore a hat with a low brim, and his cloak was muffled up around his face so that she could not make out any of his features. His hands were hidden deep within the folds of his cloak. Noticing her scrutiny, he strolled over to her.

"Ah, our lovely guest is awake!" he said.

His voice was very like a croak, and Alethia could not place the accent. She fought down her fear, and managed to reply with some energy: "No thanks to you, I'm sure! I do not like people who abduct me and then whisk me off to nowhere. Where are we, where are you taking me, and what do you intend to do with me when you get there? Oh, and by the way, who are you?"

The cloaked leader threw back his head and laughed. It was not a pleasant sound, and Alethia was glad when he stopped abruptly. "So, you have spirit! I like that. It will make things more . . . interesting when we reach our destination." He paused for a moment. "I am captain of these men, and we go to Mog Ograth in Lithra. I think the Lord of Brenn will pay well for the return of his daughter, safe and unharmed, don't you?"

Alethia looked at him contemptuously. "Not at all," she said freezingly. "And I like you less than before. Furthermore, I doubt if your instructions include starving me to death. I am ravenous!" She started at another burst of laughter, then had to stifle a scream as the Lithmern leader bowed mockingly and walked away. For as he bent she saw clearly into the dark space between the hat brim and the cloak. There was nothing there, only shadows.

Apparently her final comment had made some impression, for presently one of the men brought Alethia a piece of hard bread. She thought that he looked nicer than the others; he seemed younger, barely thirty, and he did not have any of the scars that the rest of the party seemed to flaunt. When she looked at his eyes, however, Alethia felt chilled. They were brown and cold, and remote as the icy blue peaks of the Kathkari mountains, as though their owner roamed in other fields. She did not try to speak to him.

Eating with her hands tied was awkward, but she managed. As she ate, Alethia considered carefully the little she had learned. That her kidnappers were Lithmern she did not doubt. Though she had never seen one of the raiders, she was familiar with the descriptions that filtered constantly back to Brenn, and these men fit. She was positive that the Lithmern leader had not told her the real purpose behind her kidnapping, but no likely alternatives occurred to her. Alethia abandoned that line of thought and turned her attention to the cords binding her hands and feet.

The awkward movements of eating gave her an excuse to study the knots from several angles without arousing suspicion. Well before she had finished the bread, Alethia had decided that she could untie her hands by using her teeth. Unfortunately the maneuver would occupy no little time, and she was constantly watched by one or another of the men. Alethia concluded that she must wait for a more suitable opportunity, and concentrated on eating.

She finished her scanty meal and leaned back against the tree. The forest was a place men shunned and she had never before been within it, though she had lived her whole life in its shadow. It was surprisingly pleasant to lie listening to the birds as they began their morning chorus. She felt relaxed; quite relaxed, in fact. Her eyes closed, and she slept.

Alethia was awakened abruptly by the sound of harsh cries. Her eyes flew open. Green daylight poured through the branches of the trees, making deep shadows on the forest floor. The fire was out, and it was nearly noon. All of the Lithmern raiders except the captain were scattered on the floor of the clearing, sleeping so soundly that they might have been drugged. Even the horses stood with their heads down.

The Lithmern leader was stumbling painfully from one man to another, shouting and shaking them in a futile attempt to arouse them. Eventually, he moved in her direction, and Alethia closed her eyes and tried to breathe more slowly. She heard his footsteps come closer and stop by her side. He was apparently satisfied, for after a moment she heard him walk away. When she cautiously raised her eyelids a crack, he had gone back to his men. Eventually, he gave up and reeled towards the horses, where he disappeared from view.

Hardly daring to believe her luck, Alethia raised her bound hands to her mouth, keeping careful watch for the vanished leader. It was slow work, and every minute she expected to see the captain coming back. Finally, the stubborn knots gave. With her hands free it took only a few moments more to untie her ankles, and Alethia tried to rise.

Her stiff legs would not hold her the first time she tried. By the time she gained her feet, Alethia was nearly wild with the thought that the man would return just in time to prevent her escape. As she limped past a sleeping guard at the edge of the clearing, she paused to slip his sword from its sheath, which had fortunately fallen beside and not under the man. She also plucked his dagger from his belt and thrust it through her sash. Using the sword as a cane, she started slowly off into the forest.

After some distance, walking seemed easier and she began to make better time. She had no idea which direction she was going; her one thought was to get as much distance between herself and the Lithmern as she possibly could before the inevitable pursuit began. Whatever had put her captors to sleep, she could not be sure that it would last much longer.

Alethia walked for nearly an hour. Several times the ruffled lace trimming the sleeves of her ball gown caught in bushes, and she wasted precious moments tearing free. Finally she cut the remaining fragments off with the dagger and threw them away. She was so intent on making progress that she did not see the clearing until she was almost on top of it. In the middle of the open area a man in green and blue sat before a fire with his back to her.

Alethia stopped abruptly, but the man had heard her, and he turned. At the sight of her, his eyes widened in recognition. "Alethia of Brenn! How came you to the Wyrwood, and in such a state?" She saw with relief that it was the minstrel, Tamsin, who had passed through Brenn but a few days previously and sung at her birth eve party.

"Lithmern," she said concisely. Feeling that a
further explanation was called for, she added, "I
was kidnapped."

"I take it you have escaped and pursuit is immi-
nent?" the minstrel said calmly, rising from his
seat.

"The Lithmern fell asleep; it was very strange.
As soon as their leader finds a way to wake them,
they will follow me."

Tamsin's eyebrows climbed towards his hairline,
but he kept a credible composure. "You need not
walk, my lady; Starbrow and I are at your service,"
he said, sounding like a character out of one of his
own romances. He rose and kicked some dirt over
the fire. "Pity about lunch, but it cannot be helped.
We must make do with cold fare."

"Starbrow?"

"My horse." Tamsin whistled, and a moment
later a huge chestnut with a white star on his forehead came trotting into the clearing. Tamsin
rubbed the horse's ears, and the animal snorted
contentedly.

"A noble animal, and well-trained," Alethia observed politely, feeling, absurdly, as if she too had
fallen into the minstrel's romance.

"Thank you, my lady. If you would mount, we
had best be on our way." He bowed extravagantly
and lifted her onto the saddle, then sprang lightly
up behind. With merely a touch the great horse was
off, moving surely through the trees.

Alethia found the sword she carried a little
awkward, and she was quite willing to give it up
when Tamsin commented mildly, "I should suggest
that for now we place that useful implement in one

of my bags; it would be most awkward to decapitate our mount at the beginning of the journey."

Tamsin accepted the sword and stowed it in one of the saddlebags; a neat trick while riding. From the same bag he produced cold meat and bread, part of which he handed forward to her. Alethia fell to with a will. When she finished, the minstrel passed her a water bottle and asked, "Now, we are under way and we have lunched, in a fashion. If only to pass the time and satisfy a story-teller's curiosity, will you not tell me how you came to be in such distress?"

Despite her weariness, Alethia told in short, rapid sentences the story of her kidnapping and escape. As she spoke, the minstrel's face grew grave, and he urged Starbrow to greater speed. When she finished, he was silent for a little, then spoke. "Your captors must indeed have had a pressing need to venture here; these woods do not welcome such creatures as they. And to travel so quickly . . . It will take us until midday tomorrow to reach Brenn, even if we travel most of the night."

Alethia's eyes widened. "But we only left Brenn last night! I am sure of it. How could they possibly travel so fast?" But the minstrel had no answer, and they rode on in silence.

The Wyrwood was lovely by daylight; green shadows dappled the ground and it was pleasantly cool. From time to time, Alethia heard rustling noises as some small creature, disturbed by Starbrow's passage, scampered off to safety elsewhere.

"I thought the Wyrwood was a grim and dangerous place," Alethia said after a time. "It doesn't seem nearly as unpleasant as I have been told."

"Do not be deceived, Lady," Tamsin answered dramatically. "The inhabitants of these woods keep some areas clear of deadly things, but most of the forest is as harsh as you have heard."

"Inhabitants?" Alethia said. "Outlaws and thieves, you mean."

"Those to whom this forest belongs," Tamsin corrected her. "They do not like visitors, but they will sometimes allow travelers to pass through the places they do not hold for their own. But I would not care to guess which is more dangerous: to walk among the beasts or to go uninvited into the places that are protected. It is a narrow path that travelers in these woods must walk."

"Then what are you doing here?" Alethia asked pointedly.

"Minstrels are an exception to many rules, Lady."

Alethia laughed and shook her head. "Who are these people, that make such convenient exceptions?"

"Say, rather, beings, for they are not men," the minstrel replied. "They are the Wyrds, and they are of the older days of Alkyra, when the region was just being settled and magic walked the lands freely."

"You talk as though you believe the stories you tell," Alethia laughed.

"They are no more stories than the other 'fey folk' of Lyra," Tamsin said. "The Wyrds were part of Alkyra from the very first, when Kirel was crowned. They are small in stature, but strong in magic. They gave Kirel the Shield of Law at his coronation. Though they have held apart from men for so long, their power at least remains fresh in the minds of men. No one is unaware of the dangers of these woods. The very name of the forest is proof of that."

"You've met them?" Alethia teased.

"They are real," Tamsin said. "But I have not met them. Few men knew them even in the days when Kirel and his line ruled Alkyra; none have seen them since Eirith fell."

"If no one has seen them for two hundred and fifty years, how can you be so certain they ever really existed?"

"Can you pass through their forest and doubt it?" Tamsin said. "I think you have run afoul of their magic ere now, when you left your captors sleeping."

Alethia was silent for a moment. She could not deny that something had put the Lithmern to sleep, but she was not going to attribute it to magic simply because no other explanation presented itself.

"What did you mean by 'other fey folk'?" she said finally, curious in spite of herself.

"The peoples of Lyra who have magic in their blood and bones. They are the Wyrds, the mountain-dwelling Shee, and the sea-people, the Neira. The Shee are powerful and long-lived, wise in magic and very rich. They live in the Kathkari Mountains; the original settlers of Alkyra found their cities there, and made them friends."

"I know the tale—the Shee were supposed to have helped found Alkyra," Alethia said. "But I thought they were another myth, like the firebird that fed Darneel when she was imprisoned on the mountaintop."

"The Shee are no more myth than the Wyrds," Tamsin said firmly. "They gave the Staff of Order to Kirel as a coronation gift. In return, he promised that no men would ever come to the Kathkari to settle."

"Why would anyone want to? The Kathkari Mountains are even more treacherous than the Wyrwood!"

"Some think the Shee themselves are part of the reason why. They drifted away from the other peoples of Alkyra during the ages of prosperity, and all contact with them was lost when the last of Kirel's line died in the fall of Eirith. But they are a proud people, and perhaps they prefer it that way."

Alethia nodded absently. "Are we near the river?" she asked abruptly.

"No," Tamsin replied, puzzled. "We are half a day's ride north of it, perhaps more. Why?"

"I have never seen mist linger so late in the day, except near water," Alethia said. She pointed at a dense grey fog which was coiling about Starbrow's hooves.

Tamsin sucked in his breath. "I fear this is no natural mist, but perhaps we can yet escape it. Come Starbrow! Show your paces!"

The great chestnut leapt forward, but his burst of speed was brief. In a short time the fog had risen up around the travelers, and they were forced to slow to a crawl to avoid running into trees. Alethia, looking forward, could barely make out Starbrow's ears, so dense was the mist. It was quiet, too; a dead quiet, the quiet of snow falling straight down and muffling the noise of the world, but not so friendly. The birds and smaller animals of the forest no longer sang and rustled the leaves as the travelers passed. Everything seemed to be hiding away in the grey mist.

Alethia felt detached. The world receded, melting into the shifting grey clouds around her, muffled in a great grey blanket. She felt herself falling, but even that was far away, outside of the place where she herself was. Then, small and clear, like a picture at the bottom of a deep glass, she saw the Lithmern leader, bending in concentration over a strange symbol wrought in iron, and murmuring unfamiliar words under his breath.

Just for an instant the sight held; then she recoiled and the vision passed. As it faded, she brushed the edge of something dark and greedy, and knew that it was she it sought. She started in fright, and the physical movement brought her back to herself. Alethia drew a deep breath, shuddered, and opened her eyes to see Tamsin's concerned face bending over her.

"Here, drink," he said, holding the water bottle out to her. Gratefully she accepted. After a few swallows, she felt more like herself. Tamsin watched her carefully as she drank, and reached for the bottle as soon as she finished. The grey fog was as thick as ever; Tamsin had wound Starbrow's rein about his arm to avoid losing the animal. Alethia looked at him inquiringly.

"You slipped off of Starbrow so quietly I almost lost you, and I could not wake you," the minstrel said, answering her unspoken question. "What happened?"

"I am not sure," Alethia replied. "Everything was so far away and quiet. Then I saw that Lithmern with the shadow-face, and something was looking for me . . ." Her voice trailed off, and she shivered. "I don't know. I do not understand at all," she said in a strained voice.

Tamsin was watching her with wonder. "Lady of Brenn, I do not know what else you are, but that you are more than you seem I am sure. I think I begin to see why these Lithmern are so anxious to capture you," he said. "However, if they are looking for you as you say, we had better continue, and quickly." He helped Alethia rise and once more assisted her in mounting.

As Tamsin swung onto the horse behind her, Alethia said, "You seem remarkably unshaken by these strange happenings."

"Magic and music are brother and sister," he replied as Starbrow picked his way through the fog. "The bard's craft has always been half magic; in times past minstrels and magicians were often one and the same. Perhaps it is because we must sing so frequently of the old days and the magic of them that we do not fear strangeness as do other men."

Alethia started to reply, then stopped abruptly as the dense fog suddenly dissolved. Starbrow stopped and tossed his head. Tamsin cursed under his breath. They stood at the center of a circle of grinning Lithmern with drawn swords. Facing them, his whole bearing one of triumph, stood the cloaked leader. "Ah, two fish instead of one! I am indebted to you, mistress Alethia."

# CHAPTER FIVE

As Alethia stared at the Lithmern circle in dismay, she felt Tamsin's warning hand on her arm. She stifled the angry response that rose automatically to her lips; instead, she slipped her hand under her sash to the dagger she had taken from the sleeping Lithmern. The touch of the weapon was reassuring. She felt Tamsin shift in the saddle behind her, and heard him say mildly, "Two fish can sometimes escape a net that in times past held many more."

"I think not, minstrel. We have you fast," the captain replied smugly.

Burning at the satisfaction in his voice, Alethia leaned forward on Starbrow's neck and said sweetly, "Nonetheless, perhaps we two together may do better than myself alone, captain. I hope your men had a nice nap? They seemed so tired when I left them." She smiled to herself a little wickedly at the chagrin on the dark faces, and heard a low chuckle from Tamsin. Then she felt him stiffen as the Lithmern circle closed in around them.

Alethia leaned forward and pulled her dagger free. She heard steel ring as Tamsin's sword came out of its sheath, but her attention was concentrated on the grinning circle tightening around them. So intent was she that she almost missed

48

seeing the captain draw out the twisted piece of iron she had seen or dreamt earlier.

The Lithmern leader raised his hands with a commanding gesture and hissed four words. The iron piece he held aloft began to glow with a dull red light. As it did, a heavy darkness clamped itself over Alethia, and she felt Tamsin sway in the saddle behind her. Dimly she watched the Lithmern walking toward them, their captain standing behind with the iron talisman blazing dark fire in his gloved hands. Desperately, Alethia raised one leaden arm. With the last of her strength, she threw her dagger blindly in the direction of the Lithmern captain.

The missile struck in the center of the captain's chest, just below the upraised arms. There was a puff of black smoke from the neck of his cloak, and he made a brief clutching motion before he collapsed to the ground. The flame of the talisman died as it fell from the limp gloves, and suddenly Alethia and Tamsin could see clearly again.

The remaining Lithmern fled in terror, and for a moment Alethia thought that they had seen their leader's collapse. Then she saw one of the running warriors fall, a slender wooden shaft sprouting from his back. One of the men tried to reach the horses, but the frightened animals would not allow him to mount. Another arrow found him, and he, too, fell.

More arrows came singing out of the trees around them, and suddenly the clearing was empty of Lithmern, except for four silent forms which had not reacted quickly enough. In another instant Starbrow was surrounded once more, this time by the archers who were pursuing the fleeing Lithmern.

They were only about four and a half feet high; the tallest would barely have reached Alethia's shoulder. Their eyes were bright in small, delicate-boned faces that seemed vaguely cat-like. They wore tunics of dark green, loosely belted at the waist. Where arms and legs emerged from the coarse material, they were covered by a dark brown fur, which grew more thinly on face and hands and longer and thicker over their heads. From this mane emerged two ears, shaped like a fox's but with inch-long tufts of hair at their tips. Alethia's eyes widened. Behind her she heard Tamsin's low whistle. "Wyrds!" he breathed in awe.

One of the archers turned aside and scrutinized the two for a moment. Apparently satisfied, he raised his head and gave a piping cry. His fellows stopped, and each jumped for the nearest tree. In seconds, they had all vanished as if they had never been.

The remaining archer slung his bow over his shoulder and walked over to Starbrow. He touched the animal's nose lightly, then turned. Without glancing back, he headed northwards into the trees. The horse followed; Tamsin's surreptitious tightening of the reins had no effect whatever.

Alethia and Tamsin rode in silence. Both were acutely conscious of the eerie reputation of the Wyrwood and its denizens, and neither wished to antagonize their strange rescuers.

They traveled for nearly an hour and a half. Finally their guide stopped in a glade which, to Alethia, looked exactly like every other glade they had passed through in the forest. Starbrow stopped beside the Wyrd, snorting gently. Alethia and Tamsin looked at each other uncertainly, but before they had a chance to move the Wyrd gave another high, piping call.

Almost instantly Starbrow was the center of a solemn circle of curious brown eyes. Alethia found herself uncomfortably aware of the long slender bow each Wyrd carried, and the quiver of arrows strapped conveniently to every back. One of the Wyrds stepped forward and bowed profoundly.

"Welcome to the Wyrwood. I am Grathwol, Arkon of the Wyrds of Glen Wilding," he said in their own language, in a voice that was not altogether friendly.

Alethia slid to the ground and curtsied as Tamsin dismounted. "Thank you for your welcome, sir, and for your help," she said. "Your rescue was most timely."

Grathwol's eyes flickered from Alethia to Tamsin. "I am glad you found it so. Therefore you will forgive my desire to know whom we have rescued and what business brought you to the Wyrwood."

Tamsin made one of his theatrical bows. "I am a minstrel and my name is Tamsin Lerrol; this is the Lady Alethia Tel'anh of Brenn."

The circle of Wyrds stirred for the first time, a brief rustle that could have been astonishment. Grathwol's eyes snapped back to Alethia, and he studied her narrowly for a moment. Alethia lifted her chin and stared back. The Wyrd laughed. "I see. Forgive my discourtesy; it has been a long time since we had such visitors at Glen Wilding."

He made a gesture, and all but two of the green-clad Wyrds vanished into the trees. One of the remaining Wyrds, a girl of indeterminate age, came over to stand beside Grathwol; the other took

Starbrow's bridle in hand and started to lead him away. Tamsin made half a gesture of protest. Grathwol smiled, showing pointed teeth.

"You need not fear for your horse, minstrel," the Arkon said. "Nor for yourself or your companion. Those who come from the Hall of Tears have always been welcome among us, and Mistress Alethia we have been watching for since yester eve."

"Watching for me?" Alethia said with a trace of alarm. "Why?"

"We are not totally without knowledge of things beyond our forests," Grathwol said evasively. He paused a moment, studying Alethia, then nodded slightly to himself. "I think perhaps we owe you an apology."

"I have never heard that it was customary among Wyrds to apologize for saving someone's life," Alethia said. Tamsin shot her a warning look, but the Wyrds both smiled.

"It is not for rescuing you that we apologize," the girl said, "but for being so long about it. We did not discover until this morning that the Lithmern had found a way to hide their clumsy blunderings about our woods."

"They have grown powerful indeed to dare a crossing of the Wyrwood," Grathwol growled. For a moment he seemed to have forgotten Alethia and Tamsin; then he looked back at them. "We can speak more of this later. My daughter, Murn, will guide you while you remain in Glen Wilding; I will return to hear your stories and answer your questions after you have refreshed yourselves."

Grathwol bowed, then turned and disappeared among the trees. Murn, however, remained. She eyed the two humans critically. "I think you will want to wash first," she said. "This way."

Tamsin and Alethia looked at each other. Alethia shrugged. There was no real reason not to follow; if the Wyrds wanted to harm them, there was very little Tamsin or Alethia could do to prevent them. Warily, Alethia started after Murn. A moment later she heard twigs crackling behind her as Tamsin moved to join her.

Murn led them down a narrow, barely visible path to a small brook. She waited while they rinsed the dust from their faces and hands, then brought them to another clearing. A meal of fruits, dark bread and round cheese was laid out on the ground. Alethia and Tamsin seated themselves, and Murn poured a somewhat bitter wine into carved cups. Several times during the meal Tamsin tried to question her, but Murn would only laugh and shake her head.

"Father will answer your questions when he is ready," was all she would tell them.

When they had finished eating, the Wyrd girl rose. "Now I will show you . . ." Murn stopped in mid-sentence, listening. A moment later, Grathwol appeared. The Arkon of Glen Wilding was frowning, and he carried a strange-looking, squirrel-like animal about the size of a large cat. He handed the animal to Murn with a few words in a language neither Alethia nor Tamsin understood. Murn's eyes grew wide, and she nodded. She accepted the animal and disappeared among the trees. Grathwol turned to Alethia and Tamsin.

"I apologize for this interruption," he said. "The mirrimur has brought disturbing news. I fear you may not be safe here."

"But the Lithmern are gone, aren't they?" Alethia said. "And even if they come back, surely they wouldn't try to attack Wyrds!"

"It is not swords I fear, but magic," Grathwol said. "The Lithmern have discovered . . . an important artifact. It was found in the clearing where we rescued you. They may have others as well."

"Do you mean that queer iron thing that Lithmern captain had?" Alethia asked.

"Yes," replied Grathwol with a sharp look at the girl. "They are bringing it to Glen Wilding now. What do you know of it?"

Quickly Alethia told him of her encounters with the captain. She finished with, "I am afraid that is all I can tell you. What is this thing?"

"It is a Talisman—ancient beyond imagining, and it has great power, if it can be unlocked," Grathwol replied.

"And you are certain the Lithmern know how to use it?" Tamsin said.

"There is no other way the Lithmern could have traveled so far so quickly," Grathwol said. "And how else did they hide their trail from us, and defeat our warding spells?" He gave Alethia another long, speculative look. "You must be of great value for the Lithmern to send a wielder of such power to capture you, Alethia. They would not risk the loss of such a prize, save for one of at least equal importance."

"Why would the Lithmern care about the daughter of an Alkyran noble?" Tamsin asked.

"That I do not know," Grathwol said. "Nor is it likely to be an easy thing to learn. Even if we catch one of the Lithmern who kidnapped Alethia, I doubt we could learn much from common warriors. And I do not think the Lithmern will send another party through the Wyrwood soon."

"Then you *can* protect Alethia!" Tamsin said with relief.

"Now that we are warned, I do not think the Lithmern could slip past us again," said Grathwol. "But she is *not* safe here."

"But if Alethia stays here she won't have to worry about Lithmern," Tamsin said.

"I am more worried about getting back home than I am about Lithmern," Alethia said. "Particularly if there aren't going to be any of them around for a while."

Grathwol examined Alethia for a long moment. "I will send a group of bowmen to escort you to Brenn, if you wish it," he said slowly. "I think you would arrive safely; but the city has no defense against one of the Talismans of Noron'ri."

"You seem to have some other course in mind," Alethia said thoughtfully. "Just what would you recommend?"

Grathwol smiled. "I do not wish to keep the Talisman in Glen Wilding any longer than I must. Tomorrow I will send it to Eveleth; I suggest that you go with it."

"Eveleth!" Tamsin said under his breath, so softly that Alethia almost missed the word. Grathwol smiled again.

"You may accompany Alethia, minstrel, if you desire it."

Tamsin flushed slightly. "Why are you sending the Talisman away?" he asked a little hastily. "Is it not as valuable to you as to the Lithmern?"

"It is not our manner of magic," Grathwol replied. "The Shee will know better how to deal with it."

"I really don't think I should—" Alethia started, but Grathwol interrupted with a shake of his head.

"Think on it before you give me an answer; you need not decide now. I will return shortly." He turned to leave, but Alethia caught at his arm.

"Please, would you send someone to my father to tell him I am safe?" she asked him. "I know you do not like to be seen, but there must be some way."

"It has already been done," Grathwol replied. Before Alethia could stammer her thanks, he disappeared among the trees, leaving the two travelers alone in the clearing.

Alethia caught her lower lip between her teeth and frowned. Tamsin stared after the vanished Wyrd. "This appearing and disappearing is a bit disconcerting. I suggest, lady, that we make ourselves comfortable; we seem to have much to discuss."

Alethia nodded absently as she seated herself. "What exactly is a *Talisman of Noron'ri?*" she asked abruptly. "Grathwol never did explain. Do you know?"

"The Talismans are only mentioned in one old lay, and that an unpopular one," Tamsin said thoughtfully. "Still, I think I can tell you a little."

Alethia gestured impatiently. "I am getting tired of legends that no one has ever seen and songs no one has ever heard of," she said crossly. "We seem to be running into such a large number of them!"

Tamsin laughed. "The Talismans of Noron'ri are not so unremembered as that!" he said. "The sorcerer Noron'ri made them for his followers long ago, before Alkyra was settled. There were twelve in all: three for the creatures of the sea, three for those of the land, three for the birds of the air, and three for the creatures of the depths of the world."

"You mean the Lithmern might have eleven more of those things?"

"No, for two sank with the island of the Kulseth and another was destroyed in the fires of Mount

Tyrol in the south," Tamsin said. "The other nine
have been scattered and lost for hundreds of years.
How many still exist I do not know, but it is unlikely that the Lithmern could have found more than
the one we saw."

"And now the Wyrds are sending it to the Shee,"
Alethia said. "But why do they want us to go with
it?"

"Grathwol was concerned for your safety,"
Tamsin said uncertainly.

"Why should the Wyrds care about me?"
Alethia demanded. "And if the Lithmern only had
one Talisman, why wouldn't I be safe in Brenn?"

"There is no certainty that the Lithmern have
only one of the Talismans," said a soft voice from
behind Alethia, and Murn stepped into view.

"If the Talismans are so powerful, why aren't
you keeping this one here?" Alethia said. "You
could use it, couldn't you?"

"We could use it, in a way," Murn said. "But
our magic is of the forest and the wild things, tree
and leaf and changing season, and the slow, ancient spells of earth. The Talisman is a different
type of magic, and we would have to twist it before
it could be used to help us. Twisted magics are dangerous, and the more powerful they are, the greater
the danger. The Talisman is not for us."

"Won't the Shee feel the same way?" Alethia
asked.

"The Shee are well versed in the high magic of
old," Murn said. "They are better suited to deal
with this. Even so, it will be a difficult decision;
that is why my father wishes you to go to Eveleth."

"Why?"

"To speak before the Queen of the Shee and her
Council," Murn said. "They will make the final de-

cision about the Talisman, whether it is to be destroyed or kept safe somewhere. Your story may help them decide."

Alethia stared into the forest. "I think I see," she said at last. "Still, I cannot go to Eveleth."

"Your tale might well make a difference in what the Shee will do," Murn said, frowning. "And Brenn is not safe for you."

"I am of the Noble House of Brenn, and my place is there, even if it is not safe," Alethia said. "I am willing to go to Eveleth after we reach Brenn, if you still think it necessary, but I must reassure my parents first and obtain their permission in person." Wryly, she imagined herself begging her parents' permission to seek a legend in the mountains. Who would believe her?

Murn nodded slowly. "I am sorry, but I think I understand."

"I, too, am sorry to hear your decision," Grathwol's voice said. A moment later he appeared beside his daughter. "Yet your concerns are good ones. Since your motives are true, perhaps this course is better; I have no gift of foreseeing."

"Thank you for understanding, sir," Alethia said.

Grathwol smiled. "Even so, you may travel with the Talisman for a way. I suggest you go with it to the foothills of the Kathkari and spend the night with the keeper there. A large group will travel more safely, and you can continue south to Brenn in the morning, while the Talisman goes north to Eveleth."

Alethia nodded. Grathwol went on, "Now I have preparations to make for tomorrow. Murn, show our guests to their rooms." He turned and slipped out of sight once more; hardly a leaf stirred at his passage.

"Where do you have rooms?" Alethia asked Murn curiously. "I have not seen anything even remotely like a building."

"Come, I'll show you," the girl said. She led them along a narrow path. As they walked, the trees grew closer and closer together. Then Murn turned sharply left and vanished between two massive trunks. A little hesitantly, Alethia followed, "Oh," she gasped, and stopped abruptly as Tamsin came up behind her.

They were standing at the front of a long entry room, very like those of the houses of the nobles of Alkyra. Rather than stone, however, this one was made of whole logs set upright side by side in the ground. Alethia wondered how the small Wyrds could move such enormous tree trunks, and then she realized that those were living trees, growing so close together that they formed a solid wall. The ceiling, high above, was made from strips of bark woven into the lower branches. "How do you do it?" Alethia breathed.

Murn smiled. "This hall was planted about two hundred years ago. It is not particularly old; the walls did not grow closed until about seventy-five years ago." Alethia nodded, wide-eyed.

Turning to Tamsin, the Wyrd went on, "Now I think you may understand better what I told you of our magic. It is old and slow, but sure, like the growth of the trees we care for. To hurry them would kill them or twist them into shapes that would be useless, so we use our spells to strengthen them, and to keep them growing evenly. It is our gift to the earth, and the price of our power."

"Oh." Tamsin was still too overwhelmed to say more. They followed Murn through an opening on the other side of the entry room and down a long hallway. They passed several doorways covered with heavy hangings; then Murn paused before one and swept the cloth aside. "Tamsin, this is for you."

Alethia peered inside as the minstrel stepped forward. It was a fairly small room, and the ceiling was at a normal level compared to the great height of the entry hall. Noticing the direction of her gaze, Murn said, "We do not always leave the space between the ground and the lower branches unused. We attach crosspieces to the tree trunks to support floors, and add more as the trees grow. In some places there are two or three floors that have been put on as the roof grows upward."

Alethia and Murn left Tamsin almost immediately. Murn showed the other girl to her own room and then left. Alethia fell onto the bed without bothering to remove the torn green silk she wore, and was soon deep in the dreamless sleep of utter exhaustion.

# CHAPTER SIX

It was not yet light when Alethia was awakened by a light touch on her shoulder. She sighed and opened her eyes to see Murn's serious inhuman face bending over her. "The messengers will be leaving very soon," the Wyrd girl said. "I will come for you then."

Alethia sat up. Her muscles had stiffened overnight, and she moved a little gingerly. She heard a soft sound as Murn left the room, and turned her head; the sudden movement made her wince. She slid her legs out of the bed and looked around.

On a table by the bed stood a washbasin, pitcher, and towel; beside them was a platter of honey-biscuits and a cup of cream-heavy milk. A small lamp hung from a bracket near the curtained doorway. Draped over the chair on the other side of the table was a dress of the same dark material worn by most of the Wyrds. Alethia smiled at this thoughtfulness and reached for the pitcher.

Washing and dressing took very little time. The dress proved to have a split skirt, obviously intended for riding. It was a little small and far too short, but there was a generous hem, and by taking out the stitches Alethia contrived to bring it almost down to her ankles. The only shoes she had were the spangled green dancing slippers she had been wearing when she was kidnapped. They were stained and tattered, and they looked a little strange below the dark, heavy material of the dress, but at least they were comfortable.

By the time Murn returned, Alethia was seated on the edge of the bed, nibbling at one of the biscuits. The Wyrd girl surveyed her critically. "The dress is much too short, I am afraid; it is a good thing you are slender. I am sorry we could not do better for you," she apologized.

Alethia laughed. "It will do much better than what I had," she said, indicating the stained and crumpled green silk.

"True." Murn smiled in return. "Have you eaten? Then come; they are waiting." She plucked the lamp from its hanger as she spoke, and Alethia rose and followed her out into the hallway. Murn took a different route from the one she had shown them the previous night, and by the time the two emerged into the grey pre-dawn, Alethia was thoroughly confused.

Tamsin was already there, towering over Grathwol and four of the Wyrd archers. Another Wyrd approached leading two horses. One Alethia recognized as Starbrow; the other was a brown mare. Both animals were saddled and bridled for the journey. They were followed by five shaggy ponies, who were evidently well trained, for they wore only halters and followed without benefit of a leading rein.

Grathwol nodded to the Wyrd leading the horses and took the mare's rein from him. "We have been fortunate enough to capture one of the Lithmern mounts. I hope you will not object to riding her; she is a gentle beast and one of our mounts would be . . . a little small, perhaps."

Alethia smiled. "I do not mind," she said. "What is her name?"

"She has none yet; I do not know what the Lithmern called her, but I do not think she would mind a different name," Grathwol replied. "Choose one."

"I will call her Alfand," said Alethia after a pause, reaching out to pet the horse's velvet nose.

Tamsin cleared his throat. "You said you were fortunate enough to catch one of the Lithmern horses. The others escaped, then?"

"Not all of them. We have seven other new additions to our stables." The Wyrd leader smiled a little grimly. "They would seem to like their change in ownership well. We will keep them, I think. Though they are not the type of mount we prefer, I suspect we can find a use for them."

"But what of the Lithmern themselves?" Tamsin asked with a frown.

Grathwol's eyes darkened. "Their leader is, of course, dead. Four of the men were killed immediately by our archers; three more died in the chase."

"Then three escaped," Tamsin said quietly.

"Three escaped," Grathwol confirmed. "Our only excuse is that we did not know of the Talisman at first, and sought only to drive the Lithmern out of our forests. By the time we learned of it and sought captives instead, it was too late, and they eluded us."

"You haven't given up, have you?" Alethia asked.

"No; there are still two parties tracking them," Grathwol said. "But I am afraid I have little hope for their success. The Lithmern planned well."

"But surely they won't all escape?" Alethia persisted.

"We know that at least one of them is badly wounded," Grathwol said. "But as long as one survives to reach Lithra, we have not succeeded. That is why I wish to have you safe, and the Talisman in Eveleth, as soon as possible. The Lithmern will soon learn what has happened, and I do not know what they may do then."

Tamsin nodded. "I think I begin to see," he said.

"I suggest that you leave now," Grathwol said with a piercing look at the minstrel. "It is nearly dawn, and at a comfortable pace you will barely reach the Kathkari by nightfall. These are your guides as far as the mountains; Worrel, Rarn, Anarmin, and Shallan." He waved in the general direction of the archers, who nodded formally and stepped to their ponies as Grathwol called their names.

Worrel was young, and the thick mane of hair covering his head was a rich chestnut color. Rarn was rather tall for a Wyrd, with snapping brown eyes; her fur was a tan color, with streaks of darker brown in her mane, and brown ear-tufts. The third Wyrd, Anarmin, was a uniform dark brown in color; a few threads of silver sprinkled his ear-tufts, and Alethia found herself wondering whether that was the Wyrd counterpart of greying at the temples. Shallan's fur was also dark, but his mane and ear-tufts had a reddish tinge. All four wore the deep green cloaks and tunics, and the belt and quiver of the Wyrd archers.

"Murn will also accompany you," Grathwol finished, and waved them toward their horses.

Tamsin bowed deeply to Grathwol, and with a formal farewell they mounted and departed, and were soon out of sight of the living buildings of Glen Wilding.

* * *

Maurin and Har arrived at the temporary camp of the Lithmern from which Alethia had made her escape, exhausted and worried. They had stopped but twice to rest themselves and their horses, and only for a few hours at the dead of night while waiting for the moons to rise and light their way.

Around noon of the previous day, the track had left the highway and turned north into the Wyrwood. Neither man was disheartened by the eerie reputation of the forest; by this time, their primary thought was that it would be much easier to follow the trail now that there was no chance of confusion with the tracks of the many caravans that used the roadway.

It was indeed easier to follow the Lithmern through the Wyrwood, though Maurin commented several times that the traces were unusually faint and far apart. The two noted with grim satisfaction that their deductions had been correct; the trail slanted back sharply to the west and north as soon as it entered the Wyrwood.

The two men, though tired, were still alert. They were accustomed to long rides and little sleep from their work as guards. The same could not be said, however, of the Styr horses they rode. Though both were fine animals, they had not been bred or trained for endurance. More than once Maurin wished fervently for the hardy caravan horses that had been appropriated by the two Alkyran Lords, Armin and Gahlon.

It was partly to spare their tired mounts and partly to avoid losing the trail that they were moving slowly when they reached the clearing. Har was in the lead, and he reined in abruptly as he broke through a clump of bushes near the clearing's edge.

The other horse nearly ran on top of Har's even at the slow pace they were keeping. Maurin stifled an impulse to object furiously as Har's whisper floated back to him. "It looks like a camp. Seems deserted."

Maurin drew up alongside Har. Once they were satisfied that there were no others present, they dismounted and tied their horses to a nearby sapling. Then they forced their way through the bushes and into the clearing.

"They seem to have stopped here quite a while," Maurin commented. "See, they tied their horses over there. Looks like there may have been a dozen or so."

Har poked the dead ashes of the fire. "Maurin, we must have crossed another trail somewhere and followed the wrong one. These ashes are nearly a day old; the Lithmern couldn't possibly have come this far from Brenn in a single night."

"But I'll swear we never saw a sign of anyone else, and this track goes in the right direction," Maurin said, a little puzzled. "Besides, who else would be traveling in the Wyrwood?"

Har was prowling impatiently about the clearing. "I don't know, but I still say this can't have been used by the Lithmern we have been chasing. We had better go back and see if we can pick up their trail before they get impossibly far ahead of us. We have no idea how much time we may have lost already."

Maurin nodded reluctantly, and started back toward the horses. As he passed the edge of the clearing he detoured around a clump of bushes and stopped short. Behind him he heard Har exclaiming, "Maurin! Look here!"

"No, you come look here," Maurin replied in a queer voice. Har came hurrying through the trees carrying two short pieces of rope and an empty dagger-sheath.

"I found these under that tree," he said, gesturing vaguely back toward the clearing. "They are Lithmern work, no doubt of it; maybe you weren't so far wrong after all."

"I know I'm not wrong," Maurin cut him off, and pointed. At his feet, imprinted clearly in the forest mold, was the outline of a small, narrow-heeled slipper, and caught on a twig on one side a green spangle winked dully up at them. Har stared at it for a moment. "I don't understand it," he muttered under his breath.

"Neither do I, but there it is. We are on the right trail." Maurin's eyes flashed and he almost smiled. With new energy, Har ducked back through the bushes toward the horses. Maurin meanwhile followed Alethia's footprints for a short distance. He turned as Har came up behind him with their mounts.

"It's a good clear track; we should make better time now," he said briefly as he mounted his horse. Har nodded as they started off. They rode in silence, stopping now and then to examine the tracks more closely. They saw no traces of the Lithmern, which puzzled them greatly, but several times they found bits of lace or green net to assure them that they were still on Alethia's trail.

It took them about half an hour to cover the distance it had taken Alethia a full hour or more to traverse on foot. Then they were confronted by another clearing, the cold ashes of another fire, and more hoofprints. Maurin's eyebrows rose as he surveyed the scene. "This gets stranger and stranger. I begin to think these woods deserve their reputation."

"That would really be all we need!" Har commented. "Aren't Lithmern enough to worry about?" He dismounted for a moment to study the confused tracks. "There's only one horseman this time. Well, come on; she's not here." He remounted and they continued, following the latest trail.

Gradually the trees grew denser, and they had to slow their pace slightly. A little later they stopped to rest their horses. Har had had the foresight to grab a water bottle as they left Styr Tel; this was now nearly empty, but there was enough left to wet their throats. They stood for a moment watching their horses as the animals munched hungrily on nearby bushes and low-hanging branches. Makes me wish I were a horse," Har commented.

Maurin sighed. "We will have to start again if we are going to catch up to them," he said, and started toward the horses. He had gone several paces when he heard Har's strained voice behind him. "Maurin. Don't move. There is a . . . a little brown person pointing an arrow at your head."

By the time Har had finished his sentence, the warning was no longer necessary. A dozen Wyrd archers had appeared, seemingly out of nowhere, with drawn bows and very businesslike arrows. One motioned Maurin back toward Har while another collected their horses. The remaining archers fanned out into a ring, well out of sword's reach but within easy range for their own bows.

One of the archers stepped forward. "Who are you, and what are your cities?" she demanded.

"I am Har Tel'anh of Brenn, and this is my

friend, Maurin Atuval of the Traders," Har
answered steadily.

"I see," said the same Wyrd in a skeptical tone.
She seemed to ponder for a moment, then she
raised her head and snapped several commands to
the archers in another tongue.

Turning back to Maurin and Har, the Wyrd
said, "You will come with us. If you are what you
claim, you have nothing to fear." She turned away.

Maurin and Har exchanged glances. One of the
other Wyrds gestured with his bow. Maurin
nodded, Har shrugged, and the two men started off
through the forest, surrounded by Wyrds.

The small furred people had no trouble keeping
pace with the tired horses. They rode in silence.
Twice the humans heard a high call piping through
the woods, and their guides answered in kind.

Nearly an hour and a half later, the Wyrds
stopped outside a stand of trees. Their leader sent
the piping summons ringing through the forest; a
moment later the bushes rustled softly as yet another Wyrd appeared. He spoke briefly with the
archers in the same unknown language, then
turned to the two horsemen.

He looked toward Maurin first, a long, penetrating gaze. When he seemed satisfied at last, he
turned to Har. A moment later he smiled. "They
spoke the truth," he said to the archers. He looked
back at Har. "You have the look of your sister,
Har Tel'anh."

"Alethia! How do you know about her? Where
is she? Is she safe?" Har demanded.

"Your sister spent last night with us," the Wyrd
replied. "She is quite safe; I think more detailed
explanations can wait. Will you dismount, and let
us see to your horses?"

A wave of relief swept Maurin as he swung out of the saddle, and he saw it mirrored in Har's face. Somehow, he did not doubt the Wyrd's words.

Har dismounted more slowly, and looked at the Wyrd. "That's all very well," he said pointedly. "But we still don't know where this is, or who you are. And how did my sister come to be here?"

"This is Glen Wilding, and I am Grathwol, Arkon of the Wyrds who live here," said the Wyrd patiently, with a small smile. "Now, come and dine with me; I think we have much to talk of."

Har still looked skeptical, but he followed Grathwol without further comment. The Wyrd led the two men to the great entry hall. He crossed it quickly and entered a smaller room off to one side, where a table was loaded with wild fruits, bread, honey, and several platters of cold meat. Grathwol seated himself at the head and motioned to Maurin and Har to take the two remaining seats.

Grathwol told them in detail the story of Alethia's kidnapping and escape, her meeting with Tamsin, and her second encounter with the Lithmern. When he reached the description of the Talisman of Noron'ri, Har leaned forward with an exclamation. "Could they have used that to travel two days journey from Brenn in one night?" he asked.

"Yes, and more," Grathwol replied. "They used it to summon the mists that delayed your sister and Tamsin, and they counted on its power to hide their passage from us. They very nearly succeeded," he added thoughtfully. He finished the tale with an explanation of where Alethia and Tamsin had gone and why. When he finished, Har frowned.

"I can understand why Alethia wants to get

home quickly," he said, "but she should not travel alone. Can we catch up with her before your people turn north?"

"They left early this morning," Grathwol replied. "You are only about two hours behind them; if you push your horses, you may arrive at the Ward-Keeper's cottage today, though it may be after dark when you get there."

"Our horses are tired," Har said. "But I would like to try, if it pleases you to furnish a guide."

"I can furnish you with guides, indeed, and more," Grathwol said with a gleam of satisfaction. "Fresh horses are yours to command, as soon as you have rested."

"Then we shall leave as soon as your preparations are completed," Har said firmly. "It is no reflection on your hospitality, but I do not wish to lose more time."

Grathwol smiled. "Of course." He clapped his hands and gave a few brief orders to the servitor who appeared in answer to this summons. As the Wyrd left, he turned back to the two men. "I thought I would find a use for those horses we captured! But finish your meal at your leisure; it will be a little time before they are ready."

The two men nodded in agreement, yet in a surprisingly short time they were finished. Grathwol smiled to himself and signaled again. Another Wyrd appeared to lead Maurin and Har through the halls of Glen Wilding to the place where the fresh horses waited.

Without further ado, Maurin and Har bid Grathwol thanks and farewell, and made their way out to the forest once more. Two taciturn archers were already mounted on the ponies the Wyrds preferred. An instant more and the men were astride their horses. The Wyrds stood silently watching as, for the second time that day, a party left Glen Wilding headed west toward the Kathkari.

# CHAPTER SEVEN

For the early part of the morning, Alethia rode at the back of the party with Worrel, with whom she was fast becoming friends. The two chatted easily for some time, except when Anarmin called for silence from the front of the column. Unfortunately the track they rode was barely wide enough for the two horses side by side, so when Worrel moved forward to take his turn with Rarn at the head of the party, Alethia moved back to her original position next to Tamsin.

The five Wyrds changed positions several more times during the morning. The ride was uneventful, though twice the party halted for some reason known only to their guides. Neither Alethia nor Tamsin saw or heard anything to indicate a dangerous presence or its passing, but they complied without argument to the dictates of their companions. When they came upon the fresh marks of huge claws six inches deep in the trail shortly after the second halt, their respect for the Wyrd's advice increased enormously.

Around noon Rarn and Worrel, who were riding a little in advance of the rest, halted abruptly. They had not signaled for silence, so Tamsin rode forward. "What is it?" Tamsin asked with a worried frown as he and Alethia reached them. "More trouble?"

"No," said a voice from behind him. Tamsin turned to see that Anarmin had ridden up to them and was dismounting. The Wyrd gave him a broad grin. "Not trouble. Lunch!"

Alethia laughed. Tamsin dismounted, but before he could reach Alethia to lift her from her horse, she had kicked her feet free of the stirrups and slid to the ground unaided. The Wyrds were evidently accustomed to breaking their journey at this point, for their ponies walked quietly to a nearby bush as soon as their riders were down and waited patiently to be tethered. Beneath the bush, where only a torrential rain might reach it, was a neatly stacked pile of firewood.

The Wyrds evidently did not intend to make more than a brief stay, for they did not even glance at the stacked wood. Instead, Worrel and Rarn began to unpack huge quantities of bread and slabs of cold meat and cheese from the saddlebags, while Murn spread a cloth on the ground to receive it. Anarmin disappeared into the woods even before Shallan had the horses tethered. He returned just as the other Wyrds finished laying out the meal, carrying a large honeycomb.

"The little ones are generous today!" Anarmin called as he came into sight. "See my hard-won sweets!"

"Hard-won, indeed!" Worrel grinned at him. "Stay by some time and learn the meaning of work! I'll wager you find some other excuse to be gone come time for packing up. Give it here!"

"You wrong me; indeed, you wrong me!" Anarmin responded in an injured tone. "Why! Was it not I who single handedly prepared dinner for twice this number when last we passed this way?"

"Yes, and single-handedly ate most of it, too!"

Rarn replied tartly. "Come on, we haven't got the whole day to stand about talking." Anarmin snorted, but passed the honeycomb down to Worrel, who placed it with the rest of the lunch. There was some further good-natured bickering among the Wyrds as they laid out the food, but in a short time all was ready, and the party sat down on a springy bank of moss to a meal of cold venison and cheese and dark bread spread with honey.

When they finished eating, the Wyrds packed the remains in the saddlebags once more. Despite the efficiency of the Wyrds and Anarmin's grumbles, the party again started forward nearly an hour and a half after they had stopped. Rarn set a quicker pace for the afternoon ride, and there was less talk exchanged. They rode with an air of tension, for they had passed outside the boundaries of the land known and controlled by the Wyrds of Glen Wilding, and the danger was increased.

The strained atmosphere subdued even Alethia. She rode for some time in silence beside Tamsin, and watched the shadows warily. The browns and dappled greens that had seemed cool and refreshing that morning now looked sinister and gloomy. The ground was covered inches deep in mold, built up by years of leaves rotting undisturbed, and the horses' hooves made no noise on the crumbling surface. For the most part, there was no cover between the ancient tree-trunks, but from time to time a break in the thick foliage overhead had allowed a dense group of shrubs to spring up.

The Wyrds detoured around the first two thickets, but at the third Tamsin suggested that the two horses go first to force a passage for the Wyrd's ponies. Murn was growing concerned at the extra time the detours had cost them, and she agreed.

Tamsin and Starbrow went first, and Alethia followed. Forcing a path through the dense growth was difficult even for the horses, but it was still faster than going around. When they reached the other side, Alethia turned in the saddle to observe the Wyrds as they made their way through the thicket.

Suddenly something struck her squarely in the middle of her back. The force of the blow spun her from the saddle, and she fell to the ground barely clear of the bushes. The fall knocked the wind from her, and for what seemed an eternity she lay there fighting for breath. Then she pushed herself up and looked back.

Only a few seconds had passed. Tamsin had pulled his sword free and was swinging it down in a vicious arc that ended squarely in the middle of Alfand's now empty saddle. Alethia screamed once in protest, and then there was a small squishing noise as the flat of the sword landed. The frightened mare jumped forward, but Starbrow had already moved to bar her path. The Wyrds came quickly up to them, and Anarmin and Shallan quieted the mare while the others stopped by Alethia.

Tamsin dismounted and leaned against Starbrow's side. A thick black goo dripped slowly from the end of his sword, but he did not seem to be aware of it. He looked a little white. "Alethia, are you all right?" he asked.

"I think so. What happened?" Alethia asked.

Rarn answered her. "A janaver dropped from the trees. It would have landed on your head if Tamsin had not seen it in time and pushed you out of the way. It is dead."

Alethia shuddered, and looked at the mare. She could see three of the thing's ten legs still hanging from the saddle, the claws dripping green poison. The globular, black-furred body had been smashed by Tamsin's sword. Murn and Rarn examined Alethia carefully; Anarmin performed the same office for the mare.

"She has not been touched," Rarn declared at last. "Which is fortunate; there is no antidote for a janaver's poison. Now you, minstrel."

"What?" asked Tamsin, a little dazedly.

"The blood of the janaver is as poisonous as their claws," Worrel explained, "though it does not act as fast. Did any strike you?"

Tamsin denied it, but the Wyrds were not satisfied until they had examined him themselves. This task Worrel and Anarmin performed, while Rarn and Shallan hunted through the saddlebags. Eventually they emerged with a small bottle of dark green fluid with which they carefully cleaned every drop of the janaver's blood from Alethia's saddle and Tamsin's sword.

When the Wyrds were satisfied at last, the party set off once again. "At least we aren't likely to come across another one," Worrel said as they left. "The janaver do not like to hunt close together."

"There should not have been one here," Murn murmured with a frown. "Janaver are tree-dwellers; they avoid the sun-openings and keep to the thickest parts of the Wyrwood."

"Perhaps this was one of the younger ones traveling to find a new territory of its own," suggested Shallan. "They frequently wander through unexpected areas before they become established."

"Perhaps," Murn said, but she was very thoughtful for the remainder of the ride.

The janaver were not the only danger, and the party proceeded carefully. For the rest of the afternoon, however, they saw nothing more alarming than a deer fleeing their passage. Despite the delays, they reached the first low hills of the mountains late in the afternoon. The light was fading as the Wyrds urged their companions through a maze of trees and vines. Tamsin was a little behind Alethia as she reached the top of the second hill and exclaimed, "Oh, is that where we arc going?"

Tamsin rode up beside her. "No wonder you are intimidated. I have never seen anything so dark in my life! Why, you can't see two feet in front of the horses."

Alethia looked at him in bewilderment. "I don't understand you. It is a little dark, but the path to the house is clear to see. We shall be there in a few minutes. Look, Rarn is halfway down already."

Now it was Tamsin's turn to be puzzled. "Well, I don't see anything at all," he said slowly.

"But you must!" Alethia exclaimed. "There is a little stone house ringed by a wall, with a garden and a well and all the windows lighted. And there is a stable in back. Oh, come on!"

With that she turned Alfand down the hill. Almost immediately she vanished from Tamsin's sight. Tamsin frowned and pressed Starbrow forward, but he got only a short distance. Horse and man stopped short in total blackness, unable to see anything ahead of them. Even the footfalls of Alfand sounded muffled and far away. Then, from behind them, Worrel shouted, "Jordet! Lift your curtain!"

A moment later Tamsin sat blinking in the normally dying twilight of the forest. He looked down to see Alethia a little ahead of him, waving him toward a small cottage of grey stone, just as she had described. Smoke from the chimney blew toward the hillside, bringing with it an inviting aroma of meat roasting, and the cheery glow of the windows cast a dim halo of light within the encircling wall. Somewhat bemused, Tamsin clucked to Starbrow, who shook his mane and proceeded down the hill.

Rarn and Shallan had already reached the cottage and dismounted when Alethia and Tamsin rode up with the other Wyrds. As they slid down from their horses, the door of the cottage opened and a tall young man stood framed in the doorway. Alethia could not make out his face clearly, but his voice was light and merry as he welcomed them. "What brings you here, and at such a time, my friends?"

"Tis an urgent errand to Eveleth, Jordet," Murn replied.

"An errand to Eveleth—with humans in your company?" The Shee's tone remained friendly, but his curiosity was evident.

"This is Alethia of Brenn, and a minstrel, Tamsin by name. They are bound for Brenn and we escort them this far. We had planned to stay the night, if it will not trouble you, though it is not the best of manners to come with so little warning."

"Indeed, it were small thanks for the past kindnesses of the Wyrds of Glen Wilding to let you spend the night outside this shelter, so close to the Kathkari," Jordet replied. "And it would be smaller honor to allow one of Alethia's lineage to seek refuge elsewhere."

"I thought as much," Worrel muttered under his breath.

Murn shot him a sharp look and inclined her

head. "The Keeper of the South Ward is the image of hospitality."

"Besides, I have never known that the South Ward is on any common path to Brenn," the man said. "It should make an interesting tale, I think. Now, tell me of this errand."

"Not now," Murn said. "This is not the place for such talk. We will answer your questions inside, when our ponies have been stabled."

"Very well," Jordet replied calmly. "You will not object to these others coming in, I trust? The evening air grows cold."

Without waiting for a reply, he turned to Alethia and Tamsin and motioned them into the cottage with a bow. "I must apologize for the inconvenience I caused you; if I had known you were coming I would have lifted the curtain before you arrived. It is a small spell and no hindrance to the Wyrds, but no human eyes can see in or through it. It is our major protection along the edge of these mountains, though here it is seldom needed. But come in, I keep you standing too long."

As their host led them inside, Tamsin said in a puzzled tone, "Indeed, this curtain is effective, though I do not think it would prevent a determined man from penetrating it. But how is it that Alethia could see through it when . . ." His voice trailed off as Jordet turned to face them and he and Alethia got their first clear look at the Shee Ward-Keeper.

Jordet was tall and slender, and though he was a young man his hair was white as silver. He had high cheekbones, and green eyes that tilted upward markedly under thin, straight brows. The resemblance between the Ward-Keeper and Alethia was so great that it was almost anticlimactic when he replied simply, "But Alethia and I are cousins. The Lady Isme is my father's sister. Of course the spell of the curtain would not affect her; she is half Shee."

Practically on top of Jordet's last sentence, the five Wyrds came piling through the door. "Ho, my friend, what about dinner for these weary travelers?" Anarmin sang out as he entered the room.

"I think I might manage to scrape up enough for your friends," Jordet said solemnly, "but I am afraid I cannot supply such a feast as you would like." He smiled across the small Wyrd at Alethia. "You have discovered the prodigous Wyrd appetite, no doubt."

"That is no problem," said Worrel from the doorway. With a triumphant gesture, he brought a large bag from under his cloak. This proved to contain the remains of lunch, and the Wyrds immediately set about laying it out on the table that occupied the center of the room.

By the door of the cottage was a wooden bench, and the Wyrds moved it to the table to supplement the two chairs that were already there. A fire burned brightly at the north end of the room; from the large pot suspended over it came a rich, spicy smell that made Alethia's mouth water.

Suddenly realizing how hungry she was, Alethia stepped forward to help Rarn and Worrel ransack a tall cupboard for dishes. Jordet vanished through one of the two other doorways, and a moment later the tall Shee appeared with another chair. He then went to the fireplace and, after scorching his fingers moving the pot from over the flames, announced that dinner was ready. Jordet carried the pot to the table and began dishing up steaming bowls of stew while the others seated themselves.

Alethia was burning with curiosity about her newly-discovered cousin, but her stream of questions was overruled as being of secondary importance. "For," Worrel pointed out, "Jordet's advice may save our lives yet, while I cannot say the same of your knowing more of your relations." Murn frowned, but Alethia had to admit the force of this argument.

"Now," said Jordet once the question of topic was settled, "About this mysterious errand of yours, Murn?" He passed a basket of rolls to Alethia and looked at the Wyrd woman inquiringly.

"We carry one of the nine Talismans of Noron'ri to Eveleth, along with a desire for answers to our questions," Murn said.

"A Talisman!" Jordet cried in surprise. "How have you come by such a thing?"

"I think we must begin with Alethia's story, since it was taken from the body of one of her kidnappers," Murn said. "You were notified, of course, of her kidnapping, but you will not know what has happened since then."

Jordet looked startled, then concerned. "I had heard nothing of this. There has been no messenger in days! Continue."

The Wyrds looked at each other with small frowns, but Alethia launched into her story. Jordet listened without comment, though his eyebrows rose when she described the vision she had had while riding away with Tamsin. She finished with her arrival at Glen Wilding and looked across at the Wyrds expectantly.

"Now, about your part in this?" Jordet asked.

"Two nights ago a swift came to Glen Wilding, a messenger-bird such as you of Eveleth use, with a scroll tied to its leg. The message bid us keep watch for Alethia of Brenn, kidnapped by Lithmern from her home that very eve. We sent out watchers to the western edges of the Wyrwood, where the kidnappers were most likely to pass. We had no thought then of why the Shee of Eveleth should look for the daughter of one of Alkyra's Nobles.

"At mid-morning yesterday we felt that one of our Places of Sleep had been sprung, and some went there to remove the trespassers. When they arrived, the spell had been broken by a force of great power, but enough traces remained to show that the ones who had escaped were Lithmern.

"We knew then that some powerful magic was at work to hide and protect those men, and we sent word to the searchers to bring out those skilled in finding and uncovering things hidden by magic. We came upon them just as Tamsin and Alethia encountered them, with what results you know.

"Dlasek led these two to Glen Wilding, while others pursued the survivors. Hesketh took the task of going over the bodies for some clue to their power. On most he found no more than might be expected, but when he came to the leader it was different. The body was dry and shriveled, as if it had been sucked empty, and by it . . ."

"Body?" Alethia interrupted. "But I saw him! I mean, I couldn't see him!" She turned to Jordet. "When the Lithmern kidnapped me I got a good look at him, only there wasn't anything there! Just shadows."

Murn frowned, and Jordet's eyes narrowed thoughtfully. "It could have been an illusion," he said a little dubiously. "Yes, it must have been; untrained, you are hardly capable of detecting a spell of that kind." He motioned for Murn to continue.

"Hesketh found the Talisman lying beside the body," Murn went on. "He brought it back to Glen Wilding, and the lore-masters identified it at once. Grathwol determined to send it to Eveleth where it may be nullified or kept safe, and these two with it if they would choose willingly. They have chosen not to accompany us, and so our ways part here. Tomorrow we will leave for Eveleth, with your permission; I for one do not relish this errand overmuch, though it be necessary."

"The Talismans of Noron'ri can be of great power in the wrong hands," Jordet replied. "Yet I think there are those in Eveleth who can bind it if they are not opposed. I must agree that this thing should go there as you say; still, I am not easy."

"Will you join us, then?" Anarmin inquired.

"No, though I could wish it. My duty is here," replied the young Shee. "I will gladly give you directions and whatever else you may require, but I can accompany neither of you. I think you may . . ." The sentence was interrupted by a chilling cry.

# CHAPTER EIGHT

Jordet was on his feet and out the door in an instant. Tamsin and the Wyrds reacted more slowly, and so they were behind him. Alethia stopped to snatch a candle from the table, then followed them out the door.

She could barely see Tamsin pounding up the hill with drawn sword, his long legs putting him well ahead of the shorter Wyrds. Jordet had disappeared into the darkness. From the hilltop ahead of the running figures came a second freezing scream, and with it the sound of voices shouting.

Alethia's eyes strained toward the hilltop, but it was too dark to make out anything except dim shapes. She heard Jordet's voice ring out commandingly, but she did not understand the words. Suddenly a brilliant light sprang up on the hilltop, and Alethia blinked and nearly dropped the candle.

Jordet stood, hand upraised, at the center of a bright sphere of white light. Behind him, Tamsin and Worrel stood shielding their eyes from the glare; Rarn, Anarmin, and Murn were only a few steps further away, with Shallan bringing up the rear. A little in front of Jordet, just beyond the sphere of light, the figures of two men on horseback and a shorter shape that could only be another of the Wyrds could be dimly seen in the reflected glare.

Between the newcomers and Jordet, clearly visible in the witchlight, stood a huge, grey-black monster. It topped the men on horseback by a head, and it was completely hairless. It swung its head to find the source of this interference, and Alethia saw it wince away from the light. Its eyes were large and dark, after the fashion of nightthings.

The creature voiced another cry, giving the group from the cottage a clear view of the two foot-long fangs that dropped from its wide, toothy mouth. A long arm like a gnarled tree-branch swung toward Jordet, and on the twisted claws something glistened wetly.

The Shee ignored the attack and spoke again. The thing in front of him screamed as if in pain, and withdrew a little. Jordet gestured once more, and with a final cry of hate and defiance, the thing turned and sprang back out into the darkness. The witchlight faded, and those who had stood frozen surged forward once again.

Alethia heard a confused welter of voices from above, and then they were drawing nearer. A small puff of wind blew out the flame of the candle she held, but not before she had a glimpse of the new arrivals moving down the slope. With a glad cry, Alethia threw down the dead candle and ran forward to meet her brother Har. As she reached him, Har dismounted and smiled tiredly, then turned back toward his companion.

For a moment, Alethia was hurt, not understanding; then she saw the other figure swaying in the saddle above Har. Comprehension dawned on her just as the man swayed a bit too far and fell into the waiting arms of Har and Tamsin.

The two men stumbled toward the cottage with their burden and Alethia stepped out of the way. She took one quick look back to see that one of the Wyrds had taken charge of the horses and ponies, and followed into the house. Behind her came the other Wyrds in a small mob, and the last one in the door was Jordet himself. He looked white and tired, and he sank almost immediately into a chair by the table and covered his face with his hands.

Alethia hardly noticed the background activity. By the light of the lamps in the front room she could see that the man Har and Tamsin supported was Maurin. As they helped him to the bench, Alethia saw that her brother's sleeve was stained red. She started, then saw that Har was not wounded after all; his sleeve had been stained as he helped his friend.

Curiously, the knowledge that the blood was not her brother's own did not bring the relief she would have expected. Automatically, she moved toward the fire, to the kettle of water Jordet had put on for tea after supper. She grabbed a towel hanging next to the fire to protect her hands from the hot iron handle and swung the support out so she could reach the kettle. As she brought it carefully to the table, she said, "Jordet, do you have any bandages?"

Jordet looked up and shook his head numbly.

"We will have to use something else then," Alethia said. She looked around the room, and her eye fell on a pile of folded linen on top of the cupboard. "Those napkins?"

The Shee nodded wearily, and Tamsin rose and brought them to her. She set him to tearing them into useable strips, while she herself knelt and began carefully cutting the stained and tattered remnants of Maurin's shirt away from his side.

Alethia's self-appointed task was interrupted almost immediately by the patient himself, who opened his eyes at that moment. "Alethia! This is no fit job for you," Maurin protested. He pulled away, but exhaustion and loss of blood had taken their toll, and he nearly toppled over.

"Who's to do it if I don't?" Alethia demanded, looking up. "Caring for a wounded man is fit enough task for a soldier's daughter! Hold still; you'll never stop bleeding if you keep moving around like that."

"Har . . ." Maurin's head turned to him for support. The young noble shrugged. "She's right. She *is* experienced. There are houses in Brenn where the healers take the wounded guards; they're always short-handed and Alethia goes there with Mother all the time."

Har reached for one of the napkins, but was ordered off summarily by his sister. "You look exhausted," she said as she worked. "Go eat, and then get some rest. Tamsin and I can take care of this."

"Alright," Har replied meekly, and moved around to the other side of the table. He seated himself next to Jordet, helped himself to the lukewarm stew, and began eating intently. Looking up a few moments later, he saw Jordet's eyes on him. A little green demon seemed to dance in delighted amusement within their slanted depths. Undisturbed, Har returned a smile. "I fear we put a strain upon your hospitality, sir," he said.

"Indeed not. I have not seen so much excitement in months," Jordet replied. "Besides, it is entirely proper for kin to claim shelter."

Har's jaw dropped. "Kin?"

"We are related through your mother, the Lady Isme. Can you look on me and doubt it?" Har gulped and shook his head, and Jordet went on, "In any case, my function here is the warding of this border. How could I see you so beset and not offer my help?"

Har glanced toward Alethia, but she was too busy to pay attention to the conversation. He turned back to Jordet. "What was it?" he asked in a low voice.

"It was a voll, a wight of the mountains. I have not seen one since my father killed one when I was a child, and even that was not so large." Jordet sighed. "It took nearly all my strength just to drive it away. It is a good thing that you were here where I could help you."

"I am not sure of that," said Murn's voice behind him. The group of Wyrds had ended their conference in the corner, and except for Murn, Worrel and Rarn they were leaving the cottage. Rarn surveyed the scene briefly, and after a quick word with Alethia she moved on into the north bedroom. Murn came over to the table, arriving in time to hear the last of Jordet's comments.

"What do you mean?" asked Jordet, turning to her.

"I think that if we had not come here, you would not have needed to weary yourself so dangerously against that wight, and perhaps this other one would not be hurt," Murn replied. "Nay, do not start! I have only a suspicion, and no clear ideas. But something opposes us; Krowlan brings news of strange stirrings in the forest ever since we left this morning, and I do not believe it was an accident that you had not heard of Alethia's kidnapping."

"Perhaps you are right," Jordet said. "But what then?"

Murn shrugged. "Anarmin returns with Krowlan to Glen Wilding this evening; you have not room for so many here, in any case. The rest of us remain, for the time being. Unless you have other suggestions?"

By this time, Alethia had finished cleaning and binding up the deep, ragged gashes in Maurin's side. After his initial protest, Maurin had made no further sound, but he balked when Tamsin and Alethia tried to help him to the bedroom. "I can walk without your help!" he snarled at Tamsin. Cheeks flushed, he hauled himself to his feet and swayed toward the doorway. Alethia followed, a frown of concern on her face, but she said nothing before they disappeared into the room.

Tamsin stood staring after them for a moment, then silently joined the group at the table. Outside there was a brief flurry of noise as the Wyrds left, and he looked up in surprise until Worrel explained their decision. Tamsin frowned. "Is it really safe?" he asked. "After seeing what that thing can do . . ." He nodded in the direction of the bedroom.

"It was a voll," Jordet told him. "It can do far worse than you have seen, for they can wield magic as well as force, and their wounds are often poisoned. They usually do not come this far out of the mountains; I was surprised to see this one. But you need not fear that it will remain around this area; it is not their way."

Har's face took on a worried look at this speech, and he glanced anxiously toward the closed door of the room where Alethia and Rarn were closeted with Maurin. Murn smiled reassuringly. "Do not fear for your friend," she said. "Rarn has a great deal of talent in healing." With that Har was forced to be content.

A few minutes later Rarn came out of the bedroom to find the group conversing earnestly over the cold remains of supper. "He is sleeping," she said in response to Har's look of inquiry. She stood for a moment surveying the party, then put her hands on her hips. "As you should be! I hardly need another patient on my hands, what with only Alethia to help. And another is what I'll have if you don't rest after this night's work." She glared indignantly at Jordet and Har.

"Oh, and I thought it looked like you were the one helping Alethia," murmured Worrel provocatively.

"Indeed I was, and would you have me let her wear herself out doing it all alone?" she snapped back. "Not that you would be thinking of any such thing; just look at the way you have been keeping these two sitting with your chatter, when it is as plain as the Tree they are both exhausted. You'd do better to make yourselves useful clearing up," she finished with a sweeping gesture that included Tamsin, Worrel and the cluttered table.

Tamsin shifted uncomfortably, but the small fury's attention had already turned elsewhere. Despite a few half-hearted protests, Rarn managed to shepherd Jordet and Har into the second of the back rooms, where she left them with strict instructions to go to sleep at once. She gave them one final glare and closed the door firmly behind her as she left.

In the front room, Tamsin and Worrel had taken the hint, and the dishes were being neatly stacked in a large bucket near the door. Rarn observed this with satisfaction, and informed the two men that she, Alethia and Murn would be taking turns watching over Maurin all night. Then she vanished once more into the first bedroom.

"Whew!" Tamsin commented with a chuckle. "I would sooner face a Lithmern patrol!"

"The trouble is, she is usually right," grinned Worrel sympathetically. "In any case, it looks like the floor for us tonight, my friend. And we had best turn in as well; it has been a long day's work." The two rolled themselves in their cloaks and settled in front of the fire.

"At any rate, it is only for one night," the minstrel murmured sleepily after a few minutes of trying to find a comfortable position on the stone floor. "Tomorrow for Brenn."

Midmorning of the following day found the travelers still firmly ensconsed in the cottage, and with few prospects of setting out that day. Maurin's wounds had indeed been poisoned; he was delirious with fever. Once Alethia was obliged to summon Tamsin to help keep him in bed, for he insisted that they were under attack by Lithmern and tried to get up to fight them.

The Wyrds could not delay their departure. After consulting with Jordet, Murn agreed to allow Worrel and Rarn to remain while she and Shallan went on to Eveleth with the Talisman. For this she apologized to Alethia, but getting the Talisman to Eveleth took precedence. Alethia, remembering her brief encounter with its powers, had to agree.

Rarn was more disturbed by the development of her patient's illness than she cared to show. After some thought and a conference with Alethia, she sent Har and Worrel out to gather wallas roots for an herbal concoction that she hoped would bring the fever down. Meanwhile, she and Alethia made do as best they could with cloths soaked in cold tea.

It was a good walk to the hill where Jordet had said the wallas grew. Mindful of the urgency of their errand, the two hurried on in spite of the temptation to linger in the sunlit forest. The trees here were not the enormous growths of the Wyrwood, whose branches and leaves had so completely blocked out the sunlight. Here, the forest was almost open, and frequently they passed small openings, not quite large enough to call clearings.

"There!" Worrel said suddenly, and pointed. Ahead of them the sun beat down on a hill, bare of trees but covered with a dense shrubbery of deep green, dotted with tiny, star-shaped yellow flowers. Har grinned and strode forward. In a few moments he was knee-deep in greenery, digging at the foot of a likely specimin.

"Take care not to bruise the roots," Worrel called from lower down the hill.

"I will," Har promised. He lifted the plant carefully and placed it in the bucket. Dusting his hands, he looked up and was surprised to find that his companion had vanished. "Worrel?"

"Here," came the response, but it still took Har a moment to locate him. When he did, he realized what the problem was. The deep green foliage matched the color of the Wyrd's tunic and cloak almost perfectly. Coupled with his short stature and brown fur, the Wyrd had only to step onto the shrub-covered hill to disappear almost completely. Har laughed. "Take care not to get lost!" he called down. "I doubt I could find you if you fell asleep."

"Well, I doubt if I could miss you, even if you

tried to hide," the Wyrd retorted easily. Jordet had loaned Har replacements for the bedraggled finery in which he had arrived, and he was now attired in a tan costume that stood out strikingly against the dark colors of the hillside.

"How much of this does Rarn want?" Har asked.

"She gave us each a bucket; I suspect she wants them both filled," Worrel replied. "Come, don't waste time!"

Har climbed further up the hill. There was no breeze. It was hot in the sunshine, even after he discarded his cloak, and the drone of the insects among the wallas-flowers was hypnotic. Once a wasp circled his head speculatively, but it soon departed for more profitable areas. The roots were not large, and filling the bucket took more time than Har had expected.

Straightening up from digging the last root, Har wiped his forehead and looked around for Worrel. At that moment the Wyrd's voice cut across the drowsy atmosphere of the hill from behind and above him. "Har!"

Automatically Har's head jerked in that direction. As it moved, something swished by his ear and hit the ground in front of him with a solid *thunk*. Simultaneously he heard the twang of the Wyrd's bowstring.

For a moment Har stood frozen, staring at the foot-long dagger buried halfway to its hilt in the sandy soil of the hillside. Then he turned, and was just in time to see Worrel leaping down the hill, bow in hand and another arrow already nocked. At the edge of the woods, the shrubs and lower branches of the young trees were waving in unmistakable sign of the recent, hurried passage of some large animal or person.

Har immediately started toward the Wyrd, but he was hampered by the bushy wallas plants. By the time he reached the foot of the hill, Worrel had vanished. As Har stood indecisively, the Wyrd reappeared. "He is gone," Worrel stated matter-of-factly.

"Why not follow?" Har demanded.

"First, he has a lead on us already," the Wyrd replied. "Second, we must get these herbs back to Jordet and Rarn. And third, there are hoofmarks ten feet further in. It would be folly to follow a horseman on foot."

"Oh," said Har, crestfallen.

"I think it would be wiser to return at once. And your ear is bleeding."

Har raised a hand to his head and felt something sticky. Evidently he had not escaped completely scatheless. He shrugged; it could not be more than a scratch. He wiped it clean with his handkerchief and looked back to his companion. Worrel was already up on the hill, collecting the buckets of wallas-root. As he returned, Har saw that the Wyrd had also retrieved the dagger. This he handed to Har with a single word, "Lithmern."

"What else?" Har thrust the dagger grimly into his belt, and the two started back toward Jordet's cottage. In spite of the loaded buckets they carried, they made much better time on the return journey. As they came within sight of the house, they saw to their relief that it looked as quiet and peaceful as when they had left.

Rarn met them at the door. "At last!" she exclaimed, and without ceremony took charge of their buckets. She already had a pot of water hanging over the fire, and after rinsing the dirt from the roots she tossed them whole into the boiling water. Soon the front room of the cottage was heavy with a thick, sweet odor that drove the others into the clean air outdoors.

"Ugh!" said Har, last to exit the cottage, as he waved away the last lingering traces of the aroma that had followed him. "I don't envy Maurin one bit! It's enough to make a man get well in self-defense."

"You were quick enough about your picking," Jordet commented from where he lounged against the stone wall.

"We had encouragement," Worrel replied wryly. "A Lithmern knifethrower."

"Here?" Tamsin asked incredulously. Worrel nodded.

Jordet gave the Wyrd a sharp look. "Continue," he said.

Har drew the knife from his belt and handed it hilt first to Jordet, who examined it and passed it to Tamsin. "Someone threw this at me this morning; if Worrel hadn't shouted, it would have gone through my head. He got away on a horse."

"Unquestionably Lithmern work," Jordet commented as he handed the knife to Tamsin. "It would appear that one of you was followed from Glen Wilding." He looked first at Tamsin and Worrel, then at Har.

"How could they know that we would send the Talisman on so quickly?" Worrel objected.

Har snorted. "With two parties leaving Glen Wilding within a few hours of each other, it would not be hard for anyone to guess," he said.

Worrel looked at him with disfavor. "No one can watch Glen Wilding without betraying himself," he said. "We know the forest, and we do not leave our home unguarded. There was no sign of any watcher; Murn asked before we left."

"No sign of a physical watch, perhaps," Jordet said quietly. "But should the Lithmern have a seer, that would be unnecessary. Such a one could know all your councils from a comfortable distance, and you would not be likely to guard against such a threat unsuspected." He paused for a moment, considering.

"Fortunately, the posts of the Keepers of the Wards must be protected at all times against such things," Jordet went on. "They cannot know much of what has passed since your arrival."

"Here they would seem to be relying on physical observation," Tamsin pointed out. "So they must know that Murn and Shallan left for Eveleth this morning."

"True, but is it likely that they will believe we have sent the Talisman on with only two to guard it?" Jordet said. "They must think the Talisman is still here, or they would not have attacked Har."

"You may be right," Worrel admitted. "But in that case, what can we do?"

"If they discover their error, the Lithmern will go after Murn," Jordet said. "We must convince them that the Talisman remains here, and that Murn and Shallan are only messengers. If they are watching us with magic, I think I can foster that illusion. There may be some danger, but I think I can protect you until you leave for Brenn."

"That may be sooner than you think," broke in a voice from the direction of the cottage. Heads turned to find Alethia standing in the doorway. "Maurin has drunk Rarn's potion and is resting. I had no notion anything could work so fast; the fever has left him already."

"Wyrds are healers as well as woodwise," Jordet commented. "Their manner of magic is suited to it more than ours. When do you think Maurin will be able to travel?"

"It is too early to say," Alethia replied. "Under normal circumstances, at least three days, but I have never worked with Rarn before, and it may be sooner. Is there need for haste, now that the Talisman is gone?"

It was Har who answered, explaining briefly his encounter of the morning and Jordet's suspicions. Alethia nodded. "Yes, we must go soon, and I am anxious to be home. But it would only delay us further if Maurin collapsed along the way."

"I suppose so," Jordet said with a worried frown, and on that unsatisfactory note the impromptu conference ended.

# CHAPTER NINE

Maurin was much better the following morning, and demanded loudly to get up, but this Alethia and Rarn refused to allow. They were supported by Jordet, Har and Tamsin, but it was Alethia's persuasions that finally kept Maurin in bed. Rarn nodded in satisfaction at the progress of her patient and brewed more of her potions while Alethia sat with him, but it was not until the next day that she grudgingly pronounced Maurin nearly well enough to travel.

The news was greeted with joy. It was too late to set out for Brenn at once, but Alethia, Har and Tamsin compensated by discussing at great length various improbable schemes for transporting the invalid in the greatest comfort, much to the dismay of the person in question. They were still talking when Jordet entered, frowning at a note he held.

"I am sorry to interrupt," he began, "but I am afraid I have bad news." He paused as if searching for words, then took a deep breath. "Brenn is under siege by the Lithmern, and I am recalled to Eveleth," he said baldly. "A message arrived from Eveleth by swift a few minutes ago." He handed the note to the nearest person, who happened to be Tamsin. The others crowded around the minstrel as he read aloud.

"Greetings, Keeper of the South Ward Jordet. Your services are now needed in Eveleth; come swiftly. Bring your cousins and companions as well, since Brenn is besieged by part of the Lithmern army and it is not possible for them to reach the city now. Leave at once. Prestemon, Captain, Queen's Guard."

"Under siege!" Alethia said when Tamsin had finished. "Let me see that. No, there must be some mistake!"

"Is there no way to get back to Brenn?" Har asked, turning toward Jordet.

"I do not know, but I do not think Prestemon would say such a thing if it were not true," Jordet answered. "Brenn cannot be in any great danger as yet if it is surrounded by only a part of the Lithmern army, but you would be if you attempted to gain the city. They will wait to attack until the main army arrives. That could be days or weeks."

"Or hours," Har retorted. "Or never! Allie told me how anxious the Wyrds were that she go to Eveleth. Maybe this is a ruse to get her there."

"The Shee do not need to use trickery, nor do the Wyrds," said Worrel from the doorway. Har turned angrily, but the Wyrd continued easily, "Had we wished to, we could have told your sister we were going to Brenn and simply gone to Eveleth instead. I doubt that any of you knows the woods well enough to see the deception, and it is even easier to lose one's bearing in the mountains."

"Har, it's true," Alethia said, looking up. It was impossible to say whether she spoke of the note she held or of Worrel's comments.

"Then we should ride for Lacsmer and ask Lord Armin to send aid to Brenn," Har said stubbornly.

"He may *be* in Brenn," Alethia replied sharply.

"It's only five days since the feast and he was supposed to stay for a week."

"We could still bring soldiers," Har insisted. Alethia half-nodded, but Maurin spoke up for the first time.

"Brenn is well defended against a conventional siege, Har; we looked the plans over with Lord Bracor before the Lords Armin and Gahlon arrived, remember? Brenn can hold for at least six weeks against the whole Lithmern army. But what can your soldiers, or Armin's, do against magic? If the Lithmern had one Talisman and a sorcerer who could use it, they may have more. I do not think this will be an ordinary war."

Har looked stunned; the thought had plainly not occurred to him. Alethia frowned. "Would the Shee aid Brenn? They have held apart from Alkyra for so very long." She turned toward Jordet.

"Cousin, I do not know," Jordet replied slowly. "You have kin-right among us and can claim our aid, but the Queen's Council exiled your mother for dealing with humans. Queen Iniscara might help, perhaps—I do not know her mind." He shrugged. "You can but try."

"What other choice have we?" Alethia demanded, turning to her brother, and he was forced at last to agree.

So it was that the fourth morning after their arrival at the cottage found the travelers riding north into the mountains of the Shee. Jordet provided cloaks and provisions from a seemingly inexhaustable store, and the Wyrds had their mounts, as well as Jordet's impressive white stallion, ready by first light.

All day they wound through the mountains, pausing now and then to drink from an icy stream fed by the melting snow at the top of the peaks. They camped that night in the open, beneath the stars. Rarn and Alethia insisted that Maurin rest, much as he was disinclined to do so, while Har and Tamsin helped Jordet and Worrel gather wood and care for the horses. After they had eaten, Tamsin brought out his melar and sang the ancient songs and ballads of Alkyra until the fire burned low.

The morning dawned cloudy and cold. After a hasty breakfast, they started off again. By mid-morning they were riding through a bone-chilling drizzle that penetrated even the wool of their hooded cloaks. The terrain grew steeper and rockier as they went deeper into the mountains, and the endless drizzle made the narrow paths slippery. Alethia found herself envying the ponies; they seemed to step surely no matter how slick the surface and their shaggy coats seemed to shed water effortlessly.

The rain grew worse as they went on. The wind was also rising, and the mountains seemed to be no block to it at all. Alethia gathered her sodden cloak more closely around her in a futile attempt to shut out some of the wind. She could vaguely see the figures of Tamsin and Har ahead of her, single file on the narrow trail. Although Jordet rode in the lead, he was easier to see because his white hair and the white horse he rode stood out against the dark background of the mountains and the rain.

Jordet waved the others to a halt and turned his horse easily up the steep slope of the mountain. Alethia watched in astonishment as the ghostly white figure and its rider faded above her. Har, directly in front of her, waved his arm and she obligingly rode closer.

"What is he doing?" Alethia shouted, trying to

make herself heard over the wind. Har shook his head and leaned backward, and she repeated the question as loudly as she could.

"Don't know," Har shouted back. "Turn her head into the mountain." It took Alethia a moment to make sense of this cryptic utterance, but when she did she tugged at Alfand's rein. The horse shifted slightly in compliance, and Alethia found that the new position seemed to lessen the force of the driving rain. Further conversation was impossible, and Alethia could only sit and wait miserably for Jordet to return.

A few moments later Alethia saw a flash of white as Jordet reappeared beside Tamsin. It was impossible to hear what he said, but she saw Tamsin nod and dismount. Leading his horse, he turned up the mountain and vanished from her sight almost immediately. Har followed in the same way, and Alethia rode forward.

As she reached the point where the others had turned off, she saw a steep path, barely visible on the rocky mountainside, forking out from the main trail on which they had been riding. Jordet was positioned at the fork to make sure that no one missed it. In the rain and with such uncertain footing it was obvious that the horses would have to be led, and with a little sigh Alethia dismounted and began pulling Alfand upward.

It was hard work climbing against the wind and without what little shelter the mountainside had provided on the lower path. Ahead of her she saw Har disappearing among a tangled pile of huge boulders, and she hurried her horse as much as she was able to keep from losing him altogether. A moment later she, too, was among the rocks.

Alethia staggered for a moment as the wind she

had been braced against was suddenly blocked. From her left came a merry whistle. Turning, she saw Har and Tamsin unsaddling their horses in the mouth of a large, shallow cave. Gratefully, she joined them. In a few minutes more, the entire company was gathered in the cave, wringing out their cloaks and unsaddling their horses.

"How did you know about this place?" Alethia asked Jordet.

The Shee grinned. "I've made enough trips through these mountains to learn where the good bolt-holes are!" he replied. "There are a lot of caves in this section of the Kathkari, though; it isn't hard to find one when you have to if you know where to look."

Rarn looked up. "So far, so good, but you'd be wise to think about finding some firewood so we can dry ourselves out. We haven't any spare cloaks, and these are soaked. Not you," she added as Maurin started to rise. "You're wet enough now. I'll not have you catching a chill on top of everything else!"

"Nay, we needn't all go!" Jordet said hastily as Maurin scowled. "Come cousin!"

Har grinned, and the two men moved back out into the storm. The others set to work unpacking the blankets and rubbing down the horses and ponies with whatever dry scraps of cloth they could find. By the time Har and Jordet returned carrying armloads of twisted brush, the animals at least were tolerably comfortable.

"I am afraid it will take some time to get a fire going," Jordet said, dumping an armload of glistening black branches at one side of the cave mouth. "The wood is rather wet," he added unnecessarily.

"Well, can't you use some of your magic to start it?" Alethia asked.

The young Shee frowned. "No," he said shortly.

Alethia was quite ready to argue with him, but Maurin spoke before she could reply. "Perhaps you should let me make the fire. Traders know no magic, but we do have a few tricks to use on wet wood!"

Without waiting for an answer, Maurin went over to the pile of branches and began sorting them. The others watched as he laid out the wood that suited him, and then began whittling on one of the drier pieces. Soon he had a pile of relatively dry shavings, and he pulled out a small firebox and took from it tinder and flints. In a shorter time than Jordet expected, a warm fire was burning and the party huddled around it thankfully.

The storm began to let up in mid-afternoon, but Jordet vetoed Har's suggestion that they continue on. "Mountain storms can be tricky," he said, "and this is the best shelter in the area. It will be worth the extra time on the road to be sure of missing another cloudburst." True to his prediction, the rain began again shortly before nightfall, and the travelers could only be glad they had not ventured further.

Alethia awoke a little after dawn and sat up. The others were still asleep; Har, Tamsin, Maurin and Worrel lying in a row at the mouth of the cave and Rarn next to her, a discreet distance from the others. Jordet was nowhere to be seen, and his stallion was missing from among the horses.

Carefully, so as not to wake Rarn or the others, Alethia rose and tiptoed out of the cave. The sky was clear and the first rays of the sun poured over the mountains to the east. Gathering her cloak about her, for the air was crisp, Alethia walked slowly through the tangled pile of boulders that had sheltered them from the wind the day before.

Just at the edge of the rock pile she met Jordet, riding up the steep little path to the cave. "Good morning!" she greeted him. "Where have you been?"

"Checking out the road ahead," Jordet replied, dismounting. Privately, Alethia felt that the narrow trails they had followed for the past two days could hardly be called roads, but she did not comment. "I am afraid we will have to backtrack and take the lower trail," Jordet continued as they walked together back toward the cave. "The trail is washed out up ahead, and we cannot get past."

"What's that?" Maurin's voice floated out of the cave toward them, followed by Maurin himself. The rain and the night spent on the hard cave floor did not seem to have hurt him at all; rather the reverse. Alethia vaguely remembered tales that the Traders prospered on hardship, and found herself more than half believing them.

"We are going to take another route," she answered Maurin's question absently. "The trail ahead of us was destroyed in the storm yesterday."

Maurin looked at Jordet, and the Shee nodded. "The other path is more difficult at first, but it is shorter," he explained. "If we start now, we should reach Eveleth tonight." This last statement was enough to whisk the travelers back into the cave to repack the few things that they had left out of the saddlebags for comfort overnight. In a surprisingly short time they were ready to go on.

Under Jordet's direction, they retraced their previous day's journey as far as the foot of the mountain, and then turned to follow the narrow ravine at its base. Sheer cliffs rose on either side; the floor of the ravine was littered with shattered slabs of rock that had torn loose from the cliffs above them. The rocks shifted treacherously underfoot, and more than once the horses stumbled, so that their progress was slow. Even the Wyrds' sure-footed ponies moved cautiously over the uncertain surface.

They had nearly reached the middle of the ravine when Alethia saw a brown heap lying on the rocks ahead of them. At first she thought it was a trick of the sun reflecting from the cliff walls, but as they drew nearer it resolved into the figure of a large brown horse lying on its side. Pinned halfway beneath it lay an unconscious man in a dark cloak, and Alethia stifled a gasp as she recognized him. It was one of her Lithmern kidnappers.

Jordet was the first to reach the fallen man. He swung down from his horse to examine him, and as the others arrived and dismounted, he looked up. "The horse is dead, but the man lives. Help me lift him."

With the assistance of Tamsin, Har and Maurin, Jordet was able to slide the Lithmern out from under the dead animal. He examined the fellow thoroughly, and announced: "There are no bones broken and no permanent harm has been done him, but he is half dead of exposure. He has evidently been lying here all night. He must have been trying to get through here yesterday, and his horse slipped in the rain."

"The more fool he," Worrel commented. "This way is hard enough in dry daylight without taking chances in such weather. I did not know that the Shee allowed human visitors—what takes him on this road, do you think?"

"Har," broke in Alethia," I know him."

"What?" Jordet straightened to face her.

"I know him," Alethia repeated. "He is one of the Lithmern who kidnapped me; I remember him well. He brought me food on that first morning." She shuddered as she remembered the cold look in his eyes. Tamsin looked at the Lithmern thoughtfully.

"I believe you said this route was faster, Jordet? Not such a fool, then; he was trying to get ahead of us," the minstrel said. "Would you say this is your vanishing knife-thrower, Har?"

Har bent over the man with an exclamation. "His sheath is empty!"

"Well, now that you know who and what he is, what do we do with him?" Rarn broke in pointedly. "Leave him? Kill him? Or bring him along?"

"Bring him along by all means," Jordet responded promptly. "I think food and drink and a warm cloak will repair what harm has been done, and he cannot do us a mischief if we keep close watch on him. He may well be able to tell us something useful when we reach Eveleth."

The others agreed, all except Alethia and Worrel, who shook his head ominously when he was overruled, but kept silent. They relieved their captive of his sword, and Jordet replaced the man's soggy cloak with his own. The Lithmern seemed to be recovering consciousness, and Har poured a cup of water from one of their water-bottles and forced it on him. After a few swallows the man choked, sputtered, and sat up.

He blinked uncertainly at his rescuers as he looked around him. Then his glance fell upon Alethia. A change came over him. His face darkened and he reached for his missing sword. Jordet stepped in front of him. "You are our prisoner," he informed the Lithmern calmly, "and we are taking you with us to Eveleth."

The man paid no attention at all to this interruption; his gaze was fixed on Alethia. He straightened and seemed to grow taller. A shadow fell on him, and he raised his hand from where he sat to point directly at Alethia. As though the words were dragged from him, he began to speak. "Asi, kalan nitranon . . ."

The little group stood frozen, except Worrel. The Wyrd was standing just behind their prisoner, and as the Lithmern began to speak he drew his dagger, reached up, and brought its hilt smartly down on the back of the man's head. As the Lithmern slumped unconscious once again, Worrel calmly replaced the weapon and turned to Jordet. "A dangerous prisoner, Ward-Keeper."

For a moment their eyes locked; then Jordet smiled. "Dangerous indeed! I fear we have underestimated these folk if even such as he can wield a spell of passage."

"You recognized it too? Well, perhaps you are right," Worrel replied. "Yet he seemed to me more one used of magic than himself a user. In any case we had best make speed to Eveleth. And I do not seek to trespass on your authority, Ward-Keeper, but I would feel myself safer were our prisoner gagged and bound."

"I'll not differ with you there!" Jordet said. "I do not seek to prove my talents against such a one; there will be better need for such power at another time and place."

"What is the need for this?" Maurin inquired as Jordet and Worrel set about binding their prisoner.

"Bound and gagged he cannot work magic,"

Worrel replied, slipping a loop of rope over the Lithmern's right hand. "And as he was about to work a spell to snatch himself and our charming companion to an unknown but probably unpleasant destination, I think our precautions are more than justified."

Alethia had been leaning against Alfand with her head down ever since the Lithmern's collapse. Now she raised her head and stared fixedly ahead of her. The pupils of her eyes were enormous. "Blindfold him," she said in a flat voice.

"What? Why?" Jordet said, looking around.

"Blindfold him. Blindfold him!" she repeated, and they could all hear the hysterical note in her voice.

"All right, Allie," Har said soothingly. "It's all right." He put an arm around her shoulders, but she shrugged it off and repeated, "Blindfold him!" Jordet frowned, but Worrel tore a strip from the bottom of his cloak and wrapped it around the Lithmern's eyes. Only when this was done did Alethia collapse, sobbing, into her brother's arms.

# CHAPTER TEN

By noon they were out of the ravine. They were just beginning another climb when a pinpoint of light darted out of nowhere and circled Jordet's head. It stopped and hovered a few feet ahead of him, and the travelers had a chance to see it clearly. It looked very like a spark rising from a fire, but it burned with a bright, silvery light that showed no sign of extinction.

Jordet smiled as the light darted off and disappeared ahead of them. "Evidently someone is looking for us."

"What was it?" Har asked.

"It is a type of spell used as a guide, a seeker. They are not hard to make, but they are difficult to maintain for any length of time. It will not be long before we meet the sender, I think."

"Are you sure it guides a friend?" Alethia asked a little nervously. She was riding at the back of the party, keeping as much distance between herself and the captive as possible, though she seemed to be recovered from the encounter.

The Shee looked thoughtful for a moment, then grinned. "My wits are gone a-begging today. No enemy would choose a spell that revealed his presence so obviously when there are easier, more secret ways. I'll wager someone from Eveleth has rid-

den to meet us; it's only a few hours travel now."
He spoke confidently, but the others were not completely convinced.

They proceeded warily despite Jordet's assurances, but there were no further signs. Half an hour later, they reached the top of the mountain and paused to let the horses rest a moment.

Halfway across the relatively flat mountaintop, a figure on horseback stood motionless beside a small fire. Jordet waved and started toward it; the others followed a bit more reluctantly. As they drew nearer, the figure resolved into a woman enveloped in a dark wool traveling cloak, whose silver-white hair and slanted green eyes proclaimed her one of the Shee.

"Greetings, Keeper of the South Ward," she said to Jordet as he halted in front of her.

"Greetings, Lady," Jordet replied formally. "What brings you alone to seek our company?"

"A story is best told in comfort," she answered. "Though time presses, it seems best to pause here, for the news I bear is difficult to ponder on horseback."

Jordet nodded and swung himself to the ground, and the others followed his example. Tamsin alone remained mounted to hand the captive Lithmern down to Har and Jordet. As she saw what they were doing, the Shee woman gave an exclamation. "What is this?"

"We, too, have a story to tell, Lady."

The travelers made themselves comfortable around the fire. Alethia, once seated, looked pointedly from Jordet to the Shee woman and back. Jordet said, "Before we begin, I think introductions are in order. This is the Lady Illeana, wizard of the Veldatha and high in the confidence of the

Council of Lord Advisors."

The others nodded, and the rest of the introductions were performed rapidly. Illeana acknowledged them coolly; then Jordet turned to her and said, "Now, tell us what message is so urgent as to bring you to meet us so close to Eveleth."

"It is not my choice, but the Lord Medilaw's that brings me here," Illeana replied. "We have learned much that you must know."

"Then speak," Jordet said.

"Nine nights ago the Lady Isme of Brenn broke the covenant of exile and sent a speaking-spell to Eveleth to ask us to keep watch for her daughter, kidnapped by Lithmern not an hour before. Though Isme broke the dictates of the Council, Queen Iniscara chose to lend what aid we might, so the message was sent on to the Glens of the Wyrds, and there the matter rested.

"Then one called Murn arrived three days ago, bringing with her a Talisman of Noron'ri. When we heard her story, Iniscara ordered the Veldatha to break the exile once more and send a speaking-spell to Isme in Brenn. Then we learned that the city was under attack, and word was sent to you to escort Alethia of Brenn to Eveleth.

"Since then the Veldatha have been working to learn more. At first it seemed simple enough; it was easy to guess what occurred at Brenn. The Lithmern found one of the Talismans of Noron'ri; how or where we do not know. Suspecting that Isme was more than she seemed, they sent to Brenn to kidnap her that she might not use her power against them in battle."

"But why would they fear mother?" Alethia asked.

Illeana looked at her contemptuously. "A full-blooded Shee, trained in magic, is more than a match for any human wizard, even with one of the Nine Talismans. Unfortunately for the Lithmern, their attempt went astray and they got Isme's child instead of Isme. The error was compounded when they lost the Talisman."

"Then Alethia is safe now that the Talisman is in your hands!" Har interrupted. "The Lithmern were never interested in her at all!"

"So we think. Therefore there is no reason for you to continue to Eveleth," Illeana said. "Lord Medilaw Robal, High Minister to the Queen, came to that conclusion this morning and sent me to you. There is a place just east of here where you can stay in safety and comfort, and it will cause less trouble if no humans come to Eveleth to disturb us."

"What of Brenn?" Har burst out. "How can we help the city by going further east?"

"What is that to me, or to the Shee?" Illeana said scornfully. "The Council has other things to concern them."

"Such as?" Jordet asked quietly, with a quelling look at Har, who had opened his mouth to retort angrily.

"Firivar sent a prophecy to the Queen this morning," Illeana answered. "Whatever it relates to is of far more importance than this little matter."

"But you do not know that Firivar has not spoken of Brenn," Jordet pointed out. "A prophecy just now seems to me to be a little too timely to be coincidence." His eyes narrowed suddenly. "Does the Queen know of your message to us?"

"I cannot say," Illeana admitted, looking disturbed. "Lord Medilaw must speak for the Queen.

But she was closeted with the foreteller when I left."

"There may have been other developments in Eveleth since you left as well," Jordet murmured. "Certainly there have been some here."

"Yes, you must tell me," Illeana said quickly. "Who, or what, is that which lies bound?"

Jordet's eyes followed hers to the Lithmern. Ignoring Har's frown, he explained the capture of the man in the ravine and his interrupted attempt at a spell of passage. Illeana listened carefully, and her lips tightened.

"We must attempt to spell-bind him," she said. "Such a magician cannot be permitted to go near Eveleth otherwise, nor can we set such a magic worker free without precaution."

"I do not know if that is wise," Jordet replied. "I have little knowledge of his ability, but it seems likely that he was one of the party that tried to kidnap Alethia using the Talisman. If so, he may be somewhat more skilled than you expect."

Illeana gestured impatiently. "Two Shee, both prepared and one a Veldatha, can easily best a human wizard. Your fears are groundless; he does not have the Talisman to aid him now."

"He may not need it. The Talismans were made by a human wizard," Jordet said softly, but he made no further objection and the two Shee walked over to the inert Lithmern. Illeana motioned to Worrel, and gave him instructions in a low voice. A moment later the Ward-Keeper straightened and motioned to Alethia.

"I think you should be back as far as you can," he said. "If Illeana is right and he has been trying to recover the Talisman, you should be in no danger, but he has attacked you once before. I doubt that he could do so successfully from within a Circle, but there is no reason to take chances."

"What are you going to do?" Alethia asked nervously as she moved away.

"We are going to try to cast a spell that will block his use of magic and bind his will. It will render him harmless, and with two of us to make the attempt it should not be difficult." His eyes were worried despite his words, and Alethia was not very reassured. She moved as far as she could and found another seat behind Tamsin and Maurin.

Illeana and Worrel completed their preparations. The Lithmern lay, still blindfolded, bound, and gagged, in the center of a circle Illeana had scratched in the hard grey soil that thinly covered the brown rocks of the mountain. Worrel crouched uneasily beside him, holding an unsheathed knife in one furred hand.

As Jordet turned back, Illeana threw back the hood of her cloak and loosened her hair to fall in silver waves over her shoulders. From under her cloak she drew a thin circlet of silver twined with gold that supported an intricate figure of silver wire; this she placed about her head, settling it firmly onto her brow.

Noticing Jordet's raised eyebrows, she smiled. "The Crown of the Veldatha is never far from me, Ward-Keeper, nor will it ever be, no matter how you may disapprove."

"I do not disapprove, merely wonder that you should bring such power out of the safety of Eveleth," Jordet replied softly.

"This is mine alone; no other can wear it without destroying it," she answered. "It is safe enough. Now come."

Jordet looked at Illeana sharply, but said nothing more. The Shee woman turned to the seated humans. "Do not stir or speak until we finish," she warned them. The two Shee walked to the edge of the circle. They stopped just outside it, Illeana at the head of the bound man and Jordet at his feet. Then they began to chant, an eerie keening sound that rose and fell in waves over the barren mountaintop.

The others watched, silent. This was the first they had seen of true magic, except during the fight with the voll, and there had hardly been time to watch carefully then. Har and Alethia felt the tug of their birthright, the magic of the Shee, and knew for the first time what they might have missed. Alethia, despite the Shee's warning, crept closer as the chant went on. Maurin sat bemused as the legends of his boyhood walked the earth in flesh before him. But Tamsin watched hungrily, with an intense longing, as the Shee wove their spell, for magic was his heart's desire.

The chant ended, and the two Shee turned outward. With their backs to the circle, faces impassive, they slowly raised their arms in a gesture that could have been summons or supplication, and as their arms rose the wind rose with them. First it was barely a stirring, then a breeze, then a strong gale that swept across the mountains and whistled around the two immobile figures towering over the circle and its occupants.

Alethia shivered and looked around uneasily. Tamsin's eyes glittered with unshed tears, and Alethia looked away quickly from the naked emotion on his face. Maurin and Har sat as if entranced.

The wind died and Jordet and Illeana turned

back toward the Lithmern and Worrel. Alethia's uneasiness grew. Nervously, she scooped up a handful of pebbles from the rocky ground and fingered them absently, occasionally dropping one softly at her feet.

Illeana gestured sharply. At that sign, Worrel, still crouched uncomfortably beside the Lithmern, slashed through the cords that bound the captive's hands and feet and leapt clear of the circle in one catlike movement. Breathing hard, he sheathed his dagger and retreated toward the ponies.

The Lithmern stirred and half rose. Only then did he pause to remove the blindfold and gag he still wore. At his first movements, Illeana and Jordet began to chant once more. This time the sound was slow and heavy, almost somber, the final chant of binding. They had barely begun when the last cloth fell away from the Lithmern's eyes and he stood free in the middle of the circle. Without warning, the man leapt for Jordet, but he was stopped short at the circle's edge by an invisible barrier. Alethia let her breath out in a soundless sigh of relief, only then aware that she had been holding it.

The slow chanting continued uninterrupted, and suddenly the Lithmern seemed to notice it for the first time. The man's eyes grew dark and remote, then he threw back his head and laughed. Peal after peal of ugly laughter rang out as a dark shadow grew around him, and then he cried in a terrible voice, "Fools! Thrice fools, to seek to bind what is bound already!"

The chant faltered and died. The Lithmern turned toward Illeana, and she flinched away from his dark, dead gaze. He spoke one hissing syllable and gestured; the Shee woman fell, stunned. The former captive whirled and repeated the spell just in time to stop Jordet, who had raised his arms for a counterattack. He laughed again as Jordet fell, and turned toward the small group of humans.

Alethia froze where she crouched behind the others, wishing desperately and hopelessly that he would not see her. The last of the stones she had been fingering was clenched in her right hand; she would not even move to let it drop lest she draw the creature's attention.

The Lithmern began to pace slowly toward the onlookers. At the edge of the circle he paused a moment and gestured; then the slow, steady progress resumed unhindered. Har and Maurin tried to rise and draw their swords, but found themselves frozen motionless. The man drew nearer, and Alethia cried out and threw up her arm to cover her eyes.

From the upraised fist came a golden glow, a soft radiance that flowed out to form a protective sphere around the kneeling girl. Alethia felt a strange sense of power, and with all her might she willed it to stop the Lithmern from reaching her.

As he arrived at the golden barrier, the Lithmern's face twisted terribly. "So, you have begun to learn!" he hissed. "So much the worse for you! You will be more useful, and you cannot escape this time. See!" He stretched out a hand and hissed again, and the shadow flowed from it, forcing the glow backward, drawing closer to the frightened girl.

Suddenly the air filled with a choking cloud of white smoke that swirled around the Lithmern, hiding him almost completely. Worrel, once more unnoticed by the man, had pulled a small bundle of herbs from his pouch, lit them, and tossed them almost at the Lithmern's feet. The cloud of smoke did not last long, but even as it cleared the air around the enchanter exploded in silver-white light. The two Shee had recovered and were attacking once more.

The black aura died as the Shee poured power into the battle. The circlet blazed on Illeana's head, and she began the spell of unbinding. The Lithmern strove with all his might to stop the ritual, but he could not outface the two Shee now that they were prepared for him. Jordet's attack occupied him almost completely, and he could not spare the effort to oppose Illeana, though he knew her for the greater danger. As the chant flowed serenely on, a change took place in him. He swayed and seemed to have trouble coordinating; it was as if he fought himself as well as the two Shee. He sank to his knees and his voice died.

Illeana reached the end of the chant and threw her arms straight upward. In a loud voice she cried, "Avoc! Nitranara helmarc elas!" The Lithmern collapsed. A darkness hovered for a moment over him, then darted toward Alethia, but she was still protected by the golden light and it could not reach her. With a faint wailing sound, hardly more than a sigh, the darkness faded and was gone.

There was complete silence on the mountaintop. Illeana and Jordet sank wearily to the ground beside the unconscious Lithmern. Alethia looked at them in wonder. She fingered the stone she still held, then slipped it into the pocket of her cloak. The others slowly began to move, as if they had been entranced; the last to stir was Tamsin. Worrel, who seemed the most himself, vanished for a moment and returned with a waterbag. This he silently offered to the two spent Shee. Illeana drank

without even looking up, but Jordet nodded his
thanks. "Well done," the Wyrd said softly.

At that Illeana raised her head and her eyes were
haunted. "Not so," she cried. "I sought to bind
what I should have sought to free, and almost were
we all undone, he was so strong."

"Do not waste time in reproaches," Jordet said
sharply. "Would you have the evil we seek to defeat take hold in our midst?"

Illeana shuddered convulsively, then with an effort grew calm. "You held him off barely, but I
loosed the cords of binding and I know their
strength and their kind. Never did I think to see
such among the living. O my friend, it is far worse
than we suspected. Far worse than anyone could
have suspected.

"The Lithmern have waked the Kaldarmaaren."

# CHAPTER ELEVEN

This announcement had varying effects on the seven listeners. Maurin simply looked puzzled. Har frowned, as if he were trying to remember something. Tamsin's eyes narrowed thoughtfully; Alethia went white and her lips pressed tightly together. Jordet froze, eyes fixed on Illeana. Only the Wyrds seemed unaffected. Worrel nodded and resumed his seat calmly; Rarn merely pursed her lips and shook her head.

The small movement seemed to break a spell. Jordet lowered his head and said tiredly, "You are sure."

"You fought him with me! How can you doubt it? But if you seek further proof, then question him in truthtrance," Illeana said, pointing at the collapsed figure of the Lithmern.

"I know you speak the truth," Jordet replied heavily, "but I never expected to see such evil wake in my lifetime."

Har shifted uncomfortably. "What are Kaldarmaaren?"

"Do not speak the name lightly!" Illeana answered sharply. "They have powers beyond your imagining, and the sound may draw their attention, though they themselves may not cross the Kathkari without help."

"But what are they?" Alethia asked.

"They are spirits of a sort, whose origin lies in times before legend," Jordet said. "They have no bodies, but they use those of living men, for a time, if the will is weak or if someone has prepared the way for them by other means. Even then, the body gradually fades into the darkness of its possessor, hence their name, which means Shadow-born. If you would name them, call them that, or Dark Men, as the Wyrds do."

"The 'man with no face' was a Shadow-born, then?" Maurin asked.

"Perhaps," Jordet said thoughtfully. "But one of the Dark Men would not need the Talisman of Noron'ri to assist his magic. Their age gives them knowledge of secrets and powers now forgotten, and better they remained so."

"But if he was not one of the Shadow-born, why couldn't I see his face?" Alethia asked. "And where did the Lithmern find them? I've never heard of Shadow-born before, not even in the old tales."

"That is not surprising," Jordet replied. "The Shadow-born were bound in silence and safety at the dawn of memory, and I believe even your minstrel could not tell you much of them."

"If the Shee bound them once, can you not do so again?" Tamsin asked the Shee. He was not entirely pleased by Jordet's last comment.

"It may be possible, if we can reach them before they gain their full strength," said Illeana. "But they were first bound over three thousand years ago, and it took the combined power of the Four Races and more; it took the power of the greatest treasures of Lyra—the Sword, the Shield, the Cup and the Staff."

"The Lost Gifts of Alkyra!" Har exclaimed.

"I thought that they were made for the first King of Alkyra, as coronation gifts," Alethia said. "How could they have been used so long ago?"

"They were indeed coronation gifts, but they are far older than that," Tamsin said with a far-away look in his eyes. "Each of the Four Races took one after the Wars of Binding, and only the Crown has greater power. They were given to Kirel at his coronation for the keeping of the peace of Alkyra, so that he would be a King for all four of the races and not only humans."

"You are well-versed, Minstrel," Jordet said. "I had not known that such ancient tales were still kept outside the Kathkari."

"You forget, perhaps, that the Hall of Tears where the minstrels gather is at least as old as the cities of the Shee," Tamsin said politely. "Still, I know little of the Wars of Binding save their name. I can tell you more of the Four Gifts, though what I know is more recent history."

"Then speak," said Illeana. "I have always wondered how you of Alkyra allowed things of such power to be lost so easily; tell me."

Har looked at her angrily, but Tamsin seemed unperturbed. "They were lost during the first invasion of the Lithmern," he said. "The Royal Family was at Lacsmer, and with them were the Crown and the Gifts. The Lithmern fell on the city without warning and killed King Cardemane and all his family, save only the youth Caruth who was not in the city. Then the Lithmern took the Crown and the Four Gifts, and sent a party to take them back to Lithra, to Mog Ograth—but they never arrived. Never again have they been seen; the party disappeared, and no one has ever found a trace of them or of the Gifts, though many have lost their lives in searching."

"Had we even one of those four, or the Crown of Alkyra, I would be more optimistic about our chances against the Shadow-born," Illeana said.

"Unfortunately, we have neither Kirel's Crown nor his coronation Gifts," Jordet said dryly. "What is our next step?"

"We must send to Eveleth at once," Illeana said with decision. "They must know what we face."

"What proof have we to offer?" Jordet demanded. "Eveleth must know, but will they believe such unlikely news?"

There was a brief silence while the unanswered question hung in the air. Then Rarn snorted. "Your proof is there; you said it yourselves," she said, waving at the still unconscious Lithmern. "Question him under truthtrance."

"Aye, if we learn nothing more than his purpose in attacking Alethia just now it will still be well worth the time," Worrel agreed. "And I'll wager he knows more of the plans for attacking Brenn than we, which must also be worth learning."

The others nodded. The wisdom of such a course was evident, and the danger was minimal now that the man had been freed of the Shadow-born's binding.

The Lithmern was beginning to stir; Worrel took a waterbag and dumped about half its remaining contents on the man's head. He gasped and spluttered, then sat up shaking glittering droplets of water from his hair. His eyes widened as he took in the nature of the people standing about him, and he scrambled to his feet.

"My undying thanks are yours," he said unexpectedly, his voice hoarse, "for your timely rescue." He tried to bow, but staggered and almost collapsed. Worrel guided him to a seat, and offered him the waterbag once more. The man drank in great gulps while the others watched in silence.

"Now that you have refreshed yourself," Illeana said sarcastically, "perhaps you will tell us who you are?"

"I am Corrim vin Halla of Karlen Gale," the man replied wearily. "I have been a prisoner of the Lithmern for four months or more, and after that the slave of that thing; I know not how long."

"Karlen Gale!" Alethia said, and the others exchanged surprised looks. Corrim vin Halla nodded once. His head did not rise again; it was as if it would be too much trouble to lift it.

Maurin drew Jordet a little aside. "Can we trust him, do you think?"

"When he is under truthtrance," Jordet replied softly, but Corrim heard. His head lifted and his eyes grew bleak.

"It were better indeed not to trust me too far," he said. "What I know I will give you freely, saving that you give me a clean death before *that* returns for me."

"Who speaks of death?" Jordet demanded. "You need not fear such if you are what you say."

Corrim shook his head. "I am free of it now, and for that I thank you," he said heavily. "But I have lived with its power. It will return for me, and when it does it will be better for you and I both if I am dead already."

"The Shadow-born cannot cross the Kathkari without a host," Illeana said. "You need not fear them while you remain in Sheleran."

The Karlen Gale man shook his head doubtfully, but remained silent. "Of course, we cannot accept you completely without more knowledge," Illeana went on, "and that is best done under truth-trance. If you are willing, we can begin."

The man's face turned grey, and it was only with obvious effort that he kept control of himself. "By your leave, is there no way other than to be again ensorcelled?" he asked hoarsely.

" 'Tis no great thing to fear," Illeana said, frowning. "You will not even know that your will is overborn, unless you try to lie. Come, now."

Corrim nodded jerkily, and walked stiff-legged to seat himself where Illeana indicated. Jordet stood behind him and murmured rapidly, making a few passes in the air. Corrim's eyes glazed. Jordet finished and came around to study the man's suddenly relaxed face for a moment, then nodded at Illeana. "Now, tell us your story," she commanded.

The tale that unwound for the fascinated listeners was not, at first, complex. Corrim had been captured by a Lithmern raiding party, and his first months had been spent as an ordinary prisoner-slave, forced to do menial labor during the day and chained at night. Then he was chosen for the Shadow-born.

He remembered the binding ceremony only vaguely, as a chill and a sibilant voice and a black fog that sank into his brain and overwhelmed him. For a long time after that he was a prisoner in his own body, aware but unable to control the simplest of his actions. He was not completely possessed, though he knew that would come when the Shadow-born used up one of their present hosts. He, and the others like him, were puppets waiting to be occupied by Shadow-born at some later date, completely trustworthy because they had no will save that of their masters.

There was little Corrim could do except cling to his sanity and hope that the Shadow-born or their wizard-masters would make a mistake that would allow him to escape, or simply die cleanly. It was a hard task, for when they wished, the Shadow-born could speak with his voice and see with his eyes in a kind of incomplete possession that was a horrible foreshadowing of what he knew was to come.

Corrim was able to give a very coherent account of Alethia's kidnapping. Jordet had been correct; the leader of the Lithmern party had not been one of the Shadow-born themselves, but one of the messenger-slaves who was very near to total possession. The Talisman of Noron'ri had been necessary to channel the creature's power to its servant. Though the Shadow-born could take possession of the man's body, they could not maintain it for more than a few minutes at such a distance until one of them took him over completely.

Corrim had been included in the party as a supplementary contact, for use in the unlikely event that something happened to the leader, who was much more firmly controlled than the Karlen Gale man. About the Shadow-born themselves, Corrim knew little. The Lithmern sorcerer-king Ninri had conjured them to aid him in conquering Alkyra; they had been weakened by their long captivity, but they were growing stronger daily.

When Corrim finished his tale, Har questioned him closely about the plans for the attack on Alkyra. The main body of the army, he learned, was still at Mog Ograth with the Lithmern wizards and the Shadow-born. It would, therefore, be at least three weeks before it could reach Brenn under the best of conditions, possibly longer. Har sat back to digest this information, and Jordet looked at Corrim gravely.

"The Lithmern do not know what they have done. It will not be long before they serve the Shadow-born, whom they summoned to be their servants. If, indeed, they do not do so already; their interests seem identical. But why do the Shadow-born want to destroy Alkyra?"

"They want to reestablish their rule over Lyra, as they ruled during the Times of Darkness," Illeana said impatiently, before Corrim could reply. "They choose Alkyra as their starting place because the Lithmern hate it and it is easy to persuade them to move against it, that is all."

"I do not think so," Worrel said. "Is it coincidence that Alkyra is bordered by the lands of the Shee and of the Wyrds? I think the Shadow-born move first to remove the last of their old enemies, the last of the ones who bound them."

There was a moment's pause as the others considered the idea. Jordet turned back to Corrim. "Could it be so?"

Corrim frowned. "Perhaps. Yet it did not seem to me that they moved from vengeance, but out of fear."

"Then they are perhaps not yet so strong that we may not bind them once more," Illeana said with more confidence than she had shown previously.

"You are wrong," said a quiet, sure voice. Heads turned toward Maurin in surprise, and Illeana lifted one eyebrow expressively. "Enlighten me," she said.

Maurin reddened slightly. "I do not mean that your people cannot bind the Shadow-born," he explained. "Only that their reason for pressing to attack Brenn must be more than fear of the Shee and the Wyrds.''

"Why?" asked Jordet.

"Because of Alethia," Maurin said. "Think on it! If the Shadow-born feared you, why would they go into the Wyrwood and risk betraying themselves too soon? Why send so strong a party to kidnap Alethia from Brenn before the attack, and why attempt to recover her and not the Talisman when both were lost? Why wouldn't the Shadow-born simply wait until their strength was at its peak and they were no longer vulnerable before attacking, unless there was something they wanted or feared more than they fear premature discovery?"

"Then you think that the Lithmern did not mistake Alethia for Isme when they kidnapped her from Styr Tel?" Worrel asked.

"What else explains their actions?" Maurin retorted.

"But why would Alethia be so valuable to them?"

"I cannot guess," Maurin replied. "But I can think of no other explanation that fits."

"Explanation?" Illeana said. "More like a fabrication! I do not find it convincing."

"Nonetheless, this is the third time the Lithmern and their creatures have tried to capture Alethia," Maurin pointed out. "That thing went straight for her as soon as it broke free of your circle. If the Shadow-born wanted Isme, why do they keep trying to recover her daughter?"

"And I still do not believe that it was entirely a coincidence that the janaver struck at Alethia," said Worrel. "If it was not, that would make four times. I am much inclined to accept your theory."

"In any case, I do not think we can remain long

in the mountains," Jordet said. Illeana frowned, and he went on, "I know that you were told to keep us from Eveleth, but the situation has now changed. None of us can heal him," he nodded at the gloomy figure of Corrim, "nor adequately protect him for more than a brief time. Though the mountains may give him some protection from the Shadow-born, I do not think that it will last once they reach their full strength."

Illeana still looked doubtful, but she nodded. "In any case, someone must take the news that the Shadow-born walk free once more, and that without delay. Very well, we shall all go. These winds blow too high for me."

# CHAPTER TWELVE

The travelers were soon on their way once more. For the rest of the day, they wound among the mountains. At twilight they had not yet reached Eveleth, but Jordet and Illeana assured them it was no more than two hours' ride. No one wanted to spend another night in the open, especially with their destination so close, and they kept on. The path gradually widened into a well-trodden road that sloped gently upward past the shadowed cliffs on either side. The two moons rose almost together, giving the white hair of the Shee a silvery sheen and lighting the road before them with a clear, cold light.

A gentle breeze, barely a stirring of the night air, came blowing down the last rise to meet them. Below her, Alethia could dimly see the rolling woods, veiled in silver light like a woman of Rathane. Above towered the immovable mountains, dark and silent, up which the small black dots of the horses and ponies crept like ants. She felt strangely peaceful for the first time since leaving Brenn.

Jordet stopped at the top of the slope and the others rode up beside him. "There," he said softly, pointing. "There is Eveleth."

They were looking out over a plateau that seemed immense. Directly before and below them rose the white spires of a city, gleaming in full moonlight. From the windows, light shone in brilliant pin-points; not the warm yellow light of candles or lamps, but a pure white light like that of the stars. The city lay within a circle of smaller lights, evenly spaced on the wall around it like beads on a necklace chain.

They looked in silence. Then, wordlessly, they applied themselves to the descent. When they stood before the gates of the city at last, Alethia was awed. Five times as high as her head they stood, yet still they seemed curiously fragile. The metal gleamed in the light of two lamps hanging from the wall on either side, and she could see carvings on the doorposts that even in the uncertain light were obviously the work of master craftsmen.

Jordet rode directly into the pool of light before the gates. "Open! Ri peri sikat!"

"Who demands entrance to the City of Lights?" said a cool voice from the top of the wall above them.

"The Keeper of the South Ward demands entrance," Jordet shouted back, with a smile.

Silent and slow as in a dream, the gates swung inward. Inside stood a Shee dressed in uniform, silver and black in the moonlight. The haughty expression on his face was belied by the warmth in his voice. "Jordet!" The warmth quickly vanished as he saw the Ward-Keeper's companions just outside the gate.

"Prestemon, there is an explanation for this," Jordet said quickly.

"Explanations must wait; we must go to the palace at once!" Illeana said behind him. She rode forward until she could be plainly seen by the guard.

"Have you run mad?" the Shee Captain demanded, looking at Jordet. "Bringing humans to our city!"

"This is the Queen's business," Illeana snapped.

Jordet nodded. "These are my *cousins,* Prestemon. This is Alethia of Brenn and her brother Har—the children of Isme. The ban against humankind need not apply to them."

"And the others? Can you claim Shee heritage for them as well, Jordet?" Prestemon spoke gently, but remained firm.

Illeana was equally firm. "This is the *Queen*'s business, Captain. It is not for you to judge. Do you question the Veldatha?"

Jordet interrupted her. "Prestemon—you must trust me."

Prestemon turned his gaze slowly from Jordet to Illeana, and back again. "Alright. I will escort you personally. But on your *life,* my friend, this had better have a good explanation."

Jordet grinned as he swung back into the saddle. "That's fair enough."

Prestemon shook his head and turned back to the gates. "Taterek! Close the gates and mind them well!"

The Shee in the gatehouse nodded his acknowledgement. The Captain seized one of the horses tethered just inside the gate, and indicated for the party to follow. "Pull your hoods up at least," he said, without turning back to them. "The less attention we attract, the better."

The buildings were clearly visible in the white light of the lanterns that hung at intervals along the streets, but none bore any resemblance to the solid stone houses of Brenn or to the wooden ones of other Alkyran towns. These were made of the same smooth white stone blocks that paved the street, and they shone ghostly amid gardens and groves of trees. From time to time, the riders heard the music of fountains.

The party turned a corner and moved slowly down a wide avenue that led directly to the palace. Ahead of them rose the silver spires of the castle, gleaming in the moonlight. The towers were visible from every part of the city, even over the tops of the tallest trees, reaching for the sky with tall, white fingers.

As they drew nearer, the rolling grounds and trees around the palace became more clearly visible, and soon they reached the foot of the long sweep of stairs leading up to the main door. On either side of the carved door-panels stood a Shee uniformed in black and silver, and as Prestemon rode up they snapped to attention.

The Captain mounted the stairs two at a time, giving orders to the guards almost as soon as he had dismounted, and disappeared through the carved doors.

One of the guards whistled as Alethia dismounted; two youths appeared in answer to the summons, and they took the reins of the horses and ponies and led them out into the shadows.

"If you will, please follow me," the second guard said politely as he swung the doors open. Illeana stepped forward at once, and the rest of the travelers followed.

Inside they were hurried down a long marble hall lined with pillars to a small chamber hung with silks and tapestries. Here the guard left them, but they did not have to wait long. Barely had they entered when they heard the sound of rapid footsteps approaching. The door opposite was thrown open, revealing Prestemon and another Shee wearing a black cloak lined in dark purple silk and carrying a silver staff. Jordet and Worrel immediately bowed; Rarn and Illeana curtsied. After a moment's hesitation, Alethia and the three men copied the others.

"Lord Medilaw Robal, High Minister to Her Majesty Queen Iniscara," announced Prestemon as the second man entered the room.

"You may go, but stay outside in case you are needed," the High Minister said as he passed the guard captain. His voice was deep, clear, and cold. Prestemon bowed and went out, closing the door behind him. "Now," Medilaw continued, "you will explain this to me, Jordet."

"My Lord," Jordet said formally, "I would first present Alethia and Har Tel'anh, Worrel n'Grath and Rarn s'Mural, Journeyman Maurin Atuval and Minstrel Tamsin Lerrol, and Corrim vin Halla." The High Minister acknowledged the introductions with narrowed eyes and looked expectantly at Jordet. "We traveled together from the South Ward in answer to the summons of the Queen."

"Yes, but why did you come all the way here?" asked Medilaw with a frown. "I thought your instructions clear enough." He looked pointedly at Illeana, who returned his gaze coolly.

"The Wearers of the Crown are not slaves, to complete a task without questioning," she replied. "It seemed best to me that they should come to

Eyeleth, and I have brought them. Will you question my judgement?"

"I fear I must," Medilaw replied angrily. "Things have not changed since this morning that you must amend my orders. There is no reason to trouble our people with humans and half-breeds."

Har's eyes narrowed dangerously. "Is it your people that will be troubled, or yourself, my Lord?" he spat. "In Alkyra at least we have the manners to give strangers a hearing before we dismiss them."

"Among yourselves you may do as you like; it is no concern of mine," Medilaw answered. "I do not see . . ."

Illeana interrupted him before he could finish the sentence. "It is plain indeed that you do not see," she said. "I am Veldatha; I am no tool for your use, my Lord. Next time perhaps you may think better before you try to use me as such."

"Even the Veldatha wizards must bow to the Queen's orders," Medilaw said.

"How could the Queen have known that you sent me to keep these folk from Eveleth when she was studying Firivar's prophecy undisturbed from midnight on?" Illeana demanded.

Medilaw's lips tightened. "The High Minister speaks for the Queen," he said. "I am still waiting for an explanation of your actions."

"My actions were in the interests of the Queen and of Eveleth," Illeana said. "I think it would be as well if the Queen and the Council knew that the Lithmern sorcerers have loosed the Shadow-born once more. Do you not?"

The High Minister paled. "The Shadow-born?" Jordet and Illeana nodded. "I . . . You could have sent one of your number with proof, rather than bring all," he said uncertainly. Then he looked up. "That is, if you have proof of this improbable assertion."

"Medilaw, for once you are a fool," said a calm voice from the doorway. Turning, they saw a Shee woman apparently of middle age, her pale hair bound back from her face by a silver circlet. Unlike all the Shee the humans had yet seen her eyes were a hazel brown flecked with green.

"Your Majesty!" Medilaw bowed deeply. The others followed suit. As his head rose, Medilaw began to speak, but the Queen cut him short.

"Have a care; do not compound your error, Medilaw," she said. "Why were these humans not brought to me at once? Why was I not even notified of their arrival? Have I not told you that the matter of Brenn is of gravest importance?"

"Your Majesty has been much occupied with preparations for the Council tomorrow," Medilaw replied austerely. "I did not wish to disturb you without cause, and so I chose to see first whether there were any need for you to be concerned."

"And was it that same concern that prompted you to send Illeana to persuade them to go elsewhere without consulting me?" the Queen asked gently.

"I wished only to relieve you of the burden of dealing with them," Medilaw replied.

"This is not the first time you have chosen to . . . relieve me of the burdens of sovereignty," the Queen replied softly. "This time, however, you might have done more damage than you realize. Still, there must be somewhere such devotion may be put to proper use. Somewhere, I think, besides the position of Minister to the Queen. Have you any suggestions? No? Think on it, then, but leave your staff with Nember. He shall be directing the Council tomorrow."

Medilaw turned white, but bowed and left without attempting to say more. Having summarily dismissed her over-ambitious minister, the Queen turned to the ring of people who had been watching this interaction with interest, and smiled graciously—though the smile did not reach her eyes. "Tell me what brings you here."

The Queen listened closely without interrupting while Jordet told the tale. She did not question him at first, but turned to Illeana. "You are sure that Corrim was controlled by the Kalder-maaren?" she asked.

"Madam, he was briefly possessed. I could not be mistaken; we were fortunate that the distance was too great for the Shadow-born to exert his full power through this one," Illeana replied. "In addition, the creature was overconfident; it was still too soon after his waking and he was weaker than he thought. Even so, he nearly defeated us; had we not been in the Kathkari where his power is weaker I think he would have won."

Iniscara's eyes narrowed, but she only nodded briefly before turning back to Jordet. "Do you concur?"

"Yes, your Majesty," said Jordet simply. Iniscara nodded again and turned to Alethia.

"The Kalder-maaren seem to be exceptionally interested in you, daughter of Isme," she said. "I am surprised you have managed to arrive here in safety."

"I think I have been very lucky, your Majesty," Alethia replied.

"That, certainly," the Queen said thoughtfully.

She looked sharply at the girl for a moment. "Were you holding any object of magic when the Shadow-born attacked?"

Alethia frowned in concentration. "No, I was just tossing pebbles," she answered.

The Queen turned abruptly to Jordet and Illeana. "Why did you not inform me?"

Illeana looked startled. "What possible importance could it be?"

"Have you forgotten all the magic you know?" the Queen asked sharply. Turning back to Alethia, she asked, "Do you still have the stones?"

"I don't . . . no, I do still have one," Alethia said. "I put it in my cloak pocket; I'd forgotten about it until now." She reached into the pocket as she spoke and dug for a moment, and brought out a small stone, about the size of a cloak button.

Her companions stared at it for a moment. It was a very ordinary looking rock. The Queen, however, did not seem disturbed by its unexciting appearance. "Do not lose it, child; you may find it useful some time," was all she said.

Privately, Alethia did not see what use a small rock could ever be, but she refrained from voicing her opinion and replaced the stone carefully in the pocket of her cloak. The Queen turned to Corrim, but questioned him only briefly. It was plain to all that the erstwhile puppet of the Shadow-born was at the edge of collapse, and Iniscara sent him away with one of the guards as soon as she finished speaking with him.

The others were questioned in more detail, and it was some time before the Queen was satisfied. Alethia was beginning to nod when the Queen finally called in another servant to take them to their rooms.

"We will speak more tomorrow," she said as she left them, her smile cold and her thoughts unreadable. Illeana and Jordet exchanged worried frowns as they departed in the servant's wake.

# CHAPTER THIRTEEN

Alethia was awakened the following morning by a young Shee girl, who brought her fresh clothes and wash water. The girl returned just as Alethia finished dressing, and led her to another room where Har, Maurin, Tamsin and Jordet were breakfasting.

"Good morning!" Alethia said as they rose to greet her. "I hope you haven't been waiting for me long."

"No, but you'll have to hurry anyway," Jordet said. "The Council of Lords will begin soon, and we must all be there before it starts. It wouldn't be wise to keep them waiting."

"Yes—but about the aid for Brenn," Har said. "How many men do you think they will send?"

"It is not at all certain that they will send any," Jordet said reluctantly. "That is one of the things the Council must decide today."

"But Queen Iniscara . . ." Alethia's voice trailed off as she mentally reviewed the previous night's conversation with the Queen of the Shee. Iniscara had never actually promised to send anyone to Brenn.

"Sheleran is not ruled by the Queen," Jordet said slowly. "In fact, the Council of Lords holds the power here. Do not expect too much."

"Sounds just as bad as home," Har said disgustedly. "A figurehead ruler governed by her council—like our regent and the Nine Families."

Jordet flushed a little. "Few lords will see an attack on Brenn as a threat to Sheleran, and many of them will fight against renewed contact between our peoples. Some will be simply disinterested in your plight. I am sorry."

There was silence for a moment. "At least that man Queen Iniscara dismissed won't be there," Alethia said finally. "If he were in charge of the Council, we wouldn't have a chance."

"Medilaw will be at the Council," Jordet replied. "He is no longer High Minister, but as a Lord Advisor he has a great deal of influence. Do not underestimate him."

"How can he be a Lord Advisor?" Har said. "I thought the Queen dismissed him?"

"Lord Nember has replaced Medilaw as High Minister, it is true," Jordet said, "but even the Queen cannot dismiss a Lord Advisor, except for treason or insanity. Medilaw has two years to go in his term of office."

"I don't think there's anything we can do about Medilaw," Maurin said as Har opened his mouth to speak again. "What else should we know about this Council?"

"Medilaw isn't the only lord who dislikes humans. If you hope to sway the Council, you must ignore their intolerance, no matter how unpleasant they are."

Har snorted. "We would have been better off going to Lacsmer the way I wanted to in the first place."

Alethia frowned at him. "If you could be polite to First Lord Orlin when he was in Brenn last year, I don't see why you can't manage to do the same for a Shee council. Particularly since it's so important to Brenn."

Before Har could reply, a guard arrived to summon them to the Council. He led the little group through the palace corridors to one end of a long hall, where he showed them to their seats. The hall was already crowded, and many of the councilors broke off their conversations to stare unabashedly and somewhat rudely as the party settled themselves in their places.

Har leaned over to Maurin. "It looks as if we are creating quite a sensation," he whispered.

"I'd be happier if we weren't," Maurin replied. "The Traders have good reasons for listening first and talking later, but it is hard to do inconspicuously if one is the center of attention."

"True, O fox. Jordet, who are these people?" Har said.

Jordet identified the councilors. The long hall was lined with Shee lords and ladies in all manner of colorful robes, which heightened the sameness of their white hair and slanted eyes. "The Council Lords wear different colors according to their rank," Jordet explained, "and the Lord Advisors wear purple, no matter what they are entitled to by birth. There are five of them; you should be able to recognize them easily when they arrive."

At that moment, Alethia spied Iniscara at the opposite end of the room, and she lost interest in Jordet's explanations. The Queen of the Shee sat on a raised throne of jet black. On her head was a delicate silver crown set with black jewels. Her garments were silver, shading into black at her feet so that she seemed a part of the throne on which she sat. The throne itself seemed to be carved from a single block of stone. The back rose high above the Queen's head, and a circle of runes unfamiliar to Alethia was inlaid upon it in silver.

To the Queen's right was a throne of identical design, but made of polished wood. In it sat Murn, and above her head the same runes shone in milky jade. On Iniscara's left was yet another throne made of crystal, with the runes inlaid in mother-of-pearl. The man seated there was robed in white, and on his deep green hair sat a thin circlet of gold. His skin was pale and faintly iridescent, like the sheen of a pearl or a fish's scales. Alethia leaned toward Jordet.

"Who is that?" she asked, nodding at the man in the crystal throne.

"He is Merissallan of the Neira," Jordet replied. "And don't ask me why the Queen invited him to be here, or Murn either! It has been a hundred years since there was a full council of all the Lords of Sheleran, and as far as I know there has never been one attended by representatives of the other races."

Alethia opened her mouth to ask another question, but before she had a chance to speak, a chime sounded through the hall. As the sound died, five Shee in purple robes moved to seat themselves at a low, curving table just in front of the three thrones. An unfamiliar Shee dressed in black and purple stepped out from behind the table and into the center of the floor. He was carrying Medilaw's silver staff, and Jordet leaned over toward Har and Alethia.

"That is Lord Nember, the new High Minister," he whispered. Alethia nodded absently as she studied Medilaw's replacement. Nember raised the staff and struck the marble floor once. A second chime went ringing through the hall, leaving an abrupt and complete silence behind it.

"Lords of Sheleran!" Nember said. "You are come to decide what course we shall take; be therefore honest and thorough in your deliberations." For the third time he struck the floor. "The Council is begun!"

The new High Minister bowed and returned to the table. There was a brief hum of voices, which died as Nember raised the staff again. "Alethia Tel'anh," he said in a cool voice, "step forward."

Alethia rose uncertainly and moved out into the hall. When she reached the center of the floor, Nember raised his staff again, and she stopped. "Alethia Tel'anh of Brenn," the High Minister said, extending the staff towards her. "You are summoned before the Queen and the assembled Lords of the Shee, to answer truly the questions we shall ask. Are you agreed to stand so?"

"I am," Alethia said, raising her chin slightly.

"Then begin by telling us how you and these other humans came to our city," Nember said.

Alethia's eyes narrowed at his phrasing, but she remembered Jordet's warning and suppressed the brief flare of anger she felt. Without preamble, she began the tale of her kidnapping and the events that followed. Several times she was interrupted by questions from one or another of the Council members before she finished.

Nember waved Alethia back to her seat at the conclusion of her tale. He turned to the Queen and bowed, then called Har forward. "Har Tel'anh of Brenn, you are summoned before the Queen and the assembled Lords of the Shee . . ."

One by one, each of the travelers was called forward to give an account of their journey. When the four humans had finished, Worrel was brought into the hall. He carried with him the Talisman of Noron'ri, which he handed to Nember before taking his place in the center of the floor. When Worrel finished his story, Nember placed the Talisman in the middle of the Lord Advisors' table, where it could be seen by all the Shee lords, then called for Corrim vin Halla.

Corrim's story sent a ripple of dismay through the audience. He was followed by Illeana, regal and imperious in the Crown of the Veldatha, who confirmed what he had said and added some speculations on the strength of the Shadow-born. Finally the Lords finished their questioning, and the High Minister rose.

"Members of the Council, you have heard the testimony. There is yet one thing lacking before your knowledge is complete." He gestured, and a black-and-silver clad guard carrying a sheet of paper came forward. "This message was sent to the Queen yesterday from Firivar the Seer," Nember went on, and nodded at the guard. The guard cleared his throat and began to read:

"To Her Majesty Iniscara, Queen of Sheleran: The Runes of Change have spoken, and these are their portents: 'An old darkness comes from the west, and if it move unopposed it will still the wind and flood and tree. Fire opposes and wind scatters; the mountains are cast down and the child of fire holds the source of power. In the end one will sit above the four once more, or all will lie in darkness.' In Service to the Queen, Firivar."

Nember nodded again and the guard bowed and left. "Lords of Sheleran!" the High Minister said. "Now it is for you to speak, and choose what course we shall take. Shall we send aid to the humans of Brenn, against the Lithmern? And what shall be done with the Talisman of Noron'ri?" The silver staff rang once more, and the High Minister seated himself.

After a moment's silence, a Shee woman robed in blue rose and bowed to the Queen. "I see no reason why we should help one set of humans against another," she said. "We have kept apart from their affairs this long; what reason now to change?"

"My lady, the Lithmern fight with magic," a young Shee lord in green said diffidently. "Is that not our concern?"

The woman in blue shrugged. "If the Alkyrans have neglected the study of sorcery, that is their concern, not ours. Are we to spend our hard-won knowledge for them?"

"Were that the only question, I would agree," said a lord robed in white. "But Firivar's prophecy speaks of an 'old darkness out of the west'; surely this refers to the Shadow-born. I think, my lords, that the Shadow-born should be our first concern, and not the human city."

"I agree," said a Shee woman robed in red. "Yet the two matters seem intertwined. Lithra has unbound the Shadow-born. Lithra is attacking Brenn, almost on our doorstep. I think our course is obvious."

"The Shadow-born are the true danger," said another lord.

"Yes, and the sooner we strike the easier they will be to deal with," said the red-clad lady. "Or would you wait until their power reaches its full strength?"

"There is strength in numbers as well as time,"

another lady said pointedly. "When they reach Brenn, the Shadow-born will be together and able to support one another. If we wait until Lithra has conquered Alkyra, the Shadow-born will be spread out, and we can deal with them one at a time."

Har shifted angrily in his seat, and leaned over toward Alethia. "They talk as if nothing mattered but their own convenience!" he whispered.

"Hush!" Alethia said. Medilaw was rising, and she wanted to hear what he said.

"My lords and ladies," Medilaw began, bowing. "In so grave a matter, let us take time to consider. The Dark Men cannot cross the Kathkari; there is no need for us to hurry. We have sat through wars among the humans before; what need to leave our land now?"

"The Shadow-born cannot cross the Kathkari, but their army can," a Shee halfway down one side of the hall said loudly.

Medilaw shrugged. "An army of humans. How should we fear them?"

"Swords do not care whether the hand that wields them is Shee or human," one of the other Lord Advisors said.

"True indeed, my lord Herre," Medilaw said. "But if you fear the humans so greatly, let us use the Talisman of Noron'ri to seal our borders against them." He waved a negligent hand at the table where the Talisman lay, and some trick of light made the iron glint ominously.

"Is it wise to keep a thing of such power that has been tainted by the Shadow-born?" one of the other lords asked.

Medilaw looked annoyed. "It would be folly to destroy what we no longer possess the knowledge to make," he said. "Besides, it is no danger to us. So long as we keep it in Eveleth, the Shadow-born cannot reach it."

"May not the Shadow-born have others?" said a Shee in yellow. "Worse, what if they discover the lost Gifts while we sit waiting? I do not like this plan of stopping and considering; wisdom sometimes must make haste."

"I do not seek to keep us from action," Medilaw said. "Only to prevent us from acting too quickly and making a grave mistake. You need not worry about the Talismans; the Lithmern can have no more of them, or the Veldatha would have detected them. Is this not so?" He turned toward Illeana, who nodded reluctantly.

"As for the Gifts," Medilaw went on, "they were lost two hundred years ago, by the same humans who now beg our aid."

"You forget, Medilaw, that we now have ties of blood in Brenn," said a Shee robed in blue, looking significantly at Har and Alethia. "Shall we abandon our own?"

"One who willfully abandoned her people may not expect aid from them in return," Medilaw replied. "Yet you are right; they have some claim on us despite their human blood. We should offer them sanctuary among us until this matter is resolved."

"What makes you think we want your sanctuary?" an angry voice interrupted.

All along the hall, heads swiveled away from Medilaw toward the far end. Alethia was on her feet, eyes blazing. "We didn't come to ask for sanctuary. We will not beg for help that is not offered freely. Keep your magic!"

There were murmurs of approval, and Medilaw

went pale with anger. He was seldom challenged, and he had not doubted his ability to sway the Council. Defiance from this slip of a half-breed girl was unthinkable. "You humans have no chance against the Shadow-born!" he cried. With some difficulty, he controlled his anger enough to shrug and say coldly, "Still, if you refuse our assistance, there is no more to be said."

"Perhaps we will surprise you," Alethia retorted. "Courage is no bad weapon against spells, or so I have learned."

"Even if you commanded the full power of the Talisman of Noron'ri and the Gifts themselves, a half-Shee like you could never hope to save your city!" Medilaw shouted.

"I suppose you know more about it than I," Alethia said sweetly. "You have no doubt studied such things; I have only managed to escape from a Shadow-born puppet wielding a Talisman, and then kill him later."

Someone chuckled. Medilaw glared about the hall, white-faced and trembling. Then he snatched up the Talisman of Noron'ri from the table in front of him. "You shall see what I know!" he cried, and raised it aloft in both hands.

The gesture was a vivid reminder of the Lithmern Shadow-captain, and Alethia stepped backward involuntarily. Maurin leapt to his feet and threw himself in front of her. Medilaw's eyes never left Alethia. His lips parted in a grimace that might have been intended as a smile, and he spoke a single word.

A muddy little cloud began to form above Medilaw's head as the Shee lords stared in frozen disbelief. Medilaw's harsh grin widened, and he raised the Talisman higher and pointed at Alethia.

The muddy cloud thickened and began to move forward.

Suddenly, Medilaw was spun around. Powerful hands wrenched the Talisman from his grasp, and the small, dark cloud shuddered and evaporated. Medilaw howled, and in blind and unthinking rage attacked the purple-clad figure that had thwarted him. It was quickly evident that the other Lord Advisor was both younger and faster than the former High Minister; he had no trouble holding the enraged man for the brief time it took the palace guards to close on the table. Medilaw quickly vanished in a wave of black and silver; a moment later, he was led away, cursing hoarsely.

In the shaken silence that followed, Iniscara spoke for the first time. "My thanks to you, Lord Advisor Herre," she said quietly. "You will not find me ungrateful."

Lord Herre bowed and seated himself at the Lord Advisors' table once more. The silence continued; the Shee lords and ladies stared at the Talisman. Then Iniscara rose to her feet, and her voice rang clearly in the still room.

"Do any of you doubt the meaning of what has just happened?" she said. Her eyes raked the hall; no one spoke.

"Then there is no longer any question what we must do," Iniscara said. "If the Shadow-born can reach even here, to touch a Lord Advisor in Council, we cannot wait to combat them at a time of our own choosing."

Heads nodded in agreement, but the Queen ignored them. She turned first to Murn and then to Merissallan. "I hope your people will join us, but if not we will not condemn you. For this will be a difficult task, and there are those here who would prevent us, as you have seen."

"I may not speak for the Wyrds," Murn said. "Yet I shall tell what I have seen and learned. I do not think they will refuse."

"The Neira will do what we can," the sea-man said. "I can speak for all of us, but I do not know how much use we may be; Brenn is a long way from the ocean."

Iniscara nodded in satisfaction. She turned back to the Shee councilors. "Three thousand horsemen will leave Eveleth at once for Brenn, with Lord Advisor Herre to command them," the Queen said. "The Talisman of Noron'ri will be destroyed immediately, lest the Shadow-born use it to work more mischief among us. You have seen and heard it."

The Shee lords and ladies bowed in acknowledgement of the Queen's commands. There was a rustle of movement; the Queen raised a hand and it checked at once.

"Lest any misunderstand me, I will do one thing more before you leave," the Queen said. "Nember!"

Imperiously, she stretched out a hand. Slowly, the High Minister rose and handed her the silver staff of his office.

Holding the staff in both hands, Iniscara raised her arms high. "I am Iniscara, Queen of Eveleth, and of Sheleran, and of the Shee! As those before me have done, so will I do! You are witnesses to this."

The Shee rose and responded with one voice, "We are witness, and will uphold the oath."

A wind swept through the hall, blowing the

Queen's robes out behind her. It grew stronger and stronger as Iniscara lowered her arms; then, as the end of the staff touched the floor, it died abruptly. "You may go," she said.

# CHAPTER FOURTEEN

There was a rustle of movement as the Shee lords and ladies rose and bowed, then turned to file slowly from the Council hall. Beside Alethia, Jordet sighed and shook his head. "This is indeed a day of wonders," he said.

"What do you mean?" Har asked.

"You saw Iniscara take up the staff and you have to ask? It has been long since a monarch of the Shee has claimed the staff and the full power of royalty," Jordet replied. "But come; if you intend to go with our troops, you must hurry."

"That many men can't possibly prepare to leave in only a few hours," Har objected. "They can't all be in Eveleth now. It will take time just to collect them."

"Don't be so sure," Jordet grinned. "I was up most of the night helping them get ready. Iniscara ordered the guard to alert a week or more ago, when word first arrived of Alethia's kidnapping; she's had them preparing to leave ever since news of the seige arrived."

Har's face lightened. "Then the Queen intended to send help to Brenn all along!"

"Perhaps," Jordet said cautiously. "But I cannot say what might have happened if Medilaw had not lost his head. However, the troops will be leaving almost at once. Are you coming?"

"Of course we're coming!" Har said.

"Then stop arguing, and let's go," said Alethia. "At the speed you're moving, Brenn may fall before we get there!"

Har looked at his sister in alarm. "Allie, there's going to be a *battle* when we get to Brenn! You can't come with us!"

"Why not?" Alethia said. "I'm almost as good an archer as you are, and it's my home, too. What else should I do?"

"You will stay with us until matters at Brenn are . . . settled," said a voice from behind Har. Har jumped and turned to find Iniscara looking at him with an unreadable expression on her face. Har gave a relieved sigh.

"If you are willing to let Alethia stay safe here, I will be very grateful, and my father also, when he learns of it," he said.

"Stay here?" said Alethia indignantly. "But . . ." She stopped short, realizing suddenly that the offer was a shrewd political move as well as a kindness on Iniscara's part, for the Shee council still did not like or trust humans. If a noble's daughter were to stay behind as a sort of hostage, Iniscara would have less trouble enacting her plan to aid the human city. Alethia was a child of one of the Noble Houses of Alkyra; she knew better than to risk offending such powerful and touchy allies. Her head turned involuntarily toward Iniscara, and their eyes met.

"You will not be disappointed in your stay here," Iniscara said softly. "And I think you will have better things to do than fighting Lithmern, for a time at least."

Alethia shivered a little as the Queen turned

away from her, toward Har. "You will go with the army to Brenn; Herre will need someone with him who can advise him about the land around the city. Your other friends shall accompany you. The Bard may stay with us if he so chooses—it is long since one of his kind passed this way."

The rest of the arrangements were quickly made. To no one's surprise Tamsin, after much thought, decided to remain in Eveleth with Alethia; the opportunity to learn more of the Shee was more than the minstrel could pass by.

Despite Har's doubts, the departing troops were ready to leave by midday. Worrel and Rarn had already left for Glen Wilding, accompanying Murn, who promised to ask her father to send some of the Wyrd archers to join the Shee on their way to Brenn. Alethia was surprised to find that Jordet would be accompanying them to act as liaison with the Wyrds. She was both pleased and saddened by the news; she was beginning to suspect that the two weeks in Eveleth might be rather lonely, and Jordet was almost the only Shee she had met who would speak to the humans without the mask of haughty indifference.

Tamsin and Alethia accompanied Jordet, Har and Maurin to the city gates, talking as they rode. The conversation was all too short, for the two humans had been positioned toward the head of the column of Shee cavalry, and they had to depart almost immediately. Maurin could not resist looking back as he and Har rode out of the city; he managed to catch one more glimpse of Alethia, framed in the open gateway, and then she vanished behind the rows of black-clad riders.

The Shee troops made good time through the mountains. Maurin was impressed by the horsemanship the Shee exhibited, as well as by their mounts. The riders made camp only when the growing darkness made further travel too dangerous, and they set off again at first light the following morning. The horses the Shee rode were trained for speed, even though the footing was often treacherous. The pace was hard, but by evening of the second day the column was out of the mountains and traveling through the Wyrwood. The going became easier, for though there were trees to wind their way through, there were no steep climbs to tire the horses, nor piles of shattered rock to slide underfoot.

On the third day, they met the Wyrds. Grathwol himself led the archers, and Murn was also among them. Though it was barely mid-morning, the two columns halted to enable the commanders to confer. Almost as soon as they dismounted, Maurin and Har were summoned to Commander Herre.

They found him seated in a hastily-erected tent with Grathwol, Murn, and several Shee. A large map was spread out in front of them, and they were studying it closely.

"—outnumber us by nearly two to one, even with the Wyrds to join us," a Shee was saying worriedly. "I don't care if they're humans; those aren't odds that I like."

Maurin saw Har frown. "Don't forget about the troops inside Brenn," he said.

The occupants of the tent looked up, and Herre motioned Har and Maurin to be seated. "More humans," muttered a Shee wearing a general's uniform, but he did not speak loudly. Maurin glanced quickly at Har, but he did not seem to have heard the remark, and Maurin relaxed.

"Some of the Lithmern troops must be on the

south side of the river," another Shee said. "If we could keep them trapped there, we would have a better chance."

"Of the ten thousand Lithmern, my scouts tell me that about a fifth are on the south side of the river," Grathwol said. "The rest are camped here, just west of Brenn and south of Brandon forest." He smiled, showing pointed teeth. "It would seem the Lithmern prefer to avoid both the Wyrwood and Brandon forest. Perhaps they do not like trees."

Herre smiled and turned toward Har. "Are there any fords near Brenn?" he asked.

"No," Har said. "We dredge regularly to keep the river deep; the bridges inside the city are the only ways to cross within half a day's ride."

"Then the Lithmern are depending on boats to keep their troops in contact," Herre said thoughtfully. "Grathwol, could your scouts get close enough to sink them before we attack?"

Grathwol snorted. "The Lithmern sentries would not notice an army at midday, much less a few Wyrds by night," he said. "Unless they have filled the river, we can sink them."

"Then we will not be quite so badly outnumbered," said the Shee who had spoken first. "Still —"

"How many Wyrds could hide in Brandon forest?" Maurin said, looking up from the map.

Grathwol snorted again. "From those sentries? All Glen Wilding, and Glen Hycroft and Glen Ravensrock besides!"

Herre looked thoughtfully at Maurin. "I think I see what you are getting at," he said. "If we charge at the camp from the east, it will push the Lithmern back against Brandon forest, and the Wyrds can pick them off with their bows. We won't get all of them, though; see, here. There will still be nearly a quarter of the Lithmern behind us, even if we succeed in cutting off the men on the other side of the river. I don't like it."

"Don't forget about the troops in Brenn," Har put in. "They won't be sitting idle during all this!"

"I don't know what the humans in the city are likely to do, and I am reluctant to count on their actions," Herre said, even more thoughtfully than before. "But I shall speak to the Veldatha who accompanied us; perhaps one of them can bespeak the Lady Isme."

Har looked at Herre blankly.

"The Lady Isme is a Shee," Herre said, speaking patiently as though to a child; "and we shall need wizards as well as warriors to win this battle. She can warn those inside the city to be ready for us."

"What of the Lithmern sorcerers?" said another of the Shee.

"Rialla assures me that the Veldatha can block any attempts to summon the Shadow-born," Herre said. "Unfortunately, they will have little energy to spare. We can look for no other help from them."

"That is unfortunate, but I expected no more," Grathwol replied gravely. "I think we are agreed, then?"

The others nodded. The meeting ended, and the combined column of Wyrds and Shee was soon moving toward Brenn once more.

As the last Shee rode out of the city gates, Alethia sighed. She looked at Tamsin, and without speaking they turned their horses and began riding back toward the palace. Alethia still more than half wished she could have accompanied the army, but before her mood could turn to depression, she saw the guard called Ferrin come running toward them. "You'll have to hurry," the young guard called between pants as soon as he was close enough to be heard. "The Queen wants to see you right away."

Alethia nodded, wondering what Iniscara could want of them now. She was even more curious when they reached the palace and found Illeana waiting in the room to which Ferrin lead them. The Shee woman looked disdainfully at Tamsin, but she made no overt objection to his presence. A moment later, the Queen herself appeared, accompanied by another Shee woman, pale and stern, whom Alethia did not recognize.

Iniscara smiled speculatively at Alethia. "I have a proposal to make to you, my dear," she said as soon as the bowing and curtsying ended. She paused. "Would you like to learn magic?"

Tamsin's jaw dropped. Alethia sat staring for a moment, then blinked. "Why should you wish to teach me?" she asked.

"It is the only way we know to determine the extent of your power," replied the unfamiliar woman beside the Queen.

"This is the Lady Clasiena. She and Illeana will be your tutors if you accept our offer," the Queen said into the silence that followed. Everyone began talking at once, except for Alethia, who sat silent. Iniscara looked at her sharply. "Well?"

"I have so many questions I don't know where to begin!" Alethia said. "I think someone should start at the beginning and explain."

Illeana raised an eyebrow. "You do not realize what an opportunity you have, girl," she said. "Else you would not quibble."

"I am not quibbling," Alethia said indignantly. "But I'm certainly not going to say yes or no until

I understand what is going on a little better."

"It will be difficult for you to understand, for you do not have the background," Illeana said condescendingly. "It has to do with Firivar's prophecy, and the Shadow-born, and the ways of magic."

"I still would like to hear what you have to say," Alethia said stubbornly.

Clasiena gave Illeana a glance that said "I told you"; Illeana shrugged. Clasiena looked at the Queen, and Iniscara nodded.

"It is difficult to know where to begin," Clasiena said, turning toward Alethia. "But I will try to explain. You have been told what the Shadow-born are?"

"Jordet said they were very powerful spirits of evil things," Alethia said. "I am not quite sure what that means."

"It means mainly that we know they have no bodies and we know they are evil," Clasiena replied. "It has been three thousand years since they were bound, and we know very little else as fact. One other thing we can add: over the years they have weakened to a fraction of their former strength; but even that is more than any one of us could face alone."

"Illeana and Jordet won out over that one on the mountaintop, didn't they?" Alethia said uneasily. Talk of the Shadow-born was still enough to unsettle her, though she was not sure why she reacted so strongly.

Before Clasiena could reply, Illeana shook her head. "We drove the creature out of Corrim, 'tis true," she said patiently. "But its grip was not strong. It was still weak from its long captivity, and it was in the Kathkari, where the Shadow-born find their magic difficult to work. Even so, it was a near thing."

"They will gain strength rapidly now," Clasiena went on. "We have a little time, perhaps, before they become so powerful that we cannot defeat them at all—but only a little."

"What does that have to do with teaching me magic?" Alethia asked.

"Do you remember the prophecy that was read at the Council this morning?" Clasiena asked. " 'The child of fire holds the source of power.' In the Elder Tongue, the language of magic, your name means 'fire-souled child.' Somehow you are a key, and we must try to prepare you as best we can."

"I don't want to have anything to do with those things!" Alethia said. "They terrify me. I'm not sure why; I'm not usually bothered by dark creepy things, but the Shadow-born scare me senseless. I am afraid I won't be much help to you. I am sorry."

"If need is there, you will find a way," Iniscara said serenely. "We will do our best to keep you away from them, since they seem so interested in obtaining possession of your person, but, if only for your own protection, we must try to teach you some magic of your own."

"I am willing to try to learn," Alethia said hesitantly. "But I cannot promise anything more, and I will only stay until there is news of Brenn and a way for me to return."

Illeana frowned, but Clasiena glanced at the Queen again, then replied, "Of course, if that is what you wish."

"I do wish it," Alethia said firmly, stifling her

own doubts about the wisdom of this project. If the Shee thought it wise for her to learn magic, she could hardly object.

"Then it is settled," Iniscara said, and rose. "I think you should begin as soon as possible. You may join her, Bard, if you like," the Queen added, turning to Tamsin as she spoke.

"What!" A startled, angry exclamation broke from Illeana. "Excuse me, your Majesty, but that's impossible!"

"There have been human sorcerers before," Clasiena said, looking warily from Illeana to the Queen. "And he *is* a Minstrel."

"What does that matter?" Illeana said. "He's a human! Do you think the Council will allow this?"

"The Lord Advisors and the Council will certainly object," Clasiena said in a troubled voice.

"Their objections no longer matter," Iniscara said calmly. "I am Queen; I have ordered this; and it will be done. This is a time of change for all the Shee; there is nothing we can do to delay it. Do you question me?"

Illeana stared at the Queen for a moment, then lowered her head and sank into a deep curtsy. "No, Your Majesty."

The Queen nodded. "See to it, then."

# CHAPTER FIFTEEN

In spite of the Queen's parting instructions, the lessons did not begin that afternoon. Instead, Tamsin and Alethia spent several hours riding through Eveleth. Alethia, accustomed to the noisy crowds of Brenn, was at first surprised by the quiet of the city. Though it was mid-afternoon, the wide streets were nearly empty. She soon adjusted to the absence of other people; indeed, she forgot it entirely in her admiration of the city.

Eveleth was even more attractive by day than by night. The houses were airy structures of slender columns and graceful arches, carefully shaped in smooth, white stone. They were surrounded by carefully kept gardens and formal parks. Alethia came to one with a fountain, and stopped her horse in surprise; three jets of water rose high in the air, then twined about each other in an intricate, loosely-woven knot before falling back into the still pool below.

"Tamsin," said Alethia, "how do they do that?"

Tamsin looked in the direction of Alethia's pointing finger and blinked. "I don't know," he said. "I wouldn't be surprised, though, if that house belongs to one of the Shee wizards."

"I thought all Shee were wizards," Alethia said.

"Are all Alkyrans farmers, or all men of Col

Sador smiths?" Tamsin said.

"Oh," said Alethia thoughtfully. She looked at the fountain again, then urged her horse forward, and they continued on in silence. They passed several more of the inexplicable fountains, and once they came to a garden where a small breeze played a tune on a curtain of tiny silver bells. Tamsin would have stood there, listening, for the remainder of the day had Alethia not reminded him that they really ought to return to the palace before night fell.

Eveleth, thought Alethia as they rode back along the way they had come, was certainly a fitting setting for the Shee. Still, she could not help comparing this city with the living buildings of Glen Wilding, and she found that she preferred the home of the Wyrds. Glen Wilding was a friendlier place.

Immediately after breakfast the next morning, Alethia and Tamsin were escorted to a room on the far side of the palace. Clasiena was waiting, and as they entered she smiled. "Be seated," she said. "We have much to talk on." They followed her instructions and looked at her expectantly.

"Magic depends on power," the Shee woman told them. "Therefore you must first learn to tap your own power and focus it. You will then be able to work small spells, but it is very draining, since you will be powering the spell with your own energy. Later we will teach you to reach out for other sources of power, and then you will really begin to work magic."

"How do we start?" asked Alethia.

"Most people require something to concentrate on, at least at first," Clasiena said. "It is better if it is something small and easy to carry. Have you anything suitable? A ring perhaps?"

Alethia's slim hands were bare of ornamentation. She felt in her pockets and pulled out a hairpin, a few coins, and a smooth round stone. The Shee woman picked out the stone and examined it carefully. "This will do," she said, and turned to Tamsin. The minstrel pulled a heavy gold ring from his finger. "Will this do for me?"

The Shee woman nodded. "Hold it in front of you, like this," she said, cupping her hands to demonstrate. "Now, concentrate. Shut out the sight of the room, the sound of my voice; see only the focus you hold."

Clasiena's voice became a drone. Alethia tried to follow her directions. At first, she found it difficult to concentrate on the pebble, but gradually Clasiena's hypnotic murmur took effect. Alethia began to feel detached, as if observing the scene from far away. From somewhere outside herself a voice was insisting, "Focus! Reach into yourself and gather your ability together!" Obediently, but with dream-like slowness, Alethia turned her attention inward.

At first it seemed as if she were once again floating in the grey fog that had surrounded her and Tamsin in the Wyrwood. The voice was urging her on, and gradually things seemed to grow lighter. A part of her mind told her that what she saw was unreal, a mental picture in familiar terms of things too strange to grasp directly. Most of her attention, though, was concentrated on the scene that was gradually growing clearer in her mind.

There were pools of light and thick ropes of shadowy emerald strung between impossible ferny trees of blood-red. Alethia floated among them, insubstantial and wondering. The prodding voice was gone, but something was still directing her gently and firmly toward the liquid light below. Alethia drifted slowly nearer, strangely reluctant, but unresisting. Finally she touched it. There was a soundless explosion of intolerable whiteness, and Alethia lost consciousness.

She came to herself lying on a couch in the study room. Clasiena, Illeana, and Tamsin were standing over her with worried expressions. Without speaking, Clasiena held out a glass of water, and Alethia took it. A moment later she looked up.

The room was the same, yet it was not. Everything seemed to be sharply defined; the chair took up *this* space, no more, and ended precisely at *that* point. Even the air seemed more emphatic, like looking through sunlit crystal. "What has happened?" Alethia asked.

Illeana started to speak, but Clasiena waved her to silence. "You were doing well with the concentration exercise, so I told you to take the next step, to turn inward and focus your abilities on something outside yourself."

Alethia nodded. "I remember hearing that," she said.

Clasiena shrugged. "I cannot tell you much more. You collapsed just before Illeana arrived; we were on the point of sending for a Healer. Tell me what it seemed like to you."

When Alethia finished her explanation, Clasiena nodded absently. "You have reached more deeply than I would have believed," she said. "The effort was perhaps too much for you. We must proceed more cautiously hereafter; I think that this will be enough for today."

Though she protested that she felt perfectly well, Alethia was overruled by the two Shee. "Put your focus away; we will try again tomorrow," Clasiena told her. Alethia realized in some surprise that her right hand was still clenched tight around the stone, and she opened her fingers to replace it in her pocket. With an exclamation she bent over it.

The stone was split in two, revealing its interior, and embedded in one fragment was a smaller stone of a deep blue, almost black. It was very smooth, almost polished; when Alethia rubbed it gently it came free and she had to close her fingers quickly to keep from dropping it. She sat down once more and carefully picked out the strange stone, putting the other fragments on the table.

The blue stone was about the size of Alethia's smallest fingertip. As she stared at it, she saw that in the center of the stone was a dim pinpoint of light. Alethia looked up. "I have never seen a stone glow before. What is this?"

Clasiena turned and gave a startled exclamation. "This was not your focus!"

"The stone split in two, and this was inside," Alethia explained. "See, there are the pieces." Clasiena bent over the table and scooped the shattered rocks toward her. She examined them carefully, then turned to the stone which had been embedded inside.

Suddenly the austere Shee woman smiled. "No wonder your attempt went so well! This is a firestone!"

"What is a firestone?" Alethia asked curiously.

"They are natural amplifiers of power," Illeana said. "They are very sensitive to power in other things, so they are sometimes used to detect spells, but their main use is to increase the power that a wizard can put into a spell. I do not know of anyone using one as a focus before; they are usually thought too dangerous for the inexperienced." The Shee seemed to agree with general opinion, for she was eyeing the stone with a disapproving frown.

Tamsin's eyes narrowed thoughtfully. "Could this explain why the Shadow-born could not reach Alethia when he attacked her on our way here?" he asked.

The two Shee exchanged startled glances. "Of course! It must have," Clasiena said. "But Alethia must have great ability to create a barrier that would hold off a Shadow-born, even with the aid of a firestone."

"I just wanted it to keep away from me," Alethia said. "I wasn't trying to *do* anything; I only wanted it to stay back."

"You must have set up a wall of pure power," Clasiena told her. "There is nothing else you could have done without training."

"It is a good thing that you are here now, where we can teach you properly," Illeana said condescendingly. "Such power can be dangerous if it is not completely controlled."

Tamsin, who had been looking at the firestone, turned to Alethia. "What did you mean when you said the stone was glowing, Alethia? I do not see it."

The Shee women turned and Tamsin handed the stone to Illeana. "I, too, see nothing," she said after looking at it for a minute, and Clasiena nodded her agreement. Alethia leaned forward. The stone lay in Illeana's palm with no hint of light.

"It was there a minute ago," Alethia said in

bewilderment, and reached for the stone. As soon as she touched it, the light returned. Illeana jerked her hand away in surprise, and immediately the light died, but as soon as Alethia touched it once more the glow rekindled. Clasiena and Tamsin tried holding the stone, but with the same results.

"It seems that by using this as a focus you have waked some power attuned to you," Clasiena said thoughtfully.

"Perhaps it is simpler than that," Illeana said. "Perhaps anyone who uses it as a focus can achieve the same results. Here, let me try." She took the stone and bent over it, concentrating as Alethia had done. A moment later she cried out, dropped the stone, and bent forward clutching her head. Clasiena hurried to her, while Alethia retrieved the stone.

"It appears that it is not so simple," Clasiena said dryly. She looked up from Illeana in sudden concern. "You did not feel anything?" she asked Alethia urgently.

"No," Alethia replied. "Nothing at all."

"Then it must have been her own power reflecting back at her," Clasiena said with some relief. "I think only you can use this as a focus now." She nodded toward the blue-black firestone.

"But why?" Alethia asked.

"I do not know," Clasiena said. "Firestones are too rare, and too little is known of them. Keep yours close; I suggest that you find some holder for it. It is too easy to misplace as it is."

"Why not have it set in a ring?" Tamsin suggested.

"A good idea!" Clasiena approved. "There are jewelers who work for the Queen; I will send one to you this afternoon." She rose and, after a brief exchange of courtesies, escorted a shaken Illeana out.

The jeweler arrived shortly after noon. He was intrigued by the stone, which he clearly valued highly. When pressed, he reluctantly agreed to deliver the ring in two days time. "But it will not be elaborate," he warned as he left. "No, it will be very plain."

The lessons resumed the following day, but no further experiments were made. Instead, Clasiena gave them a long list of rules and relationships to memorize and then repeat until they could do so instinctively. "Since magic is the art of changing the relationships between things," she told Alethia and Tamsin, "you must know what you are about before you can make a change."

Alethia found the lists boring, but she followed Clasiena's instructions. By the end of the afternoon, she was word-perfect in only half of the drills, and she found herself envious of Tamsin. The minstrel was more at home with their current tasks, and had nearly finished the list. Clasiena seemed pleased with their progress, and promised more interesting work to come.

The ring arrived next day, a small circle of silver wire with the firestone set firmly in it. The jeweler had underrated his ability; though not intricate in design, the ring was hardly plain. It fit perfectly. The back of the stone rested lightly against her finger, and Alethia noted with pleasure that the contact was enough to awaken the pinpoint of light in the heart of the stone. Thoroughly pleased, Alethia picked up the remainder of the list of rules and left to find a peaceful spot to memorize them in.

# CHAPTER SIXTEEN

Maurin stood beside his horse in the cold grey of pre-dawn, waiting. All around him were the muffled sounds of horses breathing and the occasional clink of armor as the Shee quieted their mounts. Through the screen of trees ahead, he could dimly see the beginning of the fields surrounding Brenn; the city itself was invisible in the faint light.

The Shee were positioned in the forest northeast of the city. They had managed to get so close only with the aid of a few Wyrd guides, who ambushed several Lithmern scouts before they could raise any alarm. The main body of Wyrd archers had crossed the mountains two days before to take up a position behind the Lithmern camp; if all was well, they, too, were now in place, hidden and waiting.

Off to one side of the assembled cavalry, Maurin could see the Veldatha wizards conversing with Herre. Some time later the Shee commander bowed and walked away, and the wizards began chanting and making passes in the air. A rustle of anticipation swept the line, followed closely by the signal to mount.

Tensely, Maurin checked the saddle girth one last time. As he swung into the saddle, he hoped fervently that there were no Lithmern anywhere near the edge of the woods; the noise of so many men mounting, however quietly, seemed loud enough to be heard all the way to Brenn. He settled his feet in the stirrups and looked back toward the center of the line, from which the signal to attack would come.

The light increased slowly, and Maurin chanced another look toward the wizards. Even to his untrained eye, they seemed to be reaching the end of their spell-casting; when they finished, they would only have to keep it reinforced, and then the attack would begin. The wizards lowered their hands. Maurin tensed and looked back toward the center, barely in time to note the sweeping gesture of the Shee officer commanding his portion of the line.

Almost as one the Shee cavalry began moving out of the woods and across the fields toward the Lithmern tents. They moved slowly and quietly; it was still dark enough for them to be overlooked if they traveled silently, and every minute before they were discovered meant precious ground gained. The city was visible now, its outer walls looming over the Lithmern tents clustered untidily to the west.

Ahead of them, a Lithmern sentry shouted. The Shee urged their horses to a gallop, all hope of concealment gone. The Lithmern on guard wheeled to face them, shouting to their fellows. There was a brief shock as the foremost Shee met the thin line of Lithmern sentries, then the Lithmern went down before the unexpected onslaught.

As the two lines met, Maurin raised his sword and dug his heels into the sides of his mount. A dark-haired man in Lithmern garb swung at him with a wicked-looking blade on a long pole; Maurin barely parried it in time. He hacked at another that appeared briefly by his right stirrup, but the charge carried him on before he saw whether the man fell. One of the few mounted Lithmern rode toward him, swinging wildly. Maurin stood in his stirrups and spitted the man cleanly. He barely had time to yank his sword free before the Lithmern toppled, leaving the way clear.

The Shee swept on around the city, toward the camp. Ahead, the Lithmern were beginning to stir, and Maurin realized with a shock how little time had passed since the first alarm. One of the Shee riders was already among the tents, a little ahead of the others. A Lithmern soldier carrying another of the bladed poles tried to stop him, but the Shee parried and ripped the weapon away. He rode on, controlling his mount with his knees, while he wrapped a strip of his cloak around one end of the captured pole.

By this time the rider was nearing the first of the Lithmern's dying watchfires. With a shout he thrust the end of the pole into the flames. It caught rapidly. Carrying the makeshift torch, the Shee began riding through the camp, setting fire to the tents. A Lithmern archer, belatedly realizing the threat, took aim and fired.

The Shee horseman fell, but several tents were already ablaze. A stiff breeze sprang up ahead of the attackers to fan the flames as the foremost Shee saw their advantage and exerted their powers to encourage it. The camp was in turmoil now, with men and Shee shouting and running everywhere. Among them was the Lithmern commander, trying to impart some shred of organization to the chaos among his men.

Behind the attacking Shee, a horn sounded. Maurin looked over his shoulder and cursed. The Lithmern troops which had been stationed to the east of Brenn were marching to the aid of their embattled fellows. In a few moments, they would fall upon the cavalry's rear, forcing them to turn and battle on both sides at once. Seeing his enemies' predicament, the Lithmern commander began collecting his men at the edge of the woods, where they could surround the Shee completely under cover of the smoke which was beginning to blanket the camp.

Just as the second group of Lithmern reached the Shee, another horn sounded, high and clear. In their eagerness to attack the Shee, the Lithmern troops had forgotten that behind them was an entire city; they could not have known that Bracor had been forewarned by Isme and the Veldatha and was prepared for immediate attack. The Lord of Brenn and the mounted guards of Styr Tel, supported by nearly all of the foot soldiers of Brenn, were issuing from the North Gate and attacking the Lithmern rear.

At almost the same time, a flight of arrows whirred out of the woods and into the forces that the Lithmern commander was gathering for an attack on the Shee flank. A rain of the deadly shafts began to fall on the Lithmern as the Wyrd archers opened fire from their concealed positions in the forest. A few moments later the first of the archers came into view as they began advancing in their turn.

It was too much for the Lithmern. Rumors of black magic had already taken their toll of morale among the common soldiers, who viewed the disappearance of five experienced scouts as proof of their fears. The sight of the small, furred archers with their gleaming, pointed white teeth was the last straw. Shouts of "Demons!" began to be heard above the noise of the battle, and the confusion grew worse as the men at the edge of the forest tried to flee.

The two thousand Lithmern stationed on the southside of the river were unable to cross to the battle; Grathwol's scouts had wrecked their boats during the night. They were forced to watch help-lessly as the battle became a rout. Finally, one of the officers realized that it would do no good for them to be slaughtered too, and ordered his men to withdraw before the Brenn soldiers and their unex-pected allies could finish with the main camp and cross the river.

The Shee worked their way methodically through the camp, hampered by the clouds of smoke rising from the tents. They were followed closely by the city troops, who had vanquished the Lithmern in the rear and were looking for more. Bracor, well aware of the effect that the sudden ap-pearance of the legendary Shee might have on even a well-trained veteran, had warned his men that "the Lady Isme's countrymen" were coming to aid the city. The soldiers were, therefore, somewhat prepared for the Shee.

The Wyrds were another matter. They were clearly not human; they might well be the demons the Lithmern seemed to think them. On the other hand, they were equally clearly killing Lithmern. Even so, the Brenn troops were somewhat un-nerved by the presence of the small, fierce, furry beings. By the time Bracor, Herre and Grathwol met in the middle of the Lithmern camp, more than one of the city soldiers was beginning to wonder, now that the heat of the battle was passing, just what kind of a war it was they were fighting.

* * *

The first round of fighting was over and the work of taking prisoners done when Maurin ran into Har. "What luck?" The young noble shouted when Maurin was within hailing distance.

"Fair," replied Maurin as he rode up. "Which means I am not dead, so I cannot complain too loudly of my fortune. Yourself?"

"Two of them came at me with those staffs a bit ago; a Wyrd arrow got one or I wouldn't be here," Har answered grimly. "As it is, not a scratch. Where away?"

"Herre and Bracor have decided they want some Lithmern to question. I'm to pick out the ones that look most likely to know something." Maurin frowned. "Most of the officers seem to have disappeared, and there is no trace at all of the sorcerers; I'd almost be willing to swear there were never any here."

"I don't know about sorcerers," Har said. "I can find you an officer, though, if you hurry. I just passed some Shee with one tied to a horse; they were over that way."

"Many thanks," Maurin replied wearily, and with a wave he rode off in the direction Har had indicated.

Isme was alone in the tower room when Bracor returned to Styr Tel and found her. She stood looking out over the recent battlefield with her back to the door. Bracor waited until she turned.

"No, it does not disturb me to see them again," Isme said before her husband could speak. She smiled. "Nor have I any desire to return to Eveleth. Does that content you?"

Bracor shook his head. "Sometimes I think you

know my thoughts before I do."

"After twenty-four years, how should I not?"

"And you will not be . . . uncomfortable, attending the feast tonight?"

"No. I am glad the Shee have come, and the Wyrds as well," Isme said. "Aside from the fact that they have sheltered my daughter and saved my city, it will be good to talk again to those who understand magic."

Bracor looked up quickly. "You have missed it, then."

"Magic? Of course I have missed it."

"I—" Bracor stopped. "I wish you had told me."

"It has not been so hard as you seem to think," Isme said gently. "I knew what to expect when I ran away with you. And it is not as if I have had *no* chance to practice."

Bracor blinked, considerably startled.

"There are any number of small spells that are useful in running a household," Isme said, smiling. "And there are reasons why the healers' houses in Brenn are regarded so highly; I am no Neira, but I have some skills."

Bracor nodded, but he was watching Isme closely. After a moment, he looked away. "I have spoken with Herre. There seems to be no reason why you cannot visit Eveleth again, if you wish it," he said carefully.

Isme shrugged. "I doubt that I would find Eveleth any more interesting than I did when I was young."

"You are certain?" Bracor asked, relief undisguised in his voice.

"The life of a Ward-Keeper suited me far better

than Eveleth, even before you fell down the steps into my garden," his wife replied with a soft look in her slanted eyes. "I do not pine for Eveleth; and I have harbored no regrets."

"I am glad you feel that way," Bracor said quietly.

Isme smiled, and took his hand in hers.

The feast that night was long remembered. The seige had not been lengthy enough to seriously reduce the city's provisions, and food was plentiful, but what made the feast truly unforgettable was the presence of the Wyrds and the Shee, creatures out of myth and legend, sitting at the same table as the nobles of Alkyra.

At the end of the dinner, the weary architects of the day's victory retired to a large room on the third floor of Styr Tel to discuss the events of the day. Sounds of revelry drifted up to the open windows, in sharp contrast to the formality of the company assembled there.

At the head of the long table Bracor sat with the Lady Isme, both wearing the wine-red colors of the House Tel'anh. On their right were Herre, in the full purple robes of a Lord Advisor, and the Shee General and two of his aides, imposing in the black and silver uniform of Iniscara's guards. Across from the Shee were the Alkyran Lords, Armin and Gahlon wearing the colors of their houses. Around the foot of the table sat Har, Maurin and Jordet, also in formal dress. Only Grathwol and Murn looked at all like their usual selves; the Wyrds had put away their bows and quivers for the meeting, but that was all.

"I think we may begin," Bracor said when everyone was assembled. "First, I must thank you again for your aid. It was successful beyond expectation."

"Beyond expectation, indeed," muttered Armin with an uneasy look at the Shee.

Herre smiled politely. "And I thank you for your welcome," he said formally. He paused. "I hope we might count on your assistance were we in similar straits, and the Queen agrees."

A sudden silence fell, brittle as glass. The Shee commander had just proposed a formal alliance between Eveleth and Brenn, and all eyes turned to Bracor for his response to the unexpected proposal.

"I appreciate your offer," Bracor said at last. "But I do not know if I can accept it, much as I would like to." A murmur passed through the Shee, and Bracor raised a hand. "Let me explain.

"Brenn is not a free city, but part of Alkyra, subject to the Conclave of First Lords and the Regent of Alkyra. I cannot speak for the Regent or the Conclave, and I cannot make a compact outside of our land without their approval. To do so were treason. Yet such an alliance would indeed be of benefit to both our peoples. I do not know," Bracor finished, a troubled look on his face. "I do not know."

"The Conclave be hanged!" exploded Armin. "What help have they given us against the Lithmern?"

"Little enough, tis true," Bracor replied. "But . . ."

"There can be no 'buts'!" Armin said emphatically. "Will you let the Lithmern destroy your city and us with you while the Conclave considers?"

"Armin is right," Gahlon said quietly. "And no

matter what your arguments, the First Lords will not approve this alliance. And without it, Alkyra will fall."

"What!" said several voices together. Isme leaned forward as the stir subsided. "Perhaps you could explain further, Lord Gahlon," she said calmly. "I confess, I do not see why the nobles should not agree, nor why Alkyra must inevitably fall if they do not."

"Forgive my bluntness," said Gahlon. "But it is no less than the truth. Alkyra is disintegrating. In a few more years the Regent will be totally powerless, and the last thread holding the nobles together will vanish. The country will become a hundred free cities, each warring with the others to claim as much territory as possible, while twenty nobles try to establish their right to the throne by force of arms. Already the Conclave is little more than a watchdog to keep any of the nobles from growing more powerful than his neighbors."

"But the Lithmern threaten us all!" Har burst out. "Surely they can see that!"

Gahlon shook his head gloomily. "I fear not. What they will see is that this compact provides Brenn with formidable allies, who could easily overcome any of them. I think they will even choose to believe that the Lithmern do not plan to invade, at least until the army is at their door. Then, of course, it will be too late."

Bracor's face was drawn. "It seems that either way I choose, we cannot win. If I do not accept this alliance, the Lithmern will overrun us when they return. Yet if I accept, it seems likely to throw all Alkyra into war out of fear that I am grown too powerful."

Gahlon nodded. "That is the way of it."

There was a silence. Then Isme spoke again. "Yet folly may be reasoned with; the Lithmern, never."

"True." Bracor turned to Herre in sudden decision. "I accept the alliance then; may Kirel's spirit watch over us all."

"I, too, have such a proposal to make," said Grathwol. His eyes glinted in the candlelight. "I think you will not refuse, having accepted Lord Advisor Herre."

"You are correct," Bracor said. He rose and bowed to Herre and Grathwol in turn. "I am grateful for your support; I fear what Gahlon says is true, and, alone, Brenn could not hope to stand for long against the Lithmern."

"Not quite alone; I also will support you, certainly," Gahlon said.

"And I," Armin added roughly.

Bracor nodded gravely to the two lords. "Are there no others who might be persuaded?"

Armin gave a bark of laughter. "Those close enough to fear the threat of Lithmern, perhaps. No more."

"I will see what I can do," Gahlon offered. "I think there are some who would join us. You will be too much involved here to travel, and there are Lords who trust me well enough to at least listen to what I will say."

Armin looked skeptical, but Bracor's anxious expression lightened. "Thank you again," he said. "Now, let us work out more details of these alliances. How much of your strength can you commit?"

For the next hour the talk was of the compacts

to be signed among the three Alkyran nobles, the Wyrwood, and Sheleran. Herre had been given sweeping powers by Queen Iniscara, and Grathwol was regarded as unofficial head of the loose alliance of Wyrd Glens, so both could speak with some assurance that their promises would be kept, and a framework for the alliance was quickly established.

The planning was interrupted by a knock at the door. One of the Shee soldiers entered and bowed politely. "Sirs, the Wizard Rialla has finished with the Lithmern prisoners and requests admittance."

"Bring her in," Bracor said. Rialla entered the room in a swirl of blue robes. The Crown of the Veldatha shone briefly on her forehead as she nodded and took a seat on Herre's right.

"I am sorry to have taken so long," Rialla said. "There have been difficulties."

"Indeed?" said Herre. "Of what sort?"

Rialla bit her lip. "The Lithmern officers are ensorcelled," she answered. "The soldiers know nothing worthwhile, though they have confirmed some of our guesses. But the officers . . ." Her voice trailed off.

The Shee general on her left frowned heavily. "Come, come," he said impatiently. "Surely your truthtrance can overcome any spells the Lithmern may have. Why, Illeana managed to free that young Lithmern from a Shadow-born with only the Ward-Keeper's help, and you have three Veldatha to assist you!"

The Shee woman rounded on him, and it became evident that under her calm facade she was near to hysteria. "The spell that guards them destroys their minds, General!" she hissed. "Four times have we tried truthtrance, and four men now lie below with no more wit than a drooling babe! Try your own hand at it if you will, but do not ask me to try again; I have no stomach for it!"

# CHAPTER SEVENTEEN

There was a moment of horrified silence. Rialla lowered her head and hid her face in her hands; the Shee general stared ahead unseeingly. Finally Bracor broke the silence.

"What information have you managed to obtain, then?" he asked as gently as he could.

Rialla straightened and took a deep breath. Pulling herself together, she replied, "Little enough. The common soldiers are our only source thus far, and they know nothing of the Shadow-born, only a few rumors that their King has enlisted the aid of some magicians of great power from far lands. They were told that they would attack Brenn, and that some would march northeast to meet the main army once the city had fallen."

"Northeast!" exclaimed Murn. "But that is the middle of the Wyrwood!"

"Yes," replied Rialla. "They have misunderstood, or been deliberately misled, so I can advise little trust in their claims."

"Why not?" asked Maurin.

"Because the Lithmern army cannot get into the Wyrwood without passing Brenn," Rialla replied patiently. "They cannot pass Brenn unless the city has fallen, so it makes no sense for the two parts of the army to meet there. I think perhaps the soldiers have mixed their directions; it is more likely that they should go northwest to meet the rest of their forces."

"How many of them did you question?" Maurin said.

"Four or five," said Rialla with a frown. "Why?"

"And did they all say the same?" Maurin persisted.

"Yes," said Rialla. "What is the point of that?"

"There *is* a way into the Wyrwood from the west," Maurin said.

"You know more than those who live there, of course," the Shee general said sarcastically.

The Wyrds exchanged glances, and Grathwol said, "Many things are possible. I would hear what he has to say."

"Thank you," Maurin said. He looked around the table. "There is, or was, a pass through the mountains to the north of Brenn. It was used by occasional Traders in the days when there was commerce between men and the Shee, which is how I know of it. The Lithmern may plan to use it."

The Shee general snorted his disbelief, but Grathwol looked thoughtful. "Coldwell Pass—I have heard of it. But was it not blocked long ago? And would the Lithmern know of it?"

"I do not know whether it was blocked," Maurin said. "But it may have been cleared since then. How else could the Lithmern have intended to take Alethia to Mog Ograth?"

The Wyrd nodded thoughtfully and relapsed into silence. Bracor looked at Rialla. "This puts a more serious light on your information," he said. "Are there any more details than you have told us already?"

"The armies were to meet in another month," Rialla offered after a moment's concentration. "The soldiers found it strange that their leaders looked for the city to fall within so short a time, but speculation is frowned upon in the Lithmern army."

"Obviously they expected to bring the Shadow-born to take Brenn," Herre said. "The troops were to soften the city up first, and to occupy it once it had fallen."

"Unless Alethia's escape forced the Lithmern to move up their attack," said Maurin.

"That is possible," Herre said, considering.

"Why, it is more than possible, it is likely!" broke in one of the General's aides. "Drashek is the Lithmern city closest to Alkyra, and it is five days travel from Drashek to Brenn. Five days after Alethia met the Wyrds, Brenn was attacked. What other reason could there be?"

"What will they do now, do you think?" Bracor inquired.

"With this part of their army gone, the Lithmern will have to bring the rest from the west," Herre said. "They will have other problems as well; I think the Lithmern sorcerers will soon lose control over the Shadow-born, if indeed they have not already done so. The Shadow-born will take time to make sure of their hold on Lithra and to come to stronger power, and then they will come back to attack Alkyra."

"How long?" said Gahlon, voicing the question in everyone's mind.

"I can only guess," said Herre. "But soon; a month, perhaps two."

"This time we shall be prepared!" Armin said.

"When they reach Brenn they will find more waiting than they expect."

"Why wait for them to reach Brenn?" asked
Maurin.

Silence greeted this unexpected comment. Then
Bracor leaned forward, his eyes alight. "Coldwell
Pass?" he asked. Maurin nodded, and Bracor sat
back and laughed. "Of course! It is the last thing
they will expect; with luck we may do them great
damage, and at the worst we can retreat and try to
hold them elsewhere."

The others looked puzzled, and Bracor laughed
again. "You explain," he said to Maurin. "You
thought of it first."

Maurin nodded. "It will be easier if we have a
map, I think," he said. Bracor produced one, and
Maurin spread it out on the table. "See, Lithra is
north and west, and the mountains curve down to
Brenn. If their army marches from Mog Ograth,
they will almost certainly head for Drashek, to re-
supply there. And from Drashek the route to
Brenn is . . ."

Maurin's finger traced the curve of the mountains, and stopped.

"Coldwell Pass should be right about here," the
Trader went on. "If we march north to meet them,
we can surprise them, provided we time it right."

"It may work," Har said.

"We haven't decided yet that we will try this,"
Bracor cautioned. "The hour grows late; I suggest
we return to this matter in the morning."

There were murmurs of agreement, and the Lord
of Brenn turned to Rialla. "If I may ask your aid,
Lady, I would request that you question the soldiers to try and confirm the theories you have

hcard." Rialla simply nodded. "Then, by your leave my Lords, I would end this meeting until tomorrow."

Heads nodded in agreement, but it was not so simple to put an end to the discussion, and it was some while before the room was emptied. The military men lingered to discuss Maurin's proposal and to put forward theories of their own as to the Lithmern army's probable movements.

The following day, Har and Maurin found themselves with the unenviable task of selecting possible messengers and preparing them for their respective journeys. The assembled heads of the Wyrds, the Shee, and the army of Brenn had decided that there was too little time for Gahlon to visit each of the Alkyran nobles individually, and so a team of messengers consisting of one of each race was to be sent instead. It took most of the day to find sixty men, Wyrds and Shee who were acceptable to everyone and also willing to carry such potentially explosive news to the lords of Alkyra, but by late that evening the messengers were on their way.

The Lords Armin and Gahlon, too, spent the day preparing to leave Brenn. Rialla and the other Veldatha wizards had succeeded in piecing together most of the Lithmern's movements up to the attack on Brenn, as well as some part of their future plans, from the common soldiers who had been left unprotected by the mind-destroying spell. The picture was grim enough to make the Alkyran nobles anxious to start their own preparations at home. They left the next day, each with Wyrd and Shee soldiers accompanying them as unofficial ambassadors.

Preparations for the coming battle began at once. Daily infantry drills started as soon as the grim task of disposing of the bodies around the walls was finished. Bracor, Herre, and Grathwol lost no time in setting up combination exercises with groups of soldiers, archers, and cavalry, for the process of integrating the three forces would be difficult and time was limited.

One of the first actions of the newly combined forces was to send Murn with a mixed group to the mountains around Coldwell Pass to begin preparations for the army and to send scouts out to keep abreast of the Lithmern movements. They were accompanied by one of the Veldatha, who would notify the allies if the Lithmern appeared to be moving before they were expected.

The other wizards remained in Brenn. Besides providing a means of communication with both Eveleth and Coldwell Pass, the Veldatha were experimenting cautiously with ways of piercing the black curtain that hid Lithra from their spells. Similar attempts were underway in Eveleth, and the two groups communicated daily regarding the success or failure of their various trials.

The few reports that trickled out of Lithra were highly disturbing. In the second week after the Battle of Brenn, a small group of Lithmern were intercepted at Coldwell Pass. They proved to be farmers and tradesmen, refugees fleeing the terror of the Shadow-born. Murn questioned them closely and sent them to Brenn under guard, while the little group at the pass prepared for a torrent of fugitives that never materialized.

The deficiency of refugees was nearly as disturbing as the tale the successful escapees told on reaching Brenn. Herre's guess had been correct; the Shadow-born had grown too powerful for the Lithmern sorcerers to hold. They were free at last, and rapidly converting Lithra to a mold of their own choosing.

Whispers of an army of soulless ones began to circulate. The soldiers of Brenn, who had been more than a little uneasy with the Shee and the Wyrds, began to look with more favor on their magical allies. The troops that the other nobles of Alkyra were sending would be welcome, but if they were going to face magic, the Brenn soldiers felt more comfortable with a little magic on their own side, even though the Shee soldiers were inclined to be arrogant and standoffish off the battlefield.

The return of Bracor's messengers was anxiously awaited, but the first to reappear did not bring the hoped-for promise of aid. As the negatives continued to arrive, a cold dread began to envelop the city.

The weather, too, was unseasonably cold. Farmers spat and talked of early snows, and the steward of Styr Tel shook his head anxiously and made daily checks on the great storage bins that held the city's winter supplies. The army was more cheerful; the consensus was that marching to Coldwell Pass would be much more comfortable in the cooler temperatures than in the high heat that normally prevailed.

Another event that raised the spirits of the army was the arrival of the troops from Meridel at the beginning of the third week. Gahlon wasted no time in fulfilling his part of the agreement. He also reported that he had persuaded at least two other nobles to send support, but that he considered their motives suspect.

The new arrivals were not pleased to find that the rumors of strange beings in Brenn were true. The haughty Shee and the fierce, cheerful Wyrds made them even more uneasy than they had made the army of Brenn. Despite the protests of Gahlon's officers, Bracor mingled the newcomers with some of the Shee and Wyrds almost at once. "Your men will be fighting magic," Bracor told the angry officers. "The sooner they become accustomed to seeing it about them, the better chance we have to win this war."

The veterans of the Battle of Brenn scoffed openly at the qualms of the Meridel men, which did little to improve their tempers. "You wait until you see them Lithmern marching up all long and nasty," a Brenn soldier told the newcomer with whom he was sharing evening sentry duty just outside the eastern walls. "You'll be glad then of some a them furry ones with the bows, no mistake."

"Huh," said the other man skeptically. "I ain't never going to be glad of them creatures. Or them snooty, slanty-eyed ones."

"Then you'll be heading back for Meridel afore that moon gets full again," the Brenn man said, pointing at the half circle of Elewyth that was just rising over the river. "Lord Bracor don't want nobody along what ain't friendly with them magic folks."

"You mean to say I marched here double-time from Meridel just to turn around and march back?" the other said indignantly.

"That's what I hear," the first man said.

"That ain't no way to run a war," the Meridel man said fervently. "It just ain't—what's that?"

"What?" The Brenn man spun, looking carefully around. I don't see nothing."

"I heard something, by the river," the other sentry said.

The first man looked again, then shook his head.

"You're nervy, that's what," he said. "There ain't nothing—" He stopped in mid-sentence, and his jaw dropped. The shining ribbon that was the river was swirling and boiling near the bank, though an instant before it had been calm. The surface broke, and sheets of liquid moonlight streamed from three figures standing waist deep in the shallow water near the riverbank. Each held a slender spear, and even when the water had ceased running from their shoulders, the figures seemed to gleam in the moonlight.

The two sentries stared; finally the Brenn man stepped forward. "H-halt and state your business," he said.

There was a laugh like wind on crystal chimes, and the foremost figure said, "If this is Brenn, we have business here. I am Larissalama of the Neira; I believe your Lord Bracor expects us."

"That's as may be," the sentry said austerely, having somewhat recovered from his surprise. "I'll send a message, but I can't let you into the city without I get orders."

The laugh rang once more. "Send your message; we shall wait."

Near the end of the third week of preparations, Bracor summoned Har and Maurin to his study. They arrived to find Bracor and Herre deep in conversation. Har coughed ostentatiously and Bracor looked up.

"Come in; seat yourselves," he said, waving to the other chairs. "We have been waiting."

"Not too long, I hope," Har said. "We came as soon as the message reached us."

"Commendable promptness," said Herre dryly.

Har looked at the Shee commander curiously,

then turned back to his father. "What did you want to see us about?"

"I would like you and Maurin to return to Eveleth," Bracor said. He glanced aside at Herre, who frowned but made no comment. "I want you to be escorts for Alethia when she leaves."

"There is so much to do here!" Har said, a little dismayed. "Surely she could stay until after we have finished with the Lithmern. Unless . . ." He looked at Herre.

"No, this is not my suggestion," Herre said, a bit abruptly. "Alethia is welcome in Eveleth for as long as she wishes."

"Then I would think Eveleth a safer place for her than Brenn," said Maurin diffidently.

"Eveleth may be safe, but I would prefer more distance between Alethia and the Shadow-born," Bracor replied. "Especially since the Veldatha and most of the Shee troops will be with us at Coldwell Pass, and not at Eveleth. And the Shadow-born know they can find her in Eveleth. You must remove her."

"But is Brenn likely to be any safer?" Har pointed out.

"I do not intend for you to bring Alethia to Brenn," Bracor said. "You will travel from Eveleth to Wentholm."

"I do not approve of this move," Herre put in. "But I will give you a small guard until you reach Eveleth. We have few men to spare, you understand." The Shee Commander rose and bowed gracefully. "I must go; there are other claims on my attention."

When the door had closed behind Herre, Har shook his head slightly. "But why . . ." he began, then stopped and bit his lip.

"You were chosen for the obvious reasons," Bracor said, smiling. "You have been to Eveleth, and I can trust you. I do not want Alethia to escape the Lithmern only to be held hostage by some angry Alkyran lord."

"Is that really to be feared?" Maurin asked.

"Unfortunately, I think it is," said Bracor. "I did not really believe that the Conclave of First Lords was so lost to reason that they could not see the threat that the Lithmern pose, but most of the nobles who have sent replies seem to think Brenn is the threat, not Lithra."

"Surely the Regent can make them see reason."

Bracor shrugged. "Perhaps, but it will be a month yet before we know how he sees matters, and by then it will make no difference. Either the Lithmern will be defeated, or they will be overrunning Alkyra; in either case our claims are proven."

"Have none of the lords any sense?" demanded Har.

"A few," said his father with a wry smile. "First Lord Thielen of Wentholm is sending us four thousand men; I only hope they arrive in time."

"That is why you are sending Alethia to Wentholm!" exclaimed Har in sudden enlightenment.

Bracor nodded. "Gahlon has made me cautious, and I want at least a few whom I know I can trust there. Isme and Tatia will be leaving in a few days. I have already made the arrangements."

But when the gentle Lady of Brenn was informed of her husband's plans, she flatly refused to leave the city. Tatia she had no objection to sending to a safer place, but she herself would remain in Brenn. "How would it look for the Lady of Brenn to flee before danger is even close?" she asked.

"Close!" exclaimed Bracor in exasperation. "I

would think a seige of the city more than close enough to suit you."

"But the seige has been lifted," Isme pointed out. "Besides, who will take charge of Brenn while you are gone? The city does not run itself."

Bracor sighed. "I want you and Tatia in a safer place than this," he said after a moment. "If the Lithmern defeat us at Coldwell, Brenn will be the first city to fall."

"If you are defeated at Coldwell Pass, it will not matter where I am," Isme said. "And if I am here, you will not have to leave one of the Veldatha in Brenn to let you know what is happening."

"Isme—" Bracor shook his head. "I suppose there is no help for it; I can hardly force you to go."

"I am glad you see the wisdom of my viewpoint," Isme said serenely. Her husband tried unsuccessfully to repress a smile.

"It takes very little wisdom to realize that if I did try to compel you, you would find some way out of it," Bracor said.

"Very likely," Isme said. "But send Tatia by all means." She stroked her youngest child's braids reflectively as she spoke. Tatia was seated in Isme's lap, playing with a string of colored beads, but at her mother's touch she looked up.

"Won't go," she said matter-of-factly, and returned to her beads.

"Of course you will go, Tatia," Isme said. "You would like to travel all by yourself, wouldn't you? And Wentholm is a very pretty place, and you will meet Alethia there."

" 'Lethia's not going to Wentholm," Tatia announced. "So I'm not either."

Bracor burst out laughing. "It seems no one in

this family can be convinced to move out of danger! But you at least will go to Wentholm, Tatia, if only to get you out of your mother's way."

"Won't go!" Tatia reiterated, eyeing her parents with a decidedly martial light in her eyes. Having had experience with Tatia's tantrums, Isme thought it best to postpone further discussion, and effectively ended the conversation by carrying Tatia off to bed.

Har and Maurin left for Eveleth the next day. Word of Isme's refusal to leave the city was already circulating. "And I doubt we'll have any better luck with Alethia, once she knows what we're there for," Har told Maurin as they rode through Brenn. "She can be more stubborn than Mother!"

"Alethia has a good deal of sense," Maurin said. "I don't think we'll have as much trouble as you fear."

"Sure, and every grain of sense she has will tell her that Wentholm is no safer than Eveleth, and maybe less," retorted Har. "I wouldn't be surprised if she insisted on going to Coldwell Pass to be with the army. Father must be batty to think we can persuade her." With this unfilial observation, Har turned his horse, and the two men rode out of Brenn to meet the Shee guardsmen Herre had assigned to them.

# CHAPTER EIGHTEEN

For Alethia, the next few weeks flew by on
wings. She progressed quickly from simple spells of
illusion to more difficult magic, though the teachers did not try to teach her any of the great
enchantments. She learned the basic laws of power,
as well as some of the abuses to be avoided, and for
the first time she began to understand why Jordet
had refused her request to use magic to start a fire
with wet wood on the trip to Eveleth.

The strange clarity of sight that Alethia had experienced on awakening from her attempt to use
the firestone as a focus came and went erratically,
growing more prounced as the days went by. She
soon learned that she possessed more than sharp-
ened eyesight, for when the talent awoke during
one of the lessons Alethia found that she could see
the lines of power that Clasiena was calling on to
demonstrate a simple spell.

After that, Alethia quickly discovered that she
could see power, and sometimes even the relationships that were so important to spell-casting.
The ability often enabled her to by-pass the endless
chains of rules that Illeana and Clasiena gave her
to memorize, but the spell-sight was unpredictable,
and she continued the dull chore of memorizing
Clasiena's lists.

Her Shee teachers were at first astonished by Alethia's new-found talent, but they soon began to encourage her to use it as much as she could in an attempt to discover just how she did it. Efforts to duplicate the effect by having Shee use a firestone as a focus failed completely. Several attempts to achieve similar results with Tamsin also failed, and the Shee were reluctantly forced to conclude that Alethia's mixed parentage gave her some sort of ability that neither race alone possessed.

In spite of his failure with the firestone, Tasmin, too was learning. Alethia spent much of her spare time helping him get the feel of the simple spells Clasiena and Illeana taught them, and being tutored in her turn in the long, intricate lists that the minstrel found so much easier to memorize than she. Tamsin had a knack for the spell-chants that amazed the Shee, and he was passionately interested in learning—about the Shee, about Eveleth, about magic.

At the end of the first week, news of the Battle of Brenn arrived. Almost at once, both of Alethia's teachers were summoned to assist the other Veldatha in their attempts to descry the movements of the Lithmern army. The Shee women did not, however, neglect the lessons, which surprised both Alethia and Tamsin until the minstrel remembered the importance that the Shee attached to Firivar's vague prophecy. Even so, Alethia could not help wondering whether she would have had quite as many lists to memorize if Clasiena and Illeana had not been so busy with their other duties.

Alethia's favorite spot for study was perched atop a low wall in the gardens, where she was out of sight of the palace. By the beginning of her fourth week in Eveleth, she had securely established her preference for solitude, so when her study of a singularly dull treatise was interrupted by a shout echoing across the garden, Alethia simply ignored the noise.

The shout was repeated, and this time Alethia looked up in mingled annoyance and surprise. A moment later she flung the book down from the wall and leaped after it. "Har! Maurin!"

"It's about time you saw us!" Har said as they came up to her. "What is so fascinating?"

"When did you get here?" Alethia asked, ignoring his question.

"About an hour ago," Har told her. "We've been delivering messages and seeing the horses stabled. And looking for you, I might add."

"An hour! And you let me sit here alone all that time and didn't come?" Alethia said. "I don't believe you were looking. Everyone knows I sit out here in the afternoon; you couldn't have been looking very hard, anyway."

Alethia retrieved her book, and the three started slowly back toward the palace. Alethia was full of questions about the battle, and Har and Maurin were so engrossed in answering her that none of them saw Tamsin until he was almost upon them.

"Greetings! Clasiena told me you had arrived," the minstrel said as he reached the group. He looked at Alethia. "Now you must make your decision," he said.

Maurin frowned, but Har only looked at the minstrel and said, "Decision? What decision? Father sent us to bring Alethia to Wentholm; why should she have to decide anything?"

"Wentholm!" Alethia broke in. "Why does he want me to go to Wentholm? If I am not to go to Brenn, why shouldn't I stay here?"

"We think the Lithmern army is planning to cut through the mountains at Coldwell Pass," said Maurin. "We are going to try to ambush them there, but they are very strong. If we lose, the Lithmern and Shadow-born will be within two days march of Eveleth should they turn north."

"Yes, and Father wants you further away than that," Har said. "He's sending Tatia, too; she's probably already left."

"And Mother?" Alethia asked sweetly.

"Father wanted her to go, too, but she decided to stay in Brenn," Har admitted reluctantly.

"Well, I won't go either!" Alethia said indignantly. "I'll stay here if he doesn't wish me to be in Brenn, but I can't see any point in going off to Wentholm! And I don't like First Lord Thielen anyway," she added obscurely.

"But Alethia!" Har expostulated. "The Lithmern have already tried to kidnap you once, and this time they'll have a whole army with Shadow-born in control! The Veldatha are already saying that the Shadow-born's influence is spreading into the mountains; in another week it won't be safe to travel. You must go!"

"I do not have to go," Alethia contradicted him. "I can very easily stay here in Eveleth, though I can see that I must find someone who is willing to tell me what is going on. I had not heard anything about Coldwell Pass, or ambushes, or anything."

Har cast an I-told-you-so look at Maurin, and applied himself once more to reasoning with his sister. The argument continued for hours. When he learned that the Shee were teaching Alethia magic, Maurin pointed out that the Shadow-born would be even more delighted to get their hands on her if she were partly trained, and Alethia began to weaken. The thought of the Shadow-born filled her with an unreasoning terror. Reluctantly, she agreed at last to accompany them.

Even after the fact of their departure was settled, it was three days before they were ready to leave Eveleth. The Veldatha wizards had succeeded in designing an amulet which would, they hoped, protect Corrim from the Shadow-born; without it he would almost certainly become a puppet once more as soon as he left the protection of the magicians. Corrim was anxious to leave Eveleth; the Shee were a constant reminder of things he would prefer to forget, and he was uncomfortable with the presence of magic. Even after three and a half weeks with the Shee mind-menders he seemed a broken man.

On the fourth day after their arrival, the amulet was finished, and they prepared to leave. A young Shee soldier was chosen by Prestemon to accompany them as a guide. "The mountains are easy to lose your way in, and they are dangerous for strangers," said the Shee captain. "I would give you more men if I could, but most of them are already at Coldwell Pass."

The weather was fair when the small party set out. Their Shee guide led them almost directly south, and, noting this, Maurin frowned and rode forward to speak with their guide. "I am not familiar with the Kathkari," Maurin began, "but it seems we travel south. Will this not take us to Coldwell Pass?"

"We should come out of the mountains just north of the pass," the other replied. "Does this displease you?"

"To term it so is perhaps too strong," Maurin said. "Yet I wonder if it is wise for Alethia to travel so close to Lithra."

The Shee shrugged. "This is the fastest and safest route through the Kathkari. I would not lightly chance another with so small a group; these mountains are unpredictable. Also, we shall not travel directly by the pass, but turn east through the wood once we are clear of the mountains. Will that suffice?"

Maurin nodded, though he was not completely reassured. He felt strangely uneasy, and long ago he had learned to trust such hunches. None of the others seemed at all disturbed. On the contrary, they appeared to be enjoying the ride; Corrim was even smiling a little at something Alethia was saying. Rather than speak of his vague forebodings, Maurin dropped back to the rear of the group, where he could keep watch.

His worries seemed needless, for the trip was uneventful. By night they were well into the mountains, and shortly before dark they made camp. Still, Maurin found himself prowling restlessly about during his watch later that night. There was nothing to see except small animals and an owl that swooped low over the embers of the campfire.

The morning was cold and clear. Alethia commented on the temperature as she poured water to wash in, and their guide frowned. "It is too early for frost, even here," said the Shee. "Also there is something in the air I do not like." He urged them all to hurry, and none of the travelers objected.

Camp was broken in record time. Maurin was no longer alone in his worries; the entire party seemed edgy, even the horses. Alethia continually shifted in the saddle, and several times Maurin saw Corrim's hand reach to feel the amulet he wore, as if for reassurance.

Barely an hour after they had left the campsite, their guide called a halt. "Stay here a moment," he instructed them. "There is a place a little above us that gives a good view, and I think it wise to take advantage of it today." He was gone before the others could protest, scrambling on foot up the rocky slope to disappear among the trees.

The Shee reappeared well before any of the others expected him. "We must hurry," he said as he remounted. "A storm is coming from the north—I do not like the look of it. There is a place ahead where we can shelter, if we reach it in time. Fortunately this area is full of caves."

The little group hurried on. The sky was darkening ominously and the wind was rising when the guide finally pointed to a clump of trees ahead of them. "We will have to stop here. There is an overhang behind the grove that will keep off the worst of the wind and rain. It is not as good as a cave, but better than nothing, and we shall not be able to make the one I was heading for before the storm hits."

"The horses are still fresh; we can certainly ride a little way through the storm even if it is as bad as you fear," Har objected.

"If the storm is unnatural, as I fear it is, we must be under cover when it arrives," the Shee said firmly. "Come." He nudged his horse and started forward once more.

Suddenly a loud cry came down from above them. All heads jerked upward at once, but it was a moment before any of them located the slowly growing specks in the sky above them. There were seven of them, great white birds falling like giant snowflakes. "Ride!" shouted the guide.

# CHAPTER NINETEEN

Alethia yanked on the reins, turning her horse toward the grove the Shee had pointed out and dug her heels into the animal's sides. Her mount responded with a burst of speed, and for a few moments it seemed that they would gain the shelter of the trees in time.

Then the birds ceased their slow downward spiraling and dove. Alethia heard Maurin's cry of warning and drew her dagger. Out of the corner of her eye she saw that Maurin and Har had their swords out; Tamsin and the Shee were barely behind them. Corrim, less accustomed to fighting on horseback, was still struggling with his when the birds struck.

With frightening speed, the birds swooped on the riders, slashing viciously with beak and claws and soaring again before the defenders could swing at them. Once battle was joined they were silent; only when they were safely aloft once more did they voice their raucous cry.

Two of the birds dove at the Shee. One passed just over the guide's head, slashing downward and forcing him to raise his sword and duck sideways to protect himself. Just as he did so, the second bird arrived, diving directly into his side and knocking him out of the saddle onto the ground.

Alethia did not have time to see more. One of the birds stooped toward her, and she struck up with her dagger as the bird came in. She was conscious of a great mass of white, a gust of air, and golden eyes staring into hers with surprising intelligence. Alethia ducked sidewise. She heard a tearing sound and liquid fire ran down her arm; the creature gave a scream of rage and was gone.

Another appeared to take its place before Alethia could look to see how the others fared. This time the bird swept low and slashed at Alethia's horse. The frightened animal shied and bolted. Alethia yanked desperately on the reins, but the animal had the bit between its teeth, and she could not control it.

Behind her the sounds of battle faded, until they were lost under the noise of heavy wing beats and drumming hooves. At least one of the birds was following, hoping perhaps for an easy meal when the horse tired. Alethia made fleeting mental note of the pursuit and concentrated on staying in the saddle. Her arm ached, and the horse's headlong flight threatened to throw her to the ground.

There was a sudden gust of wind, and the bird screamed and veered away. With no more warning, the storm struck. It was not the rain the travelers had expected, but snow, whipped into stinging missiles by a bone-chilling, blinding wind. In seconds, Alethia was unable to see past the horse's nose. She could only cling desperately to the saddle and hope that luck or instinct would keep her mount from falling.

The harrowing ride did not last long. The wind and snow forced the horse to slow before its strength was completely exhausted. As soon as she could control the animal again, Alethia turned it back toward what was, as nearly as she could judge, the way they had come.

It was difficult to persuade the horse to try to travel across the wind. Snow was already drifting about the horse's feet, and it was impossible to see. Alethia knotted the reins awkwardly to keep from losing them. Pulling her torn summer cloak closer around her shoulders, she bent low in the saddle, trying to present a smaller target to the biting wind.

Alethia lost track of time. Her arm was throbbing painfully, and her fingers grew numb with cold. Several times she tried breathing on them, but the warmth lasted no longer than her breath and afterwards they felt colder than before. Finally she gave it up and huddled miserably in the saddle. She had no way of knowing if they were traveling in the right direction or not, and had only her own increasing coldness by which to judge the passing of time.

The storm was now nearly a full-fledged blizzard. Alethia raised her good hand to pull at her cloak once more, and the dull glow of the firestone caught her eye. Until that moment, the thought of her new-found power had not occurred to her; she still thought of it as an impractical skill, something to play with. It had not occurred to her that it might be useful.

Trembling, Alethia brought her hand nearer her face and stared at the stone, concentrating desperately on shelter, a place to be out of the wind and snow. She had heard Clasiena and Illeana speak of guidance spells, but they were difficult and she did not know more than the fact of their existance. She had never tried, even with the firestone, to cast a spell without knowing the chants that structured its power. She knew that uncontrolled magic was dangerous and could destroy its wielder; she did not care. Blindly, she stared at the stone.

Slowly, the firestone began to glow. An image formed in the air just in front of her; a wavering picture of a dark opening in a rock wall, overgrown with bushes and with a glow of power about it. "Terrific," Alethia said aloud, "but where is it?"

The image wavered slightly, and swung to the right. Alethia pulled at the reins with unfeeling fingers, and eventually the horse turned to follow it. The semi-transparent picture faded, but the glow of the firestone grew brighter, and suddenly the horse was plowing through a large snowdrift, held in place by a clump of shrubs. A moment later, Alethia's mount stumbled and nearly fell into the interior of a small cave. Alethia slid from the saddle and collapsed unconscious to the ground.

The birds seemed to be gaining ground. Maurin was slashed in a dozen places; the others fared no better. Then, unexpectedly, one of the birds gave a cry, and the others broke away to fly rapidly back toward the cliff from which they had come.

Maurin blinked stupidly after them for a moment. Suddenly he realized what must be the cause of the flight, but as he opened his mouth to shout warning to the others the unnatural storm arrived. In seconds, the others were mere shadows, and Maurin realized that they would lose each other quickly if they did not act at once.

The Trader slid out of his saddle and stood for a moment with his horse's body between himself and the wind. Knotting the reins around his arm to keep from losing the animal, he started for the nearest shadow. This proved to be Har, who had already dismounted and was knotting his own reins in much the same fashion.

"Rope!" shouted Maurin, trying to make himself heard above the wind. "Do you have rope?" It took a couple of tries before Har understood. Once he did he produced a length from a saddlebag, and the two men tied the horses together and started in the direction of the third shape.

When they reached it, they found Tamsin trying to tie the unconscious Shee to his own saddle. Corrim was draped limply over another horse. Maurin immediately went to assist the minstrel; fortunately the guide's mount was well-trained and stood stock-still throughout the entire operation.

Har peered vainly into the gloom for another shape that might be his sister. "Where is Alethia?" Maurin shouted as he tied the other horses into the string.

"Don't know!" Har yelled back. Then he pointed. "There?"

"Maybe," Maurin answered. There did seem to be a darker area in the general direction of Har's pointing finger, but the snow was heavier already, and it was difficult to say for certain. Maurin waved Har back to the line of horses and began pulling the reluctant animals along.

They did not find Alethia, but in a few moments they were among the trees of the grove they had been heading for when the birds had attacked. The wind was partially blocked by the trees, and it was easier to move. Soon they found the overhang their guide had mentioned, and they crowded gratefully into its meager shelter.

The wind still howled so that they could barely hear each other speak. Maurin found a spot to secure the horses and was starting to unlash the Shee when he saw Har heading back out into the storm.

He dropped the rope he was holding and grabbed for his friend.

"You can't go out there again!" Maurin shouted. "You'll be lost in less than three paces!"

"Alethia's still out there somewhere!" Har said, pulling against Maurin's restraining grip. "I have to find her; she'll die if she stays out there!"

A lump of ice settled in Maurin's chest, but he said roughly, "Will it help if you die too? Going off like an idiot without even a rope! How did you expect to find us again once you got to her?"

"Maurin, please!" Har begged. "Let go! I have to find her."

"Then wait long enough to be sensible!" Maurin snapped. His hands were already busy with the saddlebags. "We have enough rope among us to reach a long way. Tie it together and take an end so you can find your way back. It won't do anyone any good to have two of you lost in that storm!"

Har looked out at the trees. The snow was falling so thickly that he could only discern the closest trunks; beyond was only a wilderness of swirling whiteness. Reluctantly, he agreed that Maurin's suggestion was necessary, but he fretted and fumed all during the time it took to knot the ropes and secure them to a large boulder. Then he grabbed the free end, tied it around his waist, and ran out into the blizzard.

Tamsin struggled with the ropes holding the Shee; Maurin crossed to the other horse and eased Corrim to the ground. The Karlen Gale man's head hung limply, and it was almost unnecessary for Maurin to feel at the throat for the non-existent pulse. With a deep feeling of regret, Maurin pulled the man's cloak to cover his head.

The first task, once the horses were securely tied,

was to set up some sort of shelter for themselves and the wounded guide. Once the Shee was more comfortably settled, they turned their attention to their own injuries. From time to time Maurin checked the lifeline to make sure the knots were still holding, but when nearly an hour had passed without any sign of Har he began to worry. Finally he turned to Tamsin.

"I'm going out after Har," he told the other man. "He may be having trouble. Don't try to come after me if I don't make it back; someone must stay with the horses."

"If you don't make it back, I might as well come after you," Tamsin said, but his tone was not reproachful. Maurin nodded reluctantly; two men helping a badly injured companion might have a chance of escaping the mountains once the storm was past, but alone it would be nearly impossible.

"I'm still going," Maurin said.

Tamsin watched him with a bleak expression, wishing there were some way he could help. If he had only had time to learn more than the simple beginner's spells the Shee had been teaching him! A seeking-spell would be particularly useful just now, or one against cold. But there was nothing he could do or say, and after a moment he nodded reluctantly. Maurin turned, grasped the rope, and stepped out into the grove.

At first the trees blocked most of the wind, but when he reached the edge of the grove Maurin was almost swept away from the lifeline. With all his strength he clung to the rope and shouted into the storm, "Alethia! Har! Alethia!" The words were swept away almost before they were uttered.

Maurin gave up shouting and lowered his head against the wind. Hand over hand, inch by painful

inch, he continued working his way along the rope.
Underneath the concentration, fear sang along the
borders of his mind in an endless chant, "Not
Alethia, not Har, not both of them. Not Alethia,
please, not both of them."

So intent was he on making progress that when
he tripped he continued on his hands and knees for
a moment. Then he realized that he had fallen and
lost the rope; almost in panic he groped behind him
for the lifeline. Instead of rope his hands found the
rough surface of a cloak, half buried in the snow,
and under it was Har, the lifeline still tied fast
around his waist.

Har was barely conscious. After one or two
futile attempts to get him to his feet, Maurin untied
the rope and lashed it around his own waist. Then,
half dragging, half carrying the smaller man, he
started back toward the shelter of the grove.
Progress became mechanical; one foot in front, haul
in the rope, drag on the other man, next foot forward.

An endless time later, Maurin reached the overhang. By this time he was crawling, stopping frequently to rest. Dimly he saw Tamsin's face above
him, full of relief. "Har," he croaked. "See to
him."

The minstrel's face vanished, and Maurin closed
his eyes. All that he wanted to do now was rest. He
couldn't rest, though; someone was shaking him.
He opened his mouth to protest, and something
warm and liquid gushed into it. He almost choked
on the first swallow, but Tamsin was insisting that
he take more.

A few more gulps of broth restored some of
Maurin's energy, and he realized how cold and
hungry he was. He tried to sit up, and Tamsin

helped him for a moment. "Finish the cup and I'll help you over to the fire," the minstrel said. "You need warmth almost as much as you need food and rest."

"How did you do it?" Maurin asked hazily.

"Don't talk," Tamsin said. "Drink!" Maurin obediently finished the broth and Tamsin helped him to his feet and guided him over to the fire he had somehow built in the Trader's absence. Har was already there, bundled in all the blankets and cloaks the minstrel could find.

Once Maurin was seated out of the wind, Tamsin returned to Har and tended the ragged slashes made by the birds. Maurin watched him for a few minutes, until the minstrel looked up and noticed his regard.

"It is a good thing these wounds are clean," Tamsin said. "At least we will not have to worry about fever and poison."

"It's as well that we were this close to shelter, too," Maurin replied. "None of us are in any condition to be wandering around in that storm." Suddenly memory hit him, and he sat bolt upright with a cry. "Alethia! She's still out there!"

Tamsin's eyes were sympathetic. "I know," the minstrel said. "I feel for her, too, but we can do no more. You are the strongest of us, and you barely made it back. Will you kill yourself trying to find her? She is strong and sensible. Perhaps she has found shelter."

Maurin collapsed with a groan. "There must be something . . ." he murmured, but he knew there was not. He was the strongest of them, and he could not simply abandon the others; they would need him if they hoped to get out of the mountains safely. Maurin subsided into his own gloomy ponderings. He did not speak again, and Tamsin did not press him, though the minstrel occasionally cast worried glances in the Trader's direction.

The storm raged for two days. The enforced idleness enabled both Maurin and Har to begin to recover from their injuries, and to regain some of the strength they had lost fighting the blizzard. The guide, however, was still unconscious. His wounds at first seemed light, and the three humans were greatly puzzled, yet it began to seem unlikely that he would survive unless he reached the healers soon.

This posed a problem. Har wanted to remain where they were, to search for his sister's body, for it seemed impossible that Alethia could have survived the storm. Maurin, tacitly acknowledged leader of the group now that the Shee was unable to function, agreed to a brief delay while he and Tamsin constructed a litter for the Shee and erected a cairn for Corrim, but he refused to jeopardize the guide's life by remaining any longer than necessary.

Finally Har capitulated. It was a subdued and wary group that set out under the leaden skies of the third day after the storm. Har was moodily silent, given to flashes of temper. Maurin rode in silence, absorbing Har's occasional remarks with the grim indifference of a granite cliff. Tamsin, riding at the rear alongside the litter, found Maurin's silence more disturbing than Har's temper, but there was nothing he could do, so he, too, kept silent.

There was no sign of the mysterious white birds, but that did not keep any of the men from casting surreptitious glances at the mountaintops when they thought the others were not looking. The weather was bitterly cold, and the men wore their clothes in layers to keep warm. The few blankets were bundled around the guide in an effort to ease the jolting of the makeshift litter and provide some warmth to the invalid.

Maurin set a slow pace, for the drifts were deep and masked treacherous footing. Several times they had to retrace their steps when snow blocked their passage. At such times Maurin was painstakingly careful not to lose track of their direction, for without a mountain-born guide to be lost was a sure death sentence.

On the second day of travel Maurin began to worry. With all the backtracking they had done he knew that they could not have come far enough to be out of the Kathkari, but he had expected to see signs that they were nearing the edge of the mountain range. When the group stopped for a moment to rest, Maurin scrambled up to a ledge and looked out over the terrain ahead. There was still no sign of an end to the mountains, and Maurin began considering whether to voice his concern to his companions.

Har forestalled him. "Look there!" the young Noble called up to him. "Are those specks travelers or deer? I can't tell at this distance; you have a better view." Har pointed through a gap in the trees.

Maurin squinted in the direction of Har's finger, to where a number of dark shapes were moving against the snow on the valley floor. "This time our luck is better; if deer carry riders, I'll eat my saddle. Come on!"

They picked their way carefully down the mountain. By the time they reached the valley floor, the riders were almost upon them, and it was obvious that they were Shee. The little group stopped and waited for them.

"Ho, Maurin!" The foremost of the Shee hailed them. "Har! We had scarcely hoped to find you this quickly, though we came in search of you!" The rider was Jordet, and Maurin found himself shaking.

When they did not return his greeting, Jordet's smile of welcome changed. He looked closely at their faces, and his eyes flew to the litter. "Not Alethia?"

"I wish it were," Maurin whispered as Jordet rode forward. "I wish it were."

# CHAPTER TWENTY

Jordet insisted on making camp where they stood. One of the men who accompanied him was a healer's apprentice, and he insisted that the man examine all of them, beginning with the guide.

Though they would not admit it, the others were glad of the chance to stop and rest, and to catch up on the news of the battle preparations. They were surprised that Jordet had ridden out in search of them.

"We knew that you planned to leave Eveleth five days ago," he explained. "When the Veldatha felt the blizzard coming they tried to warn you, but they couldn't reach your guide. Herre and Bracor were worried enough to send us out looking as soon as the storm was over."

"What do you mean, felt the storm coming?" Har asked. "I didn't think the Veldatha did weather-working; Rialla almost took my head off the one time I suggested it!"

"They don't, as a rule," Jordet said. "But the Lithmern and the Shadow-born do. This was no natural storm; that's one reason Herre was so worried."

"Was it as bad at Coldwell as it was up here?" Har asked.

"Worse," Jordet said with a shudder. "We lost

nearly a third of the supplies, and half a dozen people froze to death. Morale isn't very good, I'm afraid."

"Then the Lithmern must know we're planning to meet them at Coldwell Pass," Maurin said.

"I don't think so," Jordet said. "They had to build the storm up where their power is strongest; it just happened that Coldwell and the army was right in its path."

"Why would they send a storm to block the pass if they are planning to use it?" Har objected. "Unless they know we are there waiting for them."

"After what happened at Brenn, the Lithmern must know that the Wyrds and the Shee are involved in this," Jordet said patiently. "The storm didn't block Coldwell, but it would have made it almost impossible for any of the Shee troops to reach Brenn for weeks. Fortunately, the wizards and most of the cavalry were already at Coldwell when the storm hit."

"Then you expect the Lithmern to attack soon," Tamsin put in.

"Less than a week," Jordet said quietly. "They should reach the pass in three or four days, no more."

"Are you sure they don't know about the ambush?" Har asked again.

"Positive; the Wyrds captured a scout yesterday, and the head of the Veldatha himself questioned the man under truthtrance," Jordet replied. "He wasn't even looking for signs of people; he was simply making sure the pass was still open. Which it is, so far."

The Shee's eyes glinted wickedly, and Har looked at him suspiciously. "What do you mean?"

"Oh, we have a little surprise for them," was all

Jordet would say, and he refused to elaborate. "When we reach the pass you will find out," he said, and would answer no more of their questions.

They spent the remainder of the day camped on the valley floor. The healer's apprentice tended the three humans hovering over the unconscious Shee, occasionally applying mysterious ointments or potions. The next morning Jordet asked him if it was safe to transport the injured man, and the healer only shrugged.

"It can do him no more harm, I think; and if we can reach Coldwell in time, perhaps someone there may be able to help him. He is beyond my skill." Jordet nodded, and they began breaking camp.

It took two more days for them to reach Coldwell Pass. The cold and the drifts slowed their progress despite the expert guidance of the Shee, and they had to stop frequently to tend to the guide. Har was recovering from the initial shock of losing Alethia, though he was far from his old self. Maurin, however, blamed himself for her disappearance, and though he was no longer silent he remained withdrawn.

Jordet's first action when they reached the army was to summon a healer for the injured Shee. That attended to, he sent word to Bracor and Herre of their arrival. He did not speak of Alethia and Corrim, feeling that such news was better given in person.

Numbers of soldiers, however, had seen them ride in, and all of them could count. Anxious rumors were flying about the camp long before Bracor and Herre arrived. The two leaders were accompanied by Armin, Gahlon, and two men unfamiliar to Maurin. These were presented as the Lords Vander and Marhal, the only other Alkyran nobles who had cared to send help to the group at the pass. Theilen had sent troops as promised, but he himself remained in Wentholm.

Bracor looked toward his son. "Well?"

Har looked pleadingly at Maurin, but the Trader refused to meet his gaze. Haltingly, Har explained what had happened. Bracor's face went grey, and with the barest possible polite murmur he excused himself from the gathering. Har followed him at once, and for a few moments the others stood looking after them.

"What a pity," Lord Vander said, breaking the silence. "I hope this will not affect Lord Bracor's judgement."

"Yes," agreed Marhal with a sidelong glance at Herre. "Such a shock, so soon before a battle . . ." He let his voice trail off.

"Perhaps one of us could assist him," Vander went on. "I am sure the Lord of Brenn would not object to one of us taking some of the load from his shoulders, and he will certainly want some little time to himself, to be with his family."

Armin reddened and started to speak, but Gahlon forestalled him. "Just what did you have in mind, Lord Vander?"

"Why, it occurs to me that a great deal of Lord Bracor's time is spent making arrangements with the Wyrds and the Shee," Vander replied. "It may be distressing to him, particularly under the circumstances; I understand the Shee guide is not yet out of danger."

"What are you implying?" Armin demanded.

"But it is obvious!" Marhal said, shaking his head sadly. "Why, no one could fault Bracor for finding it a little difficult to deal with the Shee after this. Not that it was the young man's fault that his daughter was lost in the storm, of course; still, he was supposed to be guiding the group to safety."

"Yes, it almost seems better that one of us should take over that area of Lord Bracor's duties, at least until the shock has worn off," Lord Vander said blandly. He turned toward Herre. "Don't you agree?"

Herre's eyes glittered, but he responded smoothly. "Why, you seem all consideration, my Lord. I must confess that the difficulties of the situation had not occurred to me in so pressing a light." Lord Marhal could not repress a smirk of triumph, and the gleam in Herre's eyes increased.

"Your offer is a generous one," the Shee Commander went on. "I will be glad to have him appraised of it at once. Jordet!"

"Here, sir," Jordet replied promptly.

"I wish you to take a message to your uncle," Herre said. "Inform him of the kind offer these gentlemen have made, and tell him that if there is anything we can do to assist him we stand by our duty to our kindred."

"At once, Commander," Jordet said, bowing. "It will be my pleasure."

The smirk on Lord Marhal's face vanished instantly, and Lord Vander looked completely taken aback. "No, no," Vander said hastily. "It would be better to give him time to get over the shock. No need to go at once."

"But I thought that the shock was what worried you!" Herre said in mock amazement. "Well, we shall let it be for the moment; I am sure you have other duties to attend to."

The Alkyran Lords looked a bit disgruntled at this thinly veiled dismissal, but they did not quite dare to openly challenge one of the legendary Shee.

Gahlon looked relieved at the outcome, and Armin grinned openly at Herre as he left. Jordet watched them go, a little smile of amusement playing about his lips. As soon as the Lords were out of hearing, the younger Shee gave a low whistle.

"Gahlon was certainly right about them!" he exclaimed. "They are just looking for a chance to discredit Bracor and take over themselves."

"Yes, I noticed that," Herre said dryly. "I think they had conveniently forgotten that Bracor is the only one of them with family ties among the Shee."

"Well, they have been rather forcibly reminded of it," Tamsin said from the back of the tent. The minstrel came forward, frowning. "I do not mean to presume, Commander, but was that wise?"

"Perhaps not, but these Lords will not try to make trouble with me again," Herre said. "Armin and Gahlon can be trusted to keep them out of mischief until the battle; after that we will have more leisure to deal with them if necessary. Now, if you do not object, I really do have duties to attend to."

A messenger was sent to Isme the next day. Nothing more could be done. Morale in the army sank to a new low; Alethia had been beloved by her city, and though she was not known to most of the Shee or the Wyrds, the gloom that hung over the Brenn troops infected the others as well. The cold and darkness had already taken its toll; some of the Alkyran soldiers who had not fought at Brenn were already grumbling about the hazards of becoming involved with the Shee.

The reports of the Wyrd scouts that arrived that afternoon did nothing to mend matters. Now that the Lithmern army was a bare two days away, it became obvious that there were nearly three times as many of the enemy as there were of the Alkyrans and their allies. To add the finishing touch, it was soon certain that the Shadow-born were nearing the point at which the Shee wizards would be unable to contain them. When word of this reached Maurin, the Trader went to seek out Har.

He found the young Noble talking with Jordet and Tamsin. "Hello!" Har called cheerfully as he came within earshot. "Where have you been keeping yourself?"

"Have you heard Dlasek's report?" Maurin demanded, ignoring the question.

"Yes, but it won't matter," Har said.

"Won't matter! Three times as many men, and the Shadow-born as well? How can it not matter?"

Har grinned. "Tell him, Jordet."

Maurin turned to the Shee and opened his mouth. Hastily, Jordet grasped his arm and pointed down the length of Coldwell Pass. "Look there, and tell me what you see."

With a puzzled frown, Maurin turned to stare at the two-mile crack in the mountains that was Coldwell. The sides of the ravine were sheer cliffs, narrowing as they drew toward the eastern end of the pass. At the narrowest point one rock wall curved out and sloped into a ridge that almost blocked the pass completely; behind it the main part of the Alkyran armies could wait in concealment until the last minute.

"I do not see anything new," Maurin said. "What is your meaning?"

"Look up, there," Jordet said, pointing. Maurin looked. Above the sheer cliff wall rose the side of a huge mountain, crowned with snow.

"What does that have to do with Lithmern?" Maurin asked impatiently.

"As it is, nothing," Jordet replied. "But if it were to conveniently fall as they bring their army through the pass?"

Maurin's eyes widened. "It would crush their army. And block the pass forever."

Beside him, Tamsin gave a low whistle. "If it works, you will make legends with this battle," the minstrel said.

Maurin looked at Jordet with a touch of awe. "You can do this?"

"Not I," Jordet disclaimed. "But the Wyrds and the Veldatha have been spending a good deal of time up there, and they think it can be done. Two days from now they will be ready."

"I hope so," Maurin said, sobering suddenly. "In two days the Lithmern will be here."

"Already?" Jordet frowned. "I had not heard. Pardon me, but I must give this news to Rialla, if she does not know already." The Shee Ward-Keeper bowed and left, and a few moments later the others followed suit. Maurin was thoughtful for the next two days, and found himself looking more and more frequently at the imposing mountains above the pass as he went about the business of making ready for the coming battle.

Alethia recovered consciousness slowly. At first she did not know where she was; then memory flooded back and she tried to sit up and look around. It took three tries. She was terribly weak, and her left arm was almost useless. Blood from the torn shoulder had soaked her sleeve and dried to a hard crust that pulled painfully at the wound whenever she tried to move.

Finally she succeeded in propping herself upright. She was in a small cave, dark but dry. Nearby her horse stood watching. Quite sensibly, the animal showed no inclination to go back out into the raging storm. Unfortunately, it also showed no sign of coming any nearer to Alethia.

The girl put out her good hand and tried to coax the horse over. Eventually, it came, and she grabbed for the dangling loop of rein. The horse tossed its head, carrying the loop out of reach, and Alethia remembered that she had knotted the reins to keep them from sliding out of her fingers in the cold.

Gritting her teeth, Alethia lunged upright and caught the reins. She almost screamed aloud with the pain in her shoulder, but at last she had the horse. For a few moments she leaned against the animal's side, recovering; then she began to undo the buckles that held the saddle in place.

It took several tries to unfasten the girth; working one-handed was awkward, and Alethia kept jostling her shoulder painfully. Finally it was done, and Alethia gave the saddle a shove and let it crash to the floor of the cave on the opposite side of the horse. The animal jumped and shied, almost knocking her off her feet, but Alethia clung grimly to the reins until it was quiet once more. Then she unfastened the bridle and slipped the bit off. The horse moved away, and Alethia sank gratefully back to the floor of the cave.

Her next task was to investigate the saddlebags. This was easier; she could remain seated, and the fastenings were not complex, nor were the bags mobile the way the horse was. Alethia quickly found what she was looking for—blankets, water, and food.

Alethia provided water and grain for her horse before eating her own meal ravenously, then wrapped herself in the blankets and fell almost immediately into the sleep of exhaustion. Hunger woke her, but she stayed awake only long enough to satisfy it, then fell asleep once more.

When she awoke for the third time, the howling of the wind had stopped. She had no idea how long she had been lying on the floor of the cave. She was still weak, but her strength was no longer dangerously low. She looked around for the horse, and found it munching mouthfuls of green from the snow-covered bushes that screened the opening of the cave.

Alethia sat up and reached for the provisions. She ate slowly this time, and gave sparingly to her mount, noting how dangerously depleted her stock of food and grain had become. When she finished, she repacked the saddle-bag, wondering how she was going to get it back on the horse with only one arm.

There was very little she could do about her wound. She constructed a sling, using strips of her cloak; this gave the arm something to rest on and made it less painful, but it was still useless. Then she went to the mouth of the cave and peered out.

The scene was a study in shades of grey. The mountains were blanketed with snow; not clean and white, but a dingy grey in the faded light that filtered through the heavy clouds. The shapes of trees stood out in stark relief, dark grey against light, and above them grey rock poked through the snow. Nothing looked familiar in the least.

Alethia went outside cautiously, watching the sky for large birds. Her most pressing needs were fire and food. Though she knew that she could use the firestone to summon wood she was unwilling to do so, for she suspected that the effort of finding shelter by magical means was what had so exhausted her. Moreover, she was reluctant to chance using magic again so close to Lithra.

Half an hour later Alethia had found only two small sticks, and she realized that she had no choice. Exhausting herself physically plowing through the snowdrifts was just as dangerous as the energy drain of using magic. Carrying the little wood she had found, Alethia trudged back to the cave.

Standing in the shrub-covered opening, she grasped the drier of the two sticks and tried to remember Clasiena's instructions. The summoning of like to like was a spell that she had learned the day before Har's arrival in Eveleth, and she had not had a great deal of time to perfect it. When she was sure she had the spell clear in her mind, she began to grope for the power that linked her with the firestone.

At first she could not find it, and that worried her. She set the wood down carefully, and drew her hand closer to stare at the glow in the depths of the firestone ring. Suddenly it came, flooding her with so much power she could hardly handle it. Alethia cried out in protest at the searing force, and for a moment she almost lost control. She fought for balance, trying to force the power into the mold she had chosen for it. She was only partially successful; then, as suddenly as it had come, the surge of power passed.

Alethia staggered and almost fell into an absurdly huge pile of dry wood before her. She shook herself a little, feeling surprised that she was not drained after such prodigal use of power. "Like using Thoren's Sword to chop grapes!" she muttered, and reached for the firebox that held her flints.

# CHAPTER TWENTY-ONE

Alethia laid the fire a little within the mouth of the cave. The flints were awkward to use with only one hand; she wedged one between two rocks and tried striking it with the other. It didn't work very well, but eventually she got the fire lit.

With a sigh of relief, Alethia sat back, looking at the fire. As she did so, the light changed; things grew clearer and more sharply defined, and Alethia knew that the off-again, on-again spell-sight had returned, wakened perhaps by the surge of power she had felt when she used the firestone. She sighed again, wondering why the erratic gift had come now, when she did not need it, instead of a few minutes or days earlier, when she was trying to find her way through the blizzard or attempting to gather firewood. She started to rise, and as she did so she glanced out of the cave mouth. And froze.

The sky was no longer simply heavy with clouds. To her newly awakened spell-sight, it was shot with dark lightnings. Flashes of blackness leapt along a web of power that could only have been constructed by the Shadow-born. Alethia dropped the firebox and shrank back, trying to make herself as small as possible in the hope of being overlooked.

Nothing happened. Gradually she realized that she was not being hunted; if the Shadow-born had been seeking her, the tremendous power that had overwhelmed her a few minutes before would surely have attracted their attention. The lines of force were herding the clouds southward; she was seeing only a visible manifestation of a spell being cast miles away, perhaps in Mog Ograth itself. Unless she tried to tamper with the web itself, her only danger lay in blundering into the path of the spell, as she had when she was lost in the storm.

As she began to comprehend more fully what she was seeing, Alethia relaxed. She had, she realized, a tremendous advantage over the Shee wizards. As long as the spell-sight was working she would instantly know of the use of magic anywhere around her, without having to resort to detection spells which might betray her own presence. Her confidence started to return, and she glanced around for the firebox.

Only then did Alethia notice that the cave seemed to be full of light. She stopped and turned slowly, then looked quickly at the firestone. The ring was indeed glowing. The lines of power were obvious to her spell-sight, but it was not the source of the pulsing, golden light she saw.

Once more she reached out for her power, and the ring blazed in response. Suddenly she realized the source of the unexpected surge that had nearly overthrown her attempt to summon firewood; the golden glow was raw power, unchanneled. Alethia's eyes widened and she looked up to find the source of the magic.

The glow seemed stronger toward the back of the cave. Alethia walked forward and the firestone grew warm upon her finger, but she could not see anything that seemed to be the source. Patiently, she continued searching.

The cave was much deeper than she had suspected. When she reached the back wall, Alethia found that it was really only a sharp, narrow bend, partially blocked by a rockfall at some time in the past. Alethia moved a few of the rocks, then squeezed through the opening, wincing as her injured shoulder scraped against the rock walls.

She found herself in a large open area. The glow was perceptibly brighter, and she heard the sound of water dripping. The girl moved toward the noise, and the glow grew brighter still. Now she was moving in a bright haze of power, and the firestone was blazing in response. Alethia came to a halt.

She stood before a small pool; water dripped slowly into it from a ledge far above Alethia's head. Just in front of her, at the edge of the pool, lay a skeleton, covered here and there by shreds of cloth. Next to it, set carefully on a rock a little above the level of the pool, was a well-wrapped bundle that, to Alethia's spell-sensitive eyesight, seemed to glow and pulse with power.

Gingerly, Alethia stepped over the bones and picked up the bundle. She backed up a little, putting some small distance between herself and the skeleton, before she knelt to pull at the greased layers of cloth that were wrapped tightly around the thing of power.

The bundle was tied with leather thongs that had resisted well the attacks of time. The knots securing them, however, had shrunk to unyielding, stony lumps, and in the end she had to saw at them with her dagger. Finally the last layer of cloth, stiff with age, came free. Alethia choked and almost dropped the bundle as she saw what it was she held.

Gold and silver twined in intricate shapes and

spirals above a delicate circlet of gold set with opals. Precious stones flashed rainbow fire of diamond, ruby, emerald and sapphire from crystal cages that caught the light and multiplied it until the crown was ablaze. Over it all, overwhelming the beauty of the thing itself was power; power, coiling about it, fountaining from every spiral, focusing through every jewel, spilling over into every corner of the cave and filling it all with fire.

With a shiver of awe, Alethia set the crown on the cave floor. There was no doubt in her mind that she held the long-lost Crown of Alkyra; nothing else could possibly hold such power. It was easier to understand, now, why the firestone had guided her to this cave; it had been drawn by the echoes of the power of the Crown. Hadn't Clasiena said that firestones were sensitive to power in other things?

Four other treasures had disappeared at the same time as the Crown. She rose to her feet and searched thoroughly, but there was no sign of anything but the skeleton. Alethia walked slowly back to the bones and, with a grimace of distaste, began to examine them more closely.

She did not learn much. The dingy scraps of material were too coarse-woven to belong to a well-to-do or powerful man; a servant, then, or common soldier. Nearby lay a rusty knife, thin-bladed and still bearing traces of brownish stains along the edges. When she picked it up to examine it more closely, she recognized the workmanship of the Lithmern. Underneath it was a small packet wrapped in oilskin.

The light wavered, and Alethia rose hastily, holding the packet. The spell-sight was fading again, and she had nothing to see by once the glow of power disappeared. Hurriedly she snatched up cloth and crown together and headed back toward the outer part of the cave. She reached the rockfall and squeezed past just before the spell-sight vanished completely.

The fire was burning brightly, and Alethia sat down in front of it and opened the packet. It contained letters, or a diary of some kind. The pages were stiff, and they crumbled at the edges when she touched them. The writing was strange, but Alethia could recognize words here and there, and gradually she began to piece together a picture of the message she held.

A party of Lithmern had set out from Lacsmer three hundred years before to carry the Crown and the Gifts to Lithra. Alethia could not follow much of the next section; it seemed to be a list of disasters that had befallen the group. The words "injured" and "died" appeared several times, but the rest of the page was illegible. Alethia shrugged and went on.

The last page was a little clearer. The first paragraph was water-stained in spite of the protecting oilskin, and Alethia could only make out scattered phrases. The clearest were "quarreled last night," "we pursued," "killed at Coldwe" and "blocked the pass." Further down, the writing changed and was easier to read. Alethia bent over the page in fascination.

". . . had to leave the others there," the manuscript read. "The Crown is the most valuable of the treasures, so I will take it with me. Hopefully, I can find some other way through the mountains and bring a party back to Coldwell to recover the rest before the snows come."

Alethia put the note down and stared into the fire. She could almost feel sorry for the writer, the last of the convoy carrying the Gifts, dying lost and alone in a cave in the Kathkari. A thought occurred to her, and she looked at the note again. She began to grow excited; unless she was totally misreading the message, the remainder of the stolen Gifts were hidden at Coldwell Pass!

For another hour, Alethia poured over the note, trying to decipher enough of the writing to confirm her guess, but she was not successful. Finally she gave up. She put some more wood on the fire, rolled herself in the remains of her cloak and one of the blankets, and fell asleep.

She woke early the next morning. The fire was nothing but ashes, and she had to rekindle it from scratch. She ate sparingly, then took a burning branch from the fire to light her way to the inner cave, where she filled her nearly empty waterbottles from the spring. She made sure the horse was well provided for and then sat down to think.

The situation was hardly promising. She was lost in the Kathkari, severely wounded, with few remaining provisions and surrounded by hostile magic. Of course, she did have some talent for magic herself and a ring with some rather odd properties. And the Crown of Alkyra. Alethia grinned at the incongruity, then sobered. She had to get to Coldwell with the Crown, and soon. The Crown and the Gifts could be used to bind the Shadow-born; if Alethia could reach the army in time, perhaps the Veldatha could find the other gifts and use their power as it had been used in the Wars of Binding.

There was no way for her to find Har and the others. By this time they would surely have given her up for dead, and if she had not had the firestone they would have been right. She had no idea where Coldwell Pass was; the mountains were totally unfamiliar to her. Traveling south was her best hope, she decided, provided she could keep a straight path. Even if she could not find her way out of the mountains immediately, if she went south she must eventually reach the River Selyr that flowed through Brenn.

Alethia spent the early part of the morning packing the saddlebags and hoisting them onto the horse. Her arm was somewhat better, though still painful, and she wondered if the Crown had some sort of healing power. Even so, she had to rest frequently, and it was early afternoon before everything was secured to her satisfaction.

As soon as she was finished, Alethia left. The weather did not seem quite as cold, though it was still gloomy; but the torn cloak did not offer much protection. Alethia wrapped herself in one of the blankets and put the cloak on over it.

Her progress was slow. Alethia was torn between the need for haste and the fear of losing her way even more completely, or of being injured again. She was acutely conscious of the fact that the return of the Crown of Alkyra, and possibly the future of the country itself, depended on her safe arrival. On the other hand, she had the disquieting suspicion that the Shadow-born might know where the four lost Gifts were hidden, and she feared what might happen if they reached Coldwell before her.

There was little she could do to speed her journey; she could not even be entirely certain she was heading in the right direction. So she fretted whenever she was forced to retrace her steps, or to go around when the path seemed treacherous or unstable. Once at least her caution saved her life; a rock ledge collapsed onto the path ahead moments after she had turned away from the icy trail to seek safer footing. After that, she redoubled her watchfulness.

Alethia traveled for two days without finding any sign of the Wyrwood. It occurred to her several times that she could try to use the firestone to find a safe path to Coldwell, but the ever more frequent glimpses of the black power-web of the Shadow-born hovering over her made her reluctant to attempt it. Furthermore, she was not sure enough of the spell to try using magic except as a last resort.

By the third morning, cold and tired, Alethia decided to risk the firestone, in spite of the drain that she expected and her terror of detection by the Shadow-born. This time she was more cautious, and not so desperate, and the spell took far more time than it had during the storm.

When she had shaped the spell to her own satisfaction, Alethia looked up. No picture appeared in the air, and she looked around, a little puzzled. There was still nothing to be seen. Alethia moved her hand in a frustrated gesture, and the firestone flashed. She moved her hand again, more slowly and deliberately. The stone's glow brightened and dimmed again as she swung it in an arc in front of her. The brightest point of the arc seemed to be a little to the left of the direction she had been traveling in.

Reassured, Alethia set off in the new direction. By mid-morning, she had found a pathway that had clearly been traveled recently, and she struck out along it. She made good progress now that she had a clear direction and good footing, and though she met no one that day she fell asleep confident that the next day's ride would bring her to some more familiar area.

# CHAPTER TWENTY-TWO

Since dawn, Maurin had crouched behind the rockpile, watching the far end of the pass. He was cold and stiff, and he was not alone in his discomfort. Behind him he heard a muffled curse as one of the other men shifted, trying to find some part of his anatomy that was not already sore from the hours of waiting. Someone cuffed the offender back into silence, and the waiting continued.

Maurin looked toward the western end of the pass and tensed. The Lithmern were a grey river flowing into the narrow funnel of the mountains. Only a little further, Maurin thought. Only a little longer and it begins. Cautiously he signalled to the main mass of troops and cavalry, hidden behind the low ridge that he stood on. He was luckier than they; at least he could see the enemy approaching instead of waiting in ignorance, dependent on a signal from above.

For the hundredth time, Maurin checked his armor and weapons. All about him others were doing the same, shifting awkwardly to avoid sending a tell-tale gleam or clink down to the floor of the pass. Beside him a grizzled veteran grinned.

"Aye, you take proper care, lad," the man said. "Some of them, now, they'll be crow meat for not checking right." He spat into the snow.

The younger man eyed the worn leather sewn with metal rings that the other man wore and his eyebrows went up. "Are you sure that you are as well prepared as they are?" he asked, nodding toward a group of Marhal's men in chain.

"It's good enough for me, lad, and has been these many years," the veteran said. "Those staves with the blades on them can't get through the rings, and I can move a bit faster without all that extra weight. You'll see. Lithmern, bah!" He spat again. Maurin grinned and they touched clenched fists before the other man disappeared to find his place in the line that was slowly forming along the ridge.

The Lithmern army had almost reached the ridge. Maurin was light-headed with anxiety, with eagerness, with tension, with a confusing welter of familiar emotions that made the blood sing in his veins. The long wait was forgotten; these last few minutes were harder than the hours had been.

From the other side of the pass a horn sounded. Almost as one the men rose and charged down at the Lithmern, while the cavalry rode out from the concealing ridge and into the front of the Lithmern column. Behind the Shee riders, the foot soldiers of Alkyra closed their ranks and advanced.

There was a roar as the two sides met. The front part of the Lithmern column was halted, at least for the moment, and the soldiers further back milled about in confusion, unable to see what was happening in front of them. From concealed positions along the tops of the cliffs, the Wyrds rained arrows down on the exposed ranks of Lithmern. Then, from the rear of the column, there was a ripple of movement, and the soldiers shrank away as the Shadow-born advanced.

On dead black horses with madness in their eyes, fifteen shapes of darkness and shadow rode forward. Their forms continuously shifted around the edges; even the enveloping cloaks they wore could not hide it. To stare too long on those fifteen creatures made of nothing-at-all invited madness. They rode into Coldwell Pass at a slow, steady walk like a funeral march. In the center of the pass, just in front of the Alkyran lines, they stopped.

And the Shee sprang their trap.

There was a shivering, and a tremor ran through the pass itself. For a moment, nothing seemed to happen. Then, high above the Shadow-born, a mile-high slab of the rock wall began to crumble. With deceptive slowness, the avalanche came on, gathering rock, snow and speed as it came. There were screams of terror and a moment of mass confusion as half the Lithmern tried to turn back, out of the way of the deadly mass of rock.

One of the Shadow-born raised an arm, and the army stood motionless, bound in their places. His companions did not move, but about them the air grew suddenly dark and heavy. The avalanche continued, its roar drowning out all other noise. It reached the edge of the cliff and poured over it toward the floor of the pass.

The dark ring around the Shadow-born expanded rapidly. It met the leading edge of the falling wall of ice and rock fifteen feet above the heads of the Lithmern army, and held. Stone piled up above the barrier, and the first rocks were ground to a powder by the pressure from the rest of the mass. The shadow-wall darkened further in response, but still it held.

The last echoes of the avalanche died away, leaving both armies staring incredulously. For half a mile or more, the west end of the ravine was covered by an impossible bridge, a tunnel made of tons of rock and snow resting on darkness. Below it, the Lithmern army stood unharmed, save for those who had been trampled in the brief panic.

The Shadow-born hissed an order in Lithran and lowered its arm. The Lithmern shuddered and began to move again. Some of them looked upwards uneasily, but none quite dared to defy the creatures they had raised to serve them. The Shadow-born gestured again, and the Lithmern surged forward with a roar.

The Alkyrans and their allies groaned in despair. The pass was narrow enough that they could hold the Lithmern for awhile despite their smaller numbers. The Wyrd bowmen could pick off the massed Lithmern easily from their positions on the cliftops, but there were still far too many, even without the Shadow-born standing, motionless as statues, in the center of the pass.

A wave of hopelessness swept over Maurin even as he fought. So many, he thought, how can there be so many? Even without the Shadow-born to help them they can destroy us.

Suddenly the whole struggle seemed pointless. Maurin looked hopelessly from the thinning Alkyran ranks to the Lithmern, milling like grey worms in the shadow of the tons of rock suspended above them. More and more of the attackers were passing through the uneasy tunnel of rock and magic, and the invading army began to push the Alkyrans back, until they reached the narrowest part of the pass.

There the defenders held, but it was only a temporary delay. Suddenly a cry of fear went up. The Shadow-born were moving forward at last, and darkness flowed before them in a flood.

Before it reached the Alkyran lines, the wave of shadow slowed, as though something hampered it, and Maurin guessed that battle between the Veldatha and the Shadow-born was joined at last. The Shadow-born halted, and the darkness began to creep forward once more. Inch by inch it drew nearer to the Alkyrans.

The fighting came almost to a standstill. Silence fell; behind Maurin someone sobbed in terror, but he did not turn to look. Like a bird watching a snake, he stared at the shadowy border that wavered, now, only a few feet before him. Even as he watched, it gained another inch, another six. Maurin drew a shuddering breath and clutched his sword in a hand slippery with sweat.

Coruscating light flared in front of him, and for a moment Maurin was blind. He almost screamed; was this the purpose of the shadow? Behind him he heard a ragged cheer; it was not to be feared, then. He shook his head and his vision began to clear.

The Shadow-born sat unmoving, but their spell of darkness had moved back almost half the distance between them and the Alkyrans. Little darts of fire flashed across the boundary, making a net of light that held back the darkness. Behind the Shadow-born, the rest of the Lithmern had stopped advancing and were moving uncertainly.

For a few moments, time seemed to stop. The Shadow-born, motionless on their great black horses, did not gain any more ground, but they did not lose any either. Then one of the figures signaled, and the Lithmern came forward again. They stopped short of the interface between shadow and clear air, and Maurin looked at them in dismay.

They covered the canyon floor from cliff to cliff

in an unbroken mass stretching back nearly to the mouth of the pass; half the army was still inside the tunnel formed by the avalanche and the Shadow-born's spell. As he looked, the veil of shadow shivered and broke through the restraining net of light. It began to advance once more, steadily this time. The Lithmern army came behind it, moving forward at the direction of the Shadow-born. Maurin was beyond terror; he felt almost calm as he waited for the wall to reach him. His last thought before it touched him was a vague curiosity.

Cold, darkness and despair froze him where he stood. In the moment the spell swept over him, Maurin saw the loss of everything he ever loved, felt again the guilt of every mistake he had ever made and every wrong he had ever done or imagined. He saw his dimly remembered mother dying painfully in his arms. He saw Alethia screaming in terror amid the blizzard, dying slowly of thirst and exhaustion in the Kathkari because he had not found her. He saw Har hacked to pieces because he was not there to help his friend; he saw Traders from the vanished caravans dying in torment because he had not searched for them.

Maurin bowed his head in misery and self-condemnation. Just in front of him a grinning Lithmern soldier was advancing to the kill; very well, he would not resist. Death was all he deserved. The Lithmern's sword swung up and wavered mistily before him . . .

Alethia awoke early. Though it was still cold and gloomy, she was much more hopeful. Her arm was healing, and she knew she travelled in the right direction. She started off as soon as she finished eating the last of her food. She had been hoarding it carefully, but she was certain that she would find someone before nightfall who could replenish her supplies at least.

The ground rose slowly. A few hours of hard riding brought her to a ragged cliff above a maze of rockpiles, and she began to wonder whether she really was travelling in the right direction. Then, ahead of her, she heard a roar. Looking up, she saw a piece of one of the mountains go sliding away. Without stopping to think, Alethia dug her heels into the horse's sides.

The animal broke into a trot, then a gallop, and suddenly the battlefield was in sight. Alethia pulled her horse to a halt atop a low ridge that commanded a good view. She slid out of the saddle and looked down; she had no doubts that she had found Coldwell Pass.

The Alkyran army was drawn up at the foot of the ridge. Facing them, the Lithmern were emerging from the shelter of a tunnel of some sort. Alethia saw the blackness at its edges and flinched away. Only then did she see the Shadow-born themselves.

Alethia froze. Without realizing it, her hands clutched at the bulky package that contained the Crown of Alkyra, and spell-sight hit her like a wall. The ravine was dark with power. She felt the fear and pain of the men below, and suddenly realized that the Shadow-born were drawing it in, feeding on it. That is why they are so still, she thought numbly. They are feeding.

She tore her eyes away to look for the Veldatha; somehow she thought she still might reach them before the Shadow-born began their attack. The wizards were not hard to find; to her spell-sight they were a white blaze against the shadows. For a moment Alethia felt more confident; then her heart sank as she saw how small was their fire compared to the mass of darkness that was the Shadow-born. She started to remount, but even as she did she felt the Shadow-born begin their attack.

Power swept out from the creatures in a wave. The Veldatha flame met it, slowed it, but could not stop it. Alethia felt the terror of the troops below her, felt the way the dark spell fed on their fear. Then her spell-sight saw a weakness in the Shadow-born spell.

For a moment she hesitated, torn between fear of detection and fear for her friends, family and home. Then she threw all her power against the shadow-spell. Light flared as her force struck, and the shadow gave ground. Alethia pressed harder, searching for more weak spots, but the Shadow-born recovered quickly.

The spell-sight gave her an advantage, and she held them. Not alone; the Veldatha were still fighting, too, and they added their power to hers as they realized what had happened. She could see the weak spots that the wizards could only sense dimly, and she formed a wall of lightning to keep back the Shadow-born.

The creatures of darkness stopped moving and motioned the Lithmern forward. As the army surged around them, they drew more power from it. The Shadow-born reached out, and Alethia realized with a spasm of fear that she had been right; the creatures knew that the Shield, the Cup, the Sword and the Staff were somewhere in Coldwell, and they were searching for the added sources of power. Quickly, Alethia moved to block them, but the effort stretched her power too thin, and the shadows moved forward once more.

The spell reached the edge of the Alkyran army. Alethia reeled under the wave of guilt and terror and misery. For a moment she was shocked out of the linkage of power, and in that moment she saw Maurin, tall and stern, standing with his head bowed before a Lithmern soldier, about to be cut in two.

"No!" Alethia screamed, and with the instincts of desperation she raised her hands and jammed the Crown of Alkyra on her own head.

Time stopped. The world swam before her eyes as the full power of the Crown coursed through her. The mountains themselves seemed transparent; the armies below were insubstantial ghosts, frozen in mid-motion. Only the power of the Veldatha and the Shadow-born was real and tangible. As if in a dream, Alethia reached out and once more summoned the power of the Veldatha to her.

It came into her in a burst of fire. She turned toward the Shadow-born, and saw clearly on them the mark of the bindings that had held them for three thousand years. She felt a moment's doubt; even with such power, could she replace them? Once more, she reached out.

A feeling of warmth crept through her. Shapes of fire began to form in the air in front of her, and another power rose in her like a flood tide, making her very bones ache with joy. The Gifts of Alkyra had been summoned through the power of the Crown!

No longer hesitant, Alethia began rebuilding the ancient spells, following the pattern that only she could see. With great bars of power she bound the Shadow-born to the rock beneath the pass, cutting them off from the roots of their power. The struggle was intense, but brief, and the Shadow-born sank out of sight, melting into the stone.

Through his trance of despair, Maurin heard a familiar voice crying: "No!" He gasped, shaken out of the spell. His arm jerked reflexively to block the Lithmern blade. He was only partly successful; the sword bit into his side before he killed the man wielding it. He hardly noticed. "Alethia!" he shouted, looking about wildly. "Alethia?"

On the ridge overlooking the battlefield a pillar of light sprang up. It grew brighter and brighter, and the very walls of the ravine itself seemed to glow in response. Light exploded in the pass, sweeping away the dark spells of the Shadow-born. A wind sprang up, blowing off the ridge, wiping away the last shreds of the veil of misery.

The Shadow-born had vanished; fifteen black horses stood riderless in the center of the Lithmern army. Even the clouds, held in place by the black web of Shadow-born power, began to break up and dissipate. The Lithmern gave a cry of dismay that turned quickly to terror as the black wall that held back the avalanche grew insubstantial, faded, disappeared.

With a grinding roar, half a mile of stone collapsed into the pass, blocking it completely and wiping out with one stroke over half the Lithmern army. The noise of its falling drowned the screams of the men it caught and the sounds of battle alike.

As the echoes died, the Alkyrans surged forward. The Lithmern were trapped against the newly fallen rock, and they knew it. Some tried to flee toward the sides of the pass, but the archers cut them down. The main body of Lithmern, however, chose to fight, and they attacked with the desperation of men who know that they have no other hope of life.

Maurin fought with a fierce joy. He did not know how it had happened, but the Shadow-born were gone and the Lithmern no longer outnumbered the allies. More, Alethia was alive; the knowledge sang through him as he fought. He led the attack on the last of the Lithmern, who had managed to barricade themselves between the cliff and the rockslide, and he accepted their surrender at last. Only then did he go to look for Alethia.

Not content with merely binding the creatures, Alethia wove a net of power into the rock, drawing recklessly on the huge store of power at her disposal. Only when she was sure that not even a thread of darkness could creep out was she satisfied enough to stop.

The power drained away, leaving the girl suddenly exhausted. She sat down heavily and stared unseeing at the battlefield, where the Alkyrans were starting to force the Lithmern back. She could not even feel triumph. She was still sitting on the cold rocks when the crowd of wizards and lords, led by Maurin and her brother, came to find her— a drooping figure in torn and travel-stained garments with the greatest treasures of Alkyra clustered about her feet and a crown of light on her head.

# CHAPTER TWENTY-THREE

It was not until late the following day that Alethia was finally able to tell her story. The Neira healers took her in charge as soon as she reached the camp, and they refused to allow her to be disturbed by anyone until they felt she had rested enough. Har prowled restlessly around the outside of the tent for nearly an hour, but the healers remained firm.

The Crown and the Gifts were carefully wrapped and carried back to camp, where they were put under heavy guard while the survivors tried to decide what was to be done with them. The victory had taken a terrible toll, and the traditional celebrations were subdued. Lord Marhal, and Grathwol of the Wyrds, were dead; Armin was not expected to live. The prickly Shee general had been killed defending Herre, and the Commander of the Shee was badly wounded. One of Bracor's legs had been seriously hurt; only the skill of the Neira kept him from losing it. Tamsin, too, had reason to be grateful to the healers. He had been wounded in the shoulder, but the Neira assured him that it would heal cleanly. Nearly a third of the combined force of Alkyrans, Wyrds and Shee were dead, and hardly any of those remaining had escaped totally unscathed.

When the healers finally pronounced Alethia rested enough to speak, the leaders of the allied armies gathered around Herre's bedside to listen to her. In a fit of stubbornness, the Shee lord had insisted on being present, and since the Neira would not allow him to be moved, the others came to him.

Everyone who was able crowded into the tent. Rialla was there, gaunt and weary, and Murn, Arkon of Glen Wilding and leader of the Wyrds since Grathwol's death. Gahlon and Vander stood against the walls of the tent. Bracor, overruling the Neira's protests, had persuaded Har and Jordet to carry him from his own tent to Herre's. He sat next to Alethia, nursing his bandaged leg, with Har beside him. Larissalama sat between Herre and Bracor, dividing his attention between his two most difficult patients. Maurin, despite his injured side, stood near the doorway, half-hidden in the shadows behind Tamsin and Jordet.

Shadows flickered across the walls of the tent as Alethia told the assemblage about her lessons in Eveleth, the firestone, the blizzard, and the finding of the Crown. The firestone shone like a star on her finger as she spoke of the battle. When she finished, there was silence.

"So now the Crown is returned, and we shall have a ruler in place of a regent," Gahlon said with a smile. "Well, it is high time the peoples were united again."

"I suppose the Conclave of First Lords will have to choose a King now," Alethia agreed.

"Not a King, Alethia, but a Queen," Jordet's voice said from behind her. "And I do not think that the Conclave will have a choice."

Alethia looked at him and her face lost color. She did not pretend to misunderstand him. "That is absurd! I don't want to rule Alkyra!"

"You made your choice when you placed the Crown on your head," Jordet said gently.

"That was because I had no choice! I could not reach the Veldatha in time, and Maurin—" She broke off suddenly, and flushed. "I had no choice!" she repeated.

"The Crown of Alkyra may be worn by one person, and one only, so long as the wearer lives," Tamsin said in his lilting minstrel's voice. "Have you never heard Queen Carr's Lament? Her son Morrath died when he put the Crown on with his mother still living, and it broke her heart with grief."

"But the old tales say that only Kirel's line can wear the Crown!" Alethia objected. "I am not of the line of kings; I am not even of his blood."

"There was a reason that only those of Kirel's blood could wear the Crown," Rialla said. "Only his line seemed able to handle the enormous flow of power, and live. I have felt its power, and I know. I felt what you did in that battle; it would have burnt up any one of the Veldatha in spite of our training. I think, girl, that as unlikely as it seems *you* are the only one who can wear the Crown."

"Which is just as well," Gahlon said quietly. "If the First Lords had to choose someone to wear it, there would be war."

"The Shee would never bow to a puppet of the Alkyran nobles," Herre growled from his bed.

"Why should the Shee bow to anyone?" Alethia said, frowning. "You have kept apart from humans for hundreds of years!"

"Once we all were apart," Murn said quietly. "And you have brought us back. Your people fear the Shee and Wyrds already; if we do not become part of Alkyra again, how long will it be before your ambitious nobles turn their soldiers against us? Alkyra must be united. You are the one to do it."

"I can't do all that; I don't know enough about magic or politics. It is impossible!"

"You are trained as a child of the house of Brenn," her father said, "to serve Alkyra."

"The Nine Families and the Regent will never agree to it," Alethia pointed out desperately. "They already feel that the family of Brenn is too ambitious; they will never accept me as Queen."

"Some of them may not accept you," Gahlon corrected gently. "I, at least, will do so. And the Regent follows the lead of the Conclave. If you can persuade a few of the other First Lords, you need not worry about his acceptance."

"And if I can't? Unless they accept me, the First Lords certainly won't let me keep the Crown and the Gifts without fighting for them."

"Then we will fight," Herre said grimly.

"Such a war would smash all hope of reuniting the four peoples," Murn said thoughtfully. "Too many would see the Shee and the Wyrds in the army, and not the humans."

"Even so, we will fight," Herre insisted. "You yourself said that unless Alkyra is united, these Alkyran nobles will turn against us. Should we tamely hand them the Gifts and wait for them to attack?"

"But fighting with the First Lords would be just as bad as the Lithmern invading!" Alethia said. "You would have to conquer all of them, and that means nearly all of Alkyra. I won't let you do it; I'll give them the Crown myself first."

"It does not matter whether you give the nobles the Crown or not, Alethia," Gahlon said. "If the Conclave does not accept you, there will be war. But at least there is a chance to avoid it, if you agree to rule."

Alethia thought of the tired men outside the tent, who would be the ones to fight if this new war actually occurred. She thought of the maimed and wounded soldiers who had barely begun to recover from the battle with the Lithmern, and of the dead who would never recover. She did not reply.

"You have worn the Crown," Murn said sympathetically, almost as if she knew what Alethia was thinking. "Only with your death can you put this burden down."

"No!" Maurin said, under his breath.

Alethia did not hear him. She looked at the sober faces of the Shee, the Wyrds, the Neira, and the human friends about her. *Her duty as a child of the house of Brenn was to serve Alkyra*. Clearly, if she did not try to persuade the Alkyran nobles to accept her as Queen, they would fight among themselves for possession of the Crown and the Gifts. Would she really be serving her country by plunging it into war? Once more she scanned the faces around her. faces around her.

"Would you truly accept me as Queen, and your people as well?"

"We will," said Herre. "All the Shee will bow to the Crown. It was made to bind the four peoples together."

"I speak for the Wyrds, and I agree," said Murn.

"I for the Neira; I also."

"Then it seems that again I have no choice," Alethia whispered. "I will be your Queen." As her eyes fell, the firestone flared, sending the shadows dancing through the tent once more. Unnoticed, Maurin slipped out into the cold night.

# CHAPTER TWENTY-FOUR

For the rest of the week, the allied armies at Coldwell tended their wounded, buried their dead, and prepared to depart. The Lithmern prisoners were kept separate and under constant guard; with the pass blocked, they would have to go through Brenn to return to their homes once ransoms had been agreed upon. The Neira, too, were going through Brenn. The River Selyr was the closest waterway, and though they could travel overland if necessary, the sea-people preferred not to.

Most of the Veldatha had chosen to remain with the army, at Alethia's request. They were to study the Gifts and to continue Alethia's instruction in magic. Some of the Shee and the Wyrds departed on the fourth day after the battle, but many remained. In a few days, others began arriving to pay their respects to Alethia and to see the treasures of Alkyra for themselves.

Among the new arrivals was Isme. The Lady of Brenn arrived without warning on the fifth day following the battle. She listened patiently to all Bracor's reasons about why she should not have risked such a journey, then said firmly that she did not choose to remain in Brenn while her husband was lying wounded at Coldwell Pass. Since she had obviously arrived safely, Bracor found it difficult to argue convincingly. The discussion might have gone on for a long time if Alethia's entrance had not put an end to it.

"Jordet told me you had come," Alethia said as she greeted her mother. "I came straight here. Har is with Murn; I'm sure he'll come as soon as he hears you are here."

"I am sure he will," Isme agreed.

"What is he up to?" Bracor demanded.

"He's helping Murn decide how we're going to get all the Lithmern swords and armor back to Brenn," Alethia said. "We don't have enough carts for all of it."

"We shouldn't leave it to rust," Bracor said, frowning. "If the Shee could take some of it, we could—"

"—relax," Alethia interrupted. "Larissalama told you to stop worrying about things and rest, and if you don't, he'll probably keep you in that bed for a month."

"I suppose you're right," Bracor said ruefully.

"Then Alethia and I will leave and let you rest," Isme said. She rose as she spoke, and a moment later she and Alethia were outside the tent. "I would like to speak to the healer, and then we can talk. I don't know if you realize it, but I have not yet heard all of what you have been doing these past weeks."

They found Larissalama, who answered Isme's questions without hesitation. Bracor's wound was healing slowly, partly because he continued to be more active than the Neira thought desirable. Isme only nodded, but the look on her face made Alethia certain that Bracor would have far more rest for the next several days at least.

When Isme was finished with Larissalama, Alethia brought her to the small tent which had been hastily erected for her. Inside, Isme seated herself and looked at her daughter expectantly. "Now, what has been happening to you since you . . . left Brenn?"

Alethia explained. Isme listened without comment until Alethia described the finding of the firestone; then she asked what had become of it. Alethia held out her hand to display the ring, and Isme smiled.

"I am glad you kept it," she said. "I think it will be of some use to you."

"It already has been," Alethia said. "It led me to the cave where the Crown was, when I was lost in the blizzard."

Isme nodded, and Alethia went on with her story. "And now they want me to be Queen," she finished. "And I don't want to be!"

"Why not?" Isme said calmly.

Startled, Alethia looked at her mother. "I'm not sure," she said, after a moment. "It frightens me almost as much as the Shadow-born. Everything is changing. The Wyrds and the Shee are coming back into the world, and probably the Neira, too, and people will be afraid of them. The Nine Families will be in an uproar—and everyone else as well. Alkyra needs wisdom to rule here, not raw power. I feel like the Lithmern, fumbling with magic I don't understand."

"These will be difficult times," Isme agreed. She looked thoughtfully at Alethia. "What do you *want* to do?"

"I don't have a choice," Alethia said. "Because of the Crown."

"There is always a choice," Isme said firmly. "You could hide the Gifts again, or let the Regent and the First Lords continue to rule Alkyra for you, if you really wanted to. What you mean is that you don't like any of the choices any better than you like the idea of being Queen."

"I suppose you're right," Alethia said slowly. "I couldn't hide the Gifts again; they are too dangerous to risk someone like the Lithmern finding them by accident. And I couldn't just pretend to rule, because the Shee and the Wyrds won't stand for the First Lords."

Isme nodded. "You see? You seem to know all kinds of things you do not wish to do. I want to know what you *do* wish to do."

"I want—" Alethia began, and stopped. She was silent for a long time, then finally she looked up. "I think I would like to learn more about the Gifts. I know a little already, but I don't think anyone really understands them. And I'd like to learn more magic, and more about firestones. I don't think anyone really understands them, either."

"And if you do not wear the Crown, how can you study it?" Isme asked. "Do you think the nobles will let you near the Gifts if you once give them up?"

"That's true," Alethia said thoughtfully. "But even if I'm Queen, they can—" She stopped again, and her eyes narrowed. "No, they can't! I would be Queen, not Regent; the First Lords wouldn't be able to overrule me as they do him."

"When you come to them with your Crown and your Gifts, seeking fealty," Isme said, "they will see only a young and pretty woman—inexperienced, and easily manipulated. But when you are their Queen, they may learn otherwise. There is much good you can do for Alkyra, daughter."

Before Alethia could reply, they heard a flurry of

sound and Har burst into the tent. "Mother!" he said, sweeping Isme into his embrace. "I heard you were here, closeted with Alethia."

"Alethia and I have had matters to discuss," Isme said, smiling at her son. "And I'm sure you have a question or two on your mind as well . . ."

"I sure do. It's not everyday you wake up and find that you're not quite human!"

"I too am curious, mother. Why did you never tell us?"

"There is very little to tell," Isme replied. "I was Keeper of the Western Ward when I was about your age, Alethia. Your father and his brother Reidon were ambushed during a counter-raid into Lithra, you will recall; Reidon was killed, and your father sorely wounded. The part of the tale that you haven't heard before is that when he rode into the Kathkari Mountains to shake off the Lithmern, he stumbled across my cottage." Isme smiled reminiscently. "Literally stumbled; he couldn't see through the Veil spell that guards the Wards, so he fell down the stairs into my garden."

"And you took care of him and then married him?" Alethia said. "It sounds like one of Tamsin's songs!"

"That is probably the way the minstrels will sing of it in a hundred years, but it was not so simple then. He stayed until he was healed, and I helped him slip by the Lithmern, but I did not go with him then. Once or twice in the next year, when he could get away from Brenn, he came back to see me. But he did not speak of marriage until the following summer, when he had become more accustomed to being Lord of Brenn in his brother's place. By then I was ready to listen—though I knew what it would mean."

"The covenant of exile," Alethia said.

"Not merely exile, but a pledge never to speak of Eveleth or the Shee, and never to use magic openly." Isme's smile held a trace of irony and bitter memory. "The Shee were worried about the consequences, should anyone outside the mountains learn they existed."

Har grinned. "Well, there certainly have been a lot of consequences after all! Did you have to promise not to tell us, too? It might have made things a little easier, if we'd known."

"There was no need," Isme said, "and by the time you were old enough to tell, it did not seem very important any more."

"Not important!" Alethia said. "But, Mother—"

"Your lives were in Brenn; so was mine. There was no reason to think the knowledge would make any difference, except perhaps to make you curious about your heritage. Under the circumstances, that would not have been particularly . . . wise."

Alethia laughed. "I suppose not. The Shee didn't seem too anxious to have us in Eveleth even when we had a good reason for being there; I can just imagine how they'd have behaved if we'd come out of curiosity."

"I can't," Har said. "And I don't want to. But I have a few more questions."

"About the Shee?" Alethia said.

"No, about Brenn. The last I heard, there were still four or five nobles and First Lord Stethan who hadn't answered our request for troops, and I want to know whether any of them ever did."

The talk turned to affairs in Brenn. Alethia was almost glad of the change in the conversation; she wanted more time to think over some of the things her mother had said.

She had more time to ponder than she expected; the journey back to Brenn took six days. The trip itself was uneventful, but as they neared the edge of the forest the scouts brought back disturbing news of a great army of Alkyrans camped around Brenn.

As soon as the news arrived, Bracor sent messengers to Brenn to discover what had occurred. Alethia insisted on riding to the edge of the forest with them, to see Brenn for herself, accompanied by Murn and Har.

The group returned before the messengers, much excited. "The fields are full of nobles," Alethia informed her father as she dismounted. "All of the banners of the Nine Families are there, even Thielen's and Gahlon's."

"The Regent is there, too," Har said. "You can see his banners right in front of the East Gates."

"I could wish they had moved against the Lithmern as promptly," Bracor said. He turned to one of the guards who had accompanied Alethia. "Go tell Lord Herre, the Lady Murn, Lord Vander and First Lord Gahlon what you have seen, and ask them to come to us."

By the time the messengers returned, all of the leaders of the various parts of the mixed army had arrived in response to Bracor's summons. The first of the messengers bowed to them all, then handed Bracor a sealed note. Bracor opened it and began to read. "What does it say?" Har burst out.

"I am summoned by the First Lords this evening to answer charges of treason," Bracor answered without surprise. He handed the paper to Gahlon with a grimace.

"Treason is a serious matter," Lord Vander said worriedly.

"I don't think it's as bad as you fear," Gahlon said, looking up from the note, "Not all of the other First Lords support this charge; there are only four seals on this letter."

"First Lord Thielen can't support it," Alethia said. "If he did, he would be guilty too; his men were at Coldwell with us."

"Having *two* First Lords involved will only make the charge more serious," Bracor said. He shook his head. "I expected this to happen—but not so soon."

"Well, what difference does it make?" Har said impatiently. "Alethia is going to be Queen, and you haven't committed any treason against *her.*"

The Shee commander laughed. "I think this will be an interesting meeting! I hope you will not mind if I come with you, Lord Bracor?"

"We still have to convince the Conclave of First Lords that Alethia should rule Alkyra," Gahlon pointed out to Har. "I don't think that will be easy."

"Let one of them try on the Crown," Har suggested nastily. "That should settle things in a hurry."

"No!" said Alethia. "How can you joke about such a thing?" She remembered raw power coursing through the ornamental metal and shivered.

"Are you certain that this is the best time to tell them about the Gifts?" Lord Vander asked a little nervously.

"I must tell them sometime," Alethia said. "I would rather get it over with now. And they are conveniently on our doorstep."

"I think we should all go to meet with the First

Lords tonight," Murn said. "They will find it more difficult to deny your right to the throne if they realize that the Wyrds, the Shee, and the Neira have already accepted you."

Gahlon chuckled softly. "I would not miss this meeting if you offered me the Crown itself. The First Lords are going to be very annoyed."

"Will you wear the Crown?" Har asked Alethia.

"No," said Alethia, thinking again of that raw power. "Not until I must."

"You should take it with you, though," Gahlon said quickly. "And the Gifts as well. We will need them to convince the lords that you are truly meant to be Queen."

Vander frowned. "Is it wise to risk treasures of such value? The Lords could simply seize them all."

"No they can not," Alethia said. "They cannot possibly take the Gifts away from me." Her voice was quiet, but none doubted her statement.

They left camp early that evening. Murn, Maurin, Jordet and Larissalama each carried one of the four Gifts muffled under their cloaks; Alethia herself held the Crown. There was an air of great tension about the group. No one spoke.

They were met halfway to the city by nine guards, each wearing the badge of a different First Lord. The men seemed uneasy about their duty, and cast frequent glances at Murn, Herre, Jordet and Larissalama as they rode toward the large tent where the First Lords and the Regent waited.

As she entered the tent, Alethia saw a long table. Eight of the nine First Lords were seated along one side of it, with the Regent behind them. The ninth chair, Gahlon's seat, was empty, and one of the lords motioned Gahlon toward it.

"Thank you, Stethan, but I cannot take the seat you offer," Gahlon said, bowing. "If Bracor is guilty of treason, then I am also, and I cannot join you."

Alethia noticed Lord Thielen shift uncomfortably in his place midway around the table. She looked back at Gahlon, who smiled slightly as he took one of the seats on the same side of the table as Bracor and the rest of the party. Alethia suppressed an answering smile and seated herself beside her father, scanning the lords for any sign of support or sympathy.

The Regent cleared his throat officiously. "Lord Bracor, the charges against you are very grave. That is why we have come to you, instead of summoning you to the Conclave, as is the usual custom."

"The charges are obviously justified," a large blond man at the end of the table said. "Why, he has the effrontery to bring his demonic allies with him! What more proof do we need?"

"Peace, Orlin," one of the others growled. "I know your views. There has been far too much talk of demons for my taste. You forget that Lord Bracor has the right to answer the charges, and I for one would hear what he has to say!"

"Yes," said another. "I understand there are a large number of Lithmern prisoners with the army. If Lord Bracor was correct about the threat of invasion, I do not see that we can condemn his actions."

"Just what are the charges, my lords?" Bracor asked, making himself heard above the din.

"You are charged with high treason, to wit, the making of a compact outside of Alkyra, without the consent of the Conclave of the First Lords or of the Regent of Alkyra, for the purpose of enhancing your own power to the detriment of the country of Alkyra," the Regent said rapidly. "What will you answer?"

"Why, it is obvious that I cannot be guilty, my lord," Bracor said.

"How can you say so?" one of the First Lords shouted. "Your allies sit right next to you; how can you deny them?"

"I do not deny that the Wyrds, the Shee and the Neira offered me an alliance, which I accepted," Bracor said calmly. "But when Kirel founded Alkyra, he was made King by an alliance of all four of the races of Lyra, to rule over all. Therefore I have not made a compact outside of Alkyra, and the charges are void."

Several of the lords smiled in appreciation, but First Lord Stethan frowned. "Inside or outside Alkyra, it is all the same to me. What of the charge of enhancing your own might? Can you deny that you command the army that is camped out there in the forest?"

"But my father does not command the army," Alethia said softly, before Bracor could reply. "I do."

"I am afraid that Lord Bracor cannot escape through such an obvious legal fiction," Lord Orlin sneered. "Putting his daughter in command of the army is hardly believable."

"I do not command as his daughter, but in my own right," Alethia said.

"Oh?" Stethan said in tones of polite disbelief. "And what right have you to command such an army without the consent of the Conclave? Perhaps we should charge you with treason as well."

Some of the First Lords laughed. Alethia's eyes narrowed, and she rose. "This is my right," she said. She brought her hands from beneath her cloak, revealing the Crown of Alkyra.

A stunned silence fell within the tent. Alethia nodded once, and Murn, Maurin, Jordet and Larissalama rose and stepped away from the table. With simultaneous movements, they swept the wrapping from the four Gifts they carried. The silence deepened.

"I see you recognize these," Alethia said. "They were given to Kirel to help him rule the four peoples. I have found them and brought them back to Alkyra, and I will use them as he did."

"It's a trick," someone croaked.

"It is no trick," Alethia said gently. Slowly, she raised the Crown and placed it upon her own head. It burst into scintillating fire. Alethia's eyes swept the First Lords. "You know, as all Alkyra knows, what the Crown is and what it means," she said. "Only I may wear it and live; if I open the flap of this tent and step outside, every man in your armies will kneel to me, so long as I wear it."

*"Every man in the army?* No!" Heads turned as the Regent rose and stepped forward. No one spoke as he walked around the table toward Alethia; the First Lords were too astonished by the uncharacteristic note of decision in the Regent's voice, and the others waited for some sign from Alethia. Alethia stood frozen, feeling the cold knowledge of failure. The Regent must be certain indeed of the reaction of the First Lords, or he would not risk being publicly overruled.

"No," the Regent of Alkyra continued, "not every man in the army but *every man in Alkyra* shall kneel to you, and I shall be the first of them." Tears glittered in his brown eyes. Suddenly he turned to the First Lords. "I have been Regent of this land for twenty years, and my father before me, and his father," he said in a strong, clear voice. "I was sworn to hold the throne and rule the land until the Wearer of the Crown returned." He turned back to Alethia and abruptly knelt before her. "Alethia Tel'anh, you wear Kirel's Crown and you bear his coronation gifts. My oath is fulfilled."

A murmur of surprise swept the tent, changing swiftly to consternation as the First Lords realized what had happened. No matter how badly diminished the powers of the Regent had become, he still held the right to give up his authority to the rightful ruler of Alkyra. The few who, in the stress of the sudden reappearance of the Crown, had remembered that authority had expected the Regent to abide by their decision; no one had expected him to voluntarily relinquish his position.

Slowly, First Lord Thielen stood and came to kneel beside the Regent. One by one, the other First Lords followed. A few, notably the Lords Stethan and Orlin, seemed reluctant, but now that the Regent had acknowledged Alethia and relinquished his authority to her, none of them could deny her without himself committing treason.

Alethia was aware of Har's broad, half-disbelieving grin, the relief on the faces of the Shee, and Wyrds, and the stunned expressions of the First Lords. Around her the jewelled gifts glittered, filling the tent with pinpoints of prismatic color. Behind her were her inhuman friends—the proud Shee, the earthy Wyrd, the shimmering Neira—who called her Queen. And before her knelt the man who, for all the days of her childhood, she had called her ruler. The realization flooded her: now, indeed, she was truly Queen.

And the four peoples of Alkyra were united again.

# EPILOG

The coronation was set for the spring. Messengers were sent at once to every part of Alkyra and beyond, to Kith Alunel, to Col Sador, to Ciaron and Rathane, inviting the most important people of Lyra and their emissaries to be present. The ceremony would be held in Friermuth, the city closest to the center of Alkyra, and preparations began almost before the First Lords departed from the fields around Brenn.

The Queen remained in Brenn. Her most pressing concerns were with the Wyrds and the Shee, and Brenn was much more convenient for both these peoples than Friermuth. A month sped by on wings, and messengers began arriving at Styr Tel conveying variations of polite acceptance of the invitation to the coronation. The Noble House of Brenn began to think seriously about leaving for Friermuth.

Preparations for the departure were nearly complete when Har came storming into the Queen's rooms. "Alethia," he demanded, "what is the matter with Maurin? He insists that he isn't coming to Friermuth at all. Says he's going back to Master Goldar's caravan, if you please."

Alethia looked up from a sheaf of papers. "I don't know," she said. She looked down at the papers and frowned. Slowly, she pushed them away and turned thoughtfully back to Har. "I don't know," she repeated. "I've seen little of him since Coldwell Pass . . ." She gestured at the litter of documents.

"I know you are busy, Allie, with bigger problems than a moping Trader," Har said, "but I'm worried about Maurin. He's been evasive and bad tempered since we returned to Brenn, and he hasn't come near Styr Tel. I thought if perhaps it was something I'd said or done, he might have told you . . ."

"I am not privvy to Maurin's confidences," Alethia snapped. She pulled her papers back in front of her, but her brother ignored this hint that the conversation was over. "Look, Allie; you could talk to him—"

"I don't see what good that would do," Alethia said. "Besides, Maurin has made no attempt to see me, either after the battle or here in Brenn. I hardly think he'd be interested in anything I could say to him."

"Oh, is that what has made you cross?" Har sat down on the edge of the table and looked into his sister's eyes, which were identical to his own. "But you are a Queen now, Allie."

"I can hardly forget," Alethia said dryly.

"Well, I had problems enough getting Maurin to visit Styr Tel when we were just an ordinary Noble Family, because he was worried about the way it would look. Now that you're Queen of Alkyra, he's probably—"

Alethia's eyes narrowed suddenly into green diagonal slits. "Har—tell Maurin to go out to the back of the stables, at noon. Don't tell him why, but make sure he goes."

Har looked at his sister as if she'd taken leave of

her senses, then shrugged and went to find his friend. Alethia was buried back in her papers before he'd left the room, but her attention was not on them.

Maurin crossed the courtyard of Styr Tel and walked towards the old stables. He had no idea why Har wanted to meet him there, but Har had been insistent and he suspected that it had to do with his decision to leave Brenn with the caravan. Har had tried to talk him out of it, but his objections would make no difference in the end.

He turned the corner and stopped short. Har was nowhere in sight, but Alethia was standing with her arm raised, poised to throw the dagger she held at the battered san-seri target hung on the courtyard wall. Her hair was braided and wound in a crown around her head, and it shone in the sunlight. Maurin drew a deep breath and started to back away.

"Maurin, don't you dare leave without even talking to me," Alethia said without turning. Her arm came down and the dagger flew fair and true to the top of the target, completing the diamond pattern she was forming. She walked to the target and retrieved her knives, then turned and walked over to him.

"I promised you a rematch," she said, and handed him the rack of green-handled daggers. Not knowing what else to do, Maurin took his place in silence. They tossed a coin for first throw, and Alethia won.

For the first few throws, neither spoke. Alethia broke the silence. "I understand you are planning to return to the caravans."

"High Lady, it is what I am trained for," Maurin

replied, keeping his eyes on the target.

"Don't 'High Lady' me!" Alethia said. "Why are you going?"

"It is what I am trained for," Maurin repeated. His next throw went badly astray.

"That is nonsense," Alethia said flatly. She turned to face him. "When Har told me, I thought maybe you really wanted to go back to the Traders, but now I can see that you don't. Going back makes you miserable, and staying makes you miserable. Why?"

"Alethia, I can't stay," Maurin said, abandoning his pretense of calm. "Don't ask me why. Please."

"I thought so," Alethia said. "Maurin Atuval, it is your fault that I am in this mess, and if you think you can just walk away because of some misguided idea of what is proper, you are dead wrong." Alethia glared at him.

"My fault? My fault! Did I make you Queen of Alkyra?" Maurin asked bitterly.

"Yes!" Alethia retorted. "If I hadn't seen that soldier trying to chop you in half I never would have put the Crown on, and they never could have insisted that I have to keep wearing it! How can you be so blind!"

"The Queen of Alkyra can't consort with a caravan guard," Maurin said, goaded beyond caution. "What good does it do me to stay?"

"You aren't a caravan guard, you're a Journeyman Trader, and the Queen of Alkyra can do whatever the Black she pleases!" Alethia said vehemently. She glared at the Trader. "And if she wants her husband to come to her coronation, who's going to stop her?"

Maurin's jaw dropped. "Alethia . . ." he said uncertainly, "you don't mean it?"

"Am I going to have to kidnap you to convince you?" Alethia said, exasperated. "I have had first-hand experience, you know; I'm sure I could persuade Har and Jordet to do it. And Tamsin is a minstrel, so he could marry us—unless you don't want to?" she added quickly.

"Want to!" Maurin swallowed. "But what will the Nobles say?"

"I don't care!" Alethia said angrily. "I'm doing what they want; they can just live with a little bit of what I want."

A slow smile spread across Maurin's face. "Then what can I do but obey the dictates of my Queen?"

"I knew you would see it my way," Alethia said sweetly, and Maurin laughed and gathered her into his arms.

The wedding was a quiet one. The guests were few, but among them were the most prominent members of the four races, including the heroes of Coldwell Pass. Tamsin Lerrol performed the ceremony and at the wedding feast he sang a new ballad about the finding of the Crown. Alethia smiled as he sang, but when the lay described the Shadow-born, she clutched Maurin's hand beneath the table.

Two weeks later, Alethia and her family left for Friermuth. The notables of Alkyra had been gathering for some time. The nine First Nobles and the former Regent were already present, preparing for the formal recognition ceremony. Lesser nobles were arriving in a steady stream, and the non-humans were also reaching the city in increasing numbers. The citizens of Friermuth quickly became accustomed to the exotic shapes of Wyrds, Shee and

Neira passing along their streets, but even the most complacent were shaken by the arrival of Queen Iniscara and her escort. Iniscara was robed in silver and rode a horse of jet black; her guards, in their black and silver, sat astride horses white as ice. With their uniformly white hair and green eyes they presented a striking picture indeed as they rode slowly through the town to their quarters.

The foreign ambassadors began arriving soon after Alethia reached Friermuth. Blythe Kyel-Semrud, head of one of Kith Alunel's most ancient and noble families, was the first to arrive. He was followed closely by Aralyne Dohstid of Rathane, cousin to the ruler of the city and one of its most influential citizens. Prince Staryl Dundevic came from Col Sador, bringing with him the Knights of the Sword to reaffirm their long friendship with Alkyra.

It soon became apparent that there was no building in Friermuth large enough to contain the throng of people who expected to attend the coronation. A few days before the ceremony, one of the First Lords brought Alethia a list of people from which to pick and choose those who would be allowed to attend, but Alethia refused to even look at it. "I am going to be Queen of all Alkyra," she told the astonished Lord, "and I am not going to start by annoying three-quarters of the people who have come to see me."

"Someone will have to choose," the Lord replied, a trifle disgruntled. "I told you, there is no building large enough to hold all the common folk. A few representatives, perhaps, but no more."

"Then make the Nobles stand in the street as well," Alethia said calmly.

The First Lord stared. Obviously, he thought,

her new position had gone to the girl's head. Patiently, he began to repeat the objections and recommendations he had brought with him, but Alethia cut him short.

"I have told you that I am not going to allow anyone who has traveled all the way to Friermuth just to see the coronation to be turned away," she said. "Either find a place that everyone will fit, or move the Nobles."

"But there is no such place!" the harrassed Lord said. "And you can't deny the Nobles; you'll make enemies!"

Alethia smiled. "What about Starmorning Field?"

"It's certainly large enough," the First Lord said, considering. "But you can't be crowned out in the middle of a field!"

"Why not?" Alethia asked. "But of course, you can always move the Nobles."

In the end, Alethia had her way. The coronation was held in the middle of Starmorning Field, just outside Friermuth, before the largest crowd of Lords, Nobles, ambassadors, and common people ever assembled in one place in Alkyran history.

The procession that escorted Alethia from Friermuth to Starmorning Field was an impressive one. The guild representatives came first, each displaying the banner of his guild and the banner of the Lord who sponsored them. Next came the soldiers who had fought at Brenn and Coldwell. Ranks of Alkyran footsoldiers were followed by Wyrd bowmen and Shee cavalry, with the Neiran healers at the rear of the army.

The lesser Nobles of Alkyra were next, each with his escort displaying his banner and the midnight blue and gold of Alkyra. They seemed to keep coming forever; every Lord of every city in Alkyra was determined to take some part, however small, in the coronation of the country's first ruler in three hundred years, and Alethia had not allowed anyone to be left out.

The Alkyran Nobles were followed by the Lords of the Shee and the Arkons of the Wyrd Glens, excepting Murn. Next were the Nine Families of Alkyra which had supported Kirel when he founded the country and destroyed the last of the Wyrms in the Snake Mountains. The First Lords, the heads of the Nine Families, rode in the middle of their respective households.

As the Veldatha wizards rode into sight behind the Nine Families, the crowds that lined the road hushed. For many, this was the closest they had ever come to magic, and already legends were springing up around the battle at Coldwell Pass. The Veldatha were certainly impressive with their white hair and blue robes and the Crown of the Veldatha upon every head.

The visiting Lords and Princes and ambassadors were next, just before the rulers of the four peoples. Iniscara, Murn, Merissallan, and Regent Mikral rode abreast, each carrying one of Kirel's four coronation Gifts. Behind them was Reuel, the Grand Master of the Minstrels himself, with the Crown of Alkyra, and then, at last, came Alethia and Maurin in the midnight blue and gold of Alkyran royalty.

Even with all of Starmorning Field to hold them, it seemed that the people who lined the roads would never be able to fit around the raised platform where the ceremony would take place, but when the procession reached its end there was room for everyone. Alethia and Maurin mounted the steps together. Behind them came

Reuel, carrying the Crown, and the crowd quieted.

The Grand Master of the Minstrels raised the Crown above his head, and it flashed in the sunlight. In a clear voice that carried to the very edge of Starmorning Field, Reuel told again the story of Kirel the Founder and the Alliance of Wyrds, Shee, Neira and Men which became the Land of Alkyra. He ended with Kirel's Promise, sometimes called Kirel's Oath, and Alethia repeated it after him:

"By the power of the Sword will I win justice for this land; by the power of the Shield will I guard it wisely; by the power of the Cup will I hold it in mercy; by the power of the Staff will I rule it in peace. This I promise to all the people in the light of the Crown before you."

Alethia knelt, and Reuel stood motionless for a long moment with the Crown upheld. Then he lowered the Crown onto Alethia's head, and the field rang with cheers.

"Congratulations, Your Majesty," Maurin whispered to Alethia as she rose.

"I'm still not sure this was a good idea," she said dryly, in a voice so low Maurin could hardly hear it over the cheering.

"Well, it's too late to back out now, so enjoy it while you can; the work will start soon enough," her husband replied. "Speaking of which, straighten your Crown; there are people coming up to see you." Alethia suppressed laughter as she turned regally to receive the formal allegiance of the Nobles and guild-masters who were coming up the steps of the platform.

\* \* \*

*"By the power of the Sword will I win justice for this land; by the power of the Shield will I guard it wisely; by the power of the Cup will I hold it in mercy; by the power of the Staff will I rule it in peace. This I promise to all the people in the light of the Crown before you."*

## ABOUT THE AUTHOR . . . .

Patricia C. Wrede was born on March 27, 1953. Her parents were sufficiently pleased with the results that she soon (taking the grand view; taking a cosmological one, better than instantly) had three sisters [one of whom drew the map for this edition] and a brother. Then she went to Carleton College (so we skip a few details; big deal) and, while ever intending to become a writer of fantasy, pursued a B.A. in biology, obtained it, and snatched an M.A. in business administration from the University of Minnesota.

Now she lives in Minneapolis with a husband acquired about the time of the B.A., and works as a financial analyst for the Dayton-Hudson Corporation. When she is not writing or involved in the daily affairs of life, she plays guitar, sews and embroiders, and makes desultory attempts at gardening. Though she is one of the few writers of fantasy who has no cat, she likes other people's pets, and they like her—without even knowing that she's a vegetarian.

Besides *Shadow Magic*, Patricia C. Wrede is also the author of *Daughter of Witches*, another novel set on Lyra, and *The Seven Towers*.